"I'm not looking for a wife."

Cam's angry announcement pleased Annabelle.

"Why tell me?" she asked straight off.

"I should think it obvious," he explained. "We're attracted to each other, but unfortunately, you're a young lady of gentle breeding, unavailable for anything other than marriage. I therefore think it best we contrive not to be alone together."

"What you say sounds exceedingly sensible, my lord," Annabelle said sweetly. "I shall do my utmost to avoid you like the plague."

Cam's eyebrows shot up, but he held his tongue.

"Very well, then, good night," he returned stiffly. "And let me not catch you out again in such an outrageous scheme."

Annabelle smiled. "Oh, you won't catch me, my lord," she said winking at him brazenly.

WAYWARD ANGEL

VIVIAN KEITH

Harlequin Books

TORONTO • NEW YORK • LONDON
AMSTERDAM • PARIS • SYDNEY • HAMBURG
STOCKHOLM • ATHENS • TOKYO • MILAN
MADRID • WARSAW • BUDAPEST • AUCKLAND

To my husband whom I love, Keith Polasko.
For all his support, both emotional and financial,
and for being the one who truly listened.

Published July 1992

ISBN 0-373-31177-X

WAYWARD ANGEL

Printed in U.S.A.

CHAPTER ONE

MISS ANNABELLE WINTHROP'S head rested lightly against the red velvet squabs of the elegantly sprung Greywood coach-and-four. Annabelle was far too excited to sleep as did her Aunt Charlotte on the seat opposite. But then Auntie had been to London many times before—a feat Annabelle had heretofore been unable to duplicate. No longer. Annabelle smiled broadly, for at long last she, too, was headed for that great cosmopolitan metropolis.

It wasn't that Annabelle disliked the country—quite the opposite. She enjoyed scrambling over the hedgerows and lounging beneath the ancient willow trees which dotted Brierly, her Uncle William's enchanting country estate. But she was eighteen now, too old to find the same pleasure in such simple pursuits. These days, Annabelle's thoughts were more filled with the dashing young blades who dominated the Minerva Press novels she so enjoyed.

"Tripe!" That's what Uncle William called Annabelle's books; "Stuff and nonsense," her desire for a London Season. Uncle William hadn't allowed Annabelle her come-out when she was seventeen, and had almost vetoed it again this year. He was reluctant to loose the adorable hoyden who'd climbed up his trees and then into his heart. Fortuitously, Uncle William was no match for Annabelle's carefully orchestrated hysterics, nor for his wife's more subtle tactics. Misplaced pipes, burned Yorkshire pudding, stiffly starched cravats: Uncle William had lost the battle before it was earnestly begun.

So insistent had Annabelle been to make her debut this Season that she felt honour-bound not to reveal the homesickness which had begun to assail her the moment her bags were packed. A slight blush coloured Annabelle's cheeks. She should've told Uncle William how much she loved him before she left. Both he and Aunt Charlotte had been like parents to her since the death of her own mother and father when she was but a very small child. Annabelle vowed to make a great fuss over him when he joined them in London for her come-out ball.

Having soothed her guilty conscience, and with nothing else to do, Annabelle leaned over and stroked Mr. Fitzroy upon his little silver-grey head. Mr. Fitzroy opened one very large brown eye and growled. Annabelle stiffened in mock outrage and withdrew her hand. The quick-minded foxterrier then rolled upon his back and looked at her so beseechingly that she had to stifle a laugh. Annabelle continued to rebuff the dog, however, until she felt the pressure of his small paw upon her burgundy pelisse. "You little devil," she whispered, scratching him behind the ear just as he liked.

"Eh, what's that?" Aunt Charlotte queried, opening her twinkling blue eyes. She peered at Annabelle and Mr. Fitzroy somewhat myopically through her ever-present gold-rimmed quizzing glass.

"Didn't mean to wake you, Auntie," Annabelle said apologetically. "I was merely talking to Mr. Fitzroy."

"Well, I certainly hope he wasn't talking back," Aunt Charlotte replied, arranging herself more comfortably on the cushioned seat.

"Auntie, really, you know Mr. Fitzroy talks only when he has something truly important to say."

Aunt Charlotte chuckled and reached out to untie the leather flaps which she'd pulled down after lunch to cover the windows of the carriage. Bright sunlight poured through the glass, making the day seem deceptively mild. But the air outside the carriage still carried a nip of winter. The countryside was just now beginning to turn green, a few hearty spring flowers just now beginning to show colour.

As Annabelle and a newly energized Mr. Fitzroy gazed through the windows, Aunt Charlotte used the tip of her gold-studded walking-stick to rap upon the roof of the carriage. "John Coachman," she called out, "how do we progress?"

"We be passing through Sussex now, your ladyship," the coachman replied. "Not much farther to Londontown."

Annabelle felt a tingle run down her spine. Londontown!

Aunt Charlotte noted the glazed look upon her niece's face and felt her own surge of excitement. Annabelle's exuberance quite stripped away the years, until Aunt Charlotte could almost pretend that it was she who was going to London for the first time. The absurdity of such a notion made her speak more harshly than was her wont. "I hope you're prepared for a great deal of hard work, my gel. Opening the townhouse again after all these years will most certainly prove a Herculean task. Then there's all the shopping which must be done...."

A choked cough which sounded suspiciously like a giggle stopped Aunt Charlotte's tirade in mid-sentence. The older woman had the good grace to laugh. What eighteen-year-old girl minded the prospect of an enormous shopping spree?

"I shan't mind the work, Auntie," Annabelle insisted when her fit of the giggles had evaporated. "I'm just grateful for everything you and Uncle William have done for me. Why, my own parents couldn't possibly have provided as much, father being a country clergyman and all."

A thin veil of tears clouded Aunt Charlotte's eyes. Annabelle was a sweet soul. "You're a good gel," she said, patting her niece on the knee, and then added caustically, lest her niece think her growing soft, "and mind you stay that way."

Annabelle covered her aunt's hand with her own and gazed at the older woman fondly. Charlotte Greywood, the Duke of Weston's engaging only daughter, was completely white-haired now and possessed a figure considerably thickened, for Annabelle had come to Brierly long after the four Greywood boys were grown and living on their own. However, Annabelle had managed to keep her aunt on her toes these past several years, in addition to being the daughter the older woman had never had. Annabelle didn't know where she would be today if the Greywoods hadn't insisted that she come live with them. And she was truly grateful that they'd agreed to her desire for a London Season. No doubt at their age Aunt Charlotte and Uncle William would've preferred to continue rusticating in the country.

A sudden lurch of the carriage interrupted Annabelle's train of thought. Hastily she braced herself as the vehicle managed to plow through some unseen obstacle. A quick look at Aunt Charlotte, however, brought on another fit of the giggles. The turban the older woman had worn in the absence of a maid to arrange her hair had slipped down her forehead and was now resting squarely on the bridge of her nose.

"I'm blinded," Aunt Charlotte cried, struggling to push the offending article back into place.

"Only temporarily," Annabelle replied merrily as she switched seats, grabbed the turban and pulled it back, exposing her Aunt Charlotte's exquisite yet myopic blue eyes.

"I'm still blinded," Aunt Charlotte repeated frantically. "My glass—I seem to have dropped it."

Annabelle quickly lent herself to the search. A few moments later she located the missing object on the floor of the carriage. However, the quizzing glass had by then been well and truly crushed.

"I'm sorry, Auntie, but it is broken and the damage is quite irreparable," Annabelle reported, handing the unfortunate object back to the older woman.

Aunt Charlotte sighed and said, "Well, I'll just have to get another one when we reach London. Quite careless of me, really, to travel without a second."

Just then another lurch of the carriage sent Annabelle and Aunt Charlotte into each other's arms. Poor Mr. Fitzroy was deposited most rudely upon the floor.

"John Coachman, what is the meaning of this recklessness?" Aunt Charlotte demanded, pounding once again on the roof of the carriage with her walking-stick.

"Sorry, your ladyship, but it can't be helped. The spring thaw done tore up the roads something awful. There be potholes everywhere."

Aunt Charlotte snorted her displeasure, but her mind was quickly diverted by the blurry sight of Mr. Fitzroy chewing intently on something large and white beneath her feet. "Annabelle, see what that mangy cur is up to now, if you please," Aunt Charlotte directed.

"Mr. Fitzroy, how inappropriate of you!" Annabelle shrieked seconds later with genuine fury.

"What? What's he done now?" Aunt Charlotte questioned impatiently.

Annabelle's voice trembled. "Mr. Fitzroy has chewed our vouchers to Almack's," she replied in a dramatic whisper, clutching the all-important papers to her heaving bosom.

"Are they seriously damaged?" Aunt Charlotte enquired with a frown. Although she'd procured the vouchers quite easily from Sally Jersey (one of the patronesses of London's infamous marriage mart), she hardly relished the thought of demanding duplicates.

"No," Annabelle admitted, "but the envelope is decidedly dog-eared."

"It doesn't signify, child," Aunt Charlotte soothed. "We shall simply place them in a fresh envelope and no one will be the wiser."

Annabelle sighed, but her relief was short-lived, for at that precise moment the left front wheel of the Greywood coach-and-four descended into a pothole which John Coachman would later describe to his fellow servants as being the size of one very large barrel of rum.

The carriage tipped precariously. There was no saving it. John Coachman leapt clear as the sleek, black, gold-trimmed vehicle fell to its side.

On a hill not an eighth of a mile from the road upon which the Greywood carriage had been travelling sat an English gentleman mounted on a sure-footed steed named Merlin. The gentleman in question had watched the carriage making its slow progress, and had noted carefully the need to repair the road which ran parallel to his estate. Thus he was an eyewitness to the accident which occurred moments later. In fact, he'd spurred his horse forward even before the carriage hit ground. That's why Lord Camford Singletary, Earl of Westerbrook, was the first to reach the door of the fallen vehicle.

The four outriders provided by Sir William Greywood to see to the well-being of his wife and niece were hovering about the scene in various stages of shock. John Coachman sat moaning on the ground.

"Dismount immediately and assist me," Cam thundered at the outriders, who in the presence of such obvious authority hastened to comply.

The door to the carriage was then ripped open and five anxious faces peered inside. Both ladies were obviously shaken but appeared to be unharmed. "Here, let me help you," Cam said, reaching in for Aunt Charlotte. When she had been pulled to safety, he leaned forward again for the younger of the two.

Thoroughly disoriented, Annabelle felt a large pair of hands encircle her waist and without undue effort lift her from within the interior of the overturned carriage to the road outside. A handsome visage sporting black hair and light brown eyes allowed her to gently slide to the ground. For a moment Annabelle stared up at him, mesmerized, for he was very much like the heroes of her cherished romantic novels, tall and extremely broad-shouldered. But then a sudden pain in her ankle caused her to glance towards the ground as she let out a surprised squeak.

Having served as an officer in the British Army, Cam was no stranger to pain. He heard the plea for help in Annabelle's voice and immediately lifted her into his arms, noting absent-mindedly that she weighed little more than a child.

Annabelle almost swooned. The pain in her ankle was completely forgotten as she found herself crushed against the chest of this all-too-handsome man.

"Allow me to introduce myself, madam," Cam said, turning to address the older woman who was gazing about distractedly. "I'm Lord Camford Singletary, Earl of Westerbrook, and to my everlasting shame it is my stretch of road upon which your carriage has overturned. I suggest we repair to the house; I believe this young lady requires a physician."

Aunt Charlotte nodded her assent, only too happy in her befuddled state to relinquish control. "I'm Lady Charlotte Greywood and this is my niece, Miss Annabelle Winthrop. We're very grateful for your assistance."

Annabelle was so enthralled with Lord Westerbrook that she would gladly have followed the handsome earl to the ends of the earth. But when he proposed delivering her to his estate on the back of his horse, she was forced to cry foul. "I'm afraid that plan is impossible, my lord," Annabelle said, staring straight into the earl's twinkling brown eyes. "I don't care overmuch for horses."

"Don't like horses, you say?" Cam thundered, as if he hadn't heard correctly. Why, the chit was stark raving mad!

"Yes. I had a very nasty fall as a child and I've never quite got over it."

"You should've remounted at once," Cam stated firmly. "It's the only way to learn."

"Yes, I suppose you're right," Annabelle murmured, allowing her eyes to drop demurely, "but I can be most stubborn at times."

Cam snorted. "Well, then I've no choice but to seat you beside the road with your aunt, despite your injury, and ride for assistance myself."

"A most satisfactory solution, my lord," Annabelle agreed.

However, Cam had got Annabelle no farther than halfway to her destination when she emitted a startling shriek. "Oh, no, I've forgotten poor Mr. Fitzroy! Please carry me back to the carriage immediately, my lord."

"You mean there's someone else in there?" Cam asked, clearly puzzled as he turned back towards the carriage.

"Yes, indeed. My best friend in all the world."

One of Uncle William's outriders was just then lifting the unfortunate terrier out of the carriage as Cam strode forward. "That's Mr. Fitzroy?" he asked, making no effort to hide his disgust. Cam had little patience for lap-dogs.

Annabelle, who was beginning to think that Lord Westerbrook wasn't much like one of her romantic heroes after all, nodded stiffly and accepted Mr. Fitzroy's lead.

The trio had just started back towards the side of the road when Annabelle cried out again. "Oh, turn back, Lord Westerbrook, will you please? I must collect my vouchers to Almack's. I can hardly go to London without them."

"No, indeed, that would certainly be a tragedy of the first magnitude," Lord Westerbrook replied, pursing his lips firmly, but he did allow Annabelle to retrieve the all-important papers.

When Cam had at last settled the two women as comfortably as possible at the side of the road, he mounted Merlin—a magnificent charcoal grey stallion—and rode hell-bent for leather towards his estate. It was a cold day and he hadn't missed the way the two women were beginning to shiver. Then, too, Lady Charlotte was obviously not possessed of keen eyesight, and the little one was in need of medical attention.

The little one: Cam couldn't keep his thoughts from her as he pressed Merlin to the limits of the horse's endurance. Miss Annabelle Winthrop, as infuriating and naïve as the chit seemed to be, was nevertheless possessed of a certain amount of inherent charm. Though petite in stature, she was definitely not lacking in feminine curves—he'd felt those curves himself only a short while ago. Golden-brown curls, which fell about her cheeks in charming disarray, were the perfect compliment to a set of enormous, golden-brown eyes. But it was actually the set of her features which proved the chit's greatest asset, for Miss Winthrop, deservedly or not, had the face of an angel. Her magnificent eyes were set widely apart above a small, perfectly formed nose. Pink-tinged cheekbones, which hinted at Nordic ancestry, sat above two extremely prominent dimples. Full, pink lips proved a perfect foil to her creamy white skin. There could be no doubt that such an English rose would take well in London.

Cam drew quite a crowd at Westhaven as he thundered up to his estate. "Bring the carriage round, Jem," he shouted to his head groomsman. "There's been an accident on the London road. George, ride for Dr. Aimsbury if you will, and, Jenny, you'd best prepare two of the guest-rooms. Alan and Jess, mount up. I'll need you to help me right a carriage which is overturned."

The countess appeared in the doorway as the staff hurried to obey their master. "Any serious injuries, Cam?" Lady Margaret asked with a worried frown.

"No, Mother," her son replied from atop his horse, "but I'd like you to accompany me to the site, if you would. Two ladies were involved in the accident and your presence would undoubtedly soothe them."

"Of course," Lady Margaret agreed, ordering her Norwich shawl to be brought forth.

Within minutes, Lady Margaret was seated inside the estate's newest coach-and-four, bowling down the driveway in pursuit of her son.

Annabelle and Aunt Charlotte were indeed gratified to note the earl's return, for the wind was growing progressively colder and even the lap robe which Lord Westerbrook had placed upon them before he left was no great protection against the elements. Also, Annabelle's ankle was throbbing quite painfully by this time, and Aunt Charlotte was worried about the chaos which was bound to erupt among the London staff when she and Annabelle failed to arrive.

Cam lost no time in bundling the ladies into the carriage, whereupon Lady Margaret assumed control of their care. John Coachman, who had received a nasty bump on his head, was also placed inside the vehicle, despite his protests that, "It just tain't proper." Cam himself stayed behind to ascertain what could be salvaged.

Inside the carriage, Annabelle and Aunt Charlotte rubbed their hands together energetically, savouring the warmth from the heated bricks. Mr. Fitzroy curled himself into a small ball at Annabelle's feet.

"We're so sorry to intrude upon your hospitality, Lady Margaret," Aunt Charlotte said once everyone's comfort had been attended to. "I suppose we should've waited another week to set forth, until the roads had improved, but our servants and all our clothes had been sent ahead, and my niece was anxious to get her first taste of London."

Annabelle had the grace to blush, remembering the way she'd begged and pleaded for an early start.

"Nonsense, my dears," Lady Margaret stated firmly, sounding far older than her still-youthful appearance would credit. "Let's just be thankful that everyone seems to be in relatively good repair."

"Our people in London will be so worried—" Aunt Charlotte began, but Lady Margaret interrupted.

"We'll fire off a message as soon as possible," the countess promised. "But first I think we should wait to hear what the doctor has to say. Furthermore, my son Cam may have news regarding your carriage."

Aunt Charlotte nodded gratefully and let her head sink back against the squabs.

As Lady Margaret rose to arrange a lap robe on top of Aunt Charlotte, Annabelle used the opportunity to study Lord Westerbrook's mother. Obviously, he'd inherited his black hair and light brown eyes from her, but his massive frame must've come from the sire, for the countess was as diminutive as Annabelle herself. In fact, if it hadn't been for her distinctive colouring, Annabelle would've had a hard time believing Lady Margaret to be the mother of a full-grown son, for her hair was still jet-black and her skin as smooth as a babe's. Annabelle sighed and vowed to renew her weekly milk baths.

Not wanting to appear rude, Annabelle switched her focus to the windows as Lady Margaret resumed her seat. The carriage had long since departed the London road and was now making slow progress up a lengthy drive which was lined on either side by enormous old weeping willows. Annabelle felt a sudden pang of homesickness for Brierly as she watched the willows swaying gracefully in the wind. All resemblance to Brierly was lost, however, as Westhaven finally came into view. Whereas Annabelle's home was all mellow red brick, and relatively small, Westhaven was extremely large—a veritable palace of grey stone obviously constructed during Elizabethan times, for the house itself was patterned in the then-traditional E-shaped design.

Noting Annabelle's awestruck countenance, Lady Margaret smiled and said, "Ah yes, Westhaven. The old pile has been in the family since it was first constructed, hundreds of years ago."

"The old pile," Annabelle repeated stupidly.

"Said with much fondness, my dear," Lady Margaret reassured her. "I love this house with all my heart. . . ." The countess paused. "But for me it carries memories almost too painful to bear."

"Memories of your husband?" Annabelle guessed, ignoring Aunt Charlotte's sudden frown. Annabelle knew it was impolite to pry, but somehow she sensed Lady Margaret's great pain.

"Dead and buried these past two years," Cam's mother replied, making a visible effort to shake off her gloom. "But I digress. The house is yours for however long you need it. In fact, it will be nice to have guests again. Cam and I haven't entertained for quite some time."

Both Annabelle and Aunt Charlotte thanked Lady Margaret for her generosity as the carriage lurched to a stop. A footman clad in resplendent ivory livery helped the ladies to descend, carrying Annabelle into the house at the countess's direction. John Coachman was helped to the servants' quarters as the ladies repaired to the drawing-room, or the Blue Salon, as it was called.

Annabelle scarce had time to absorb the enormous marble-floored entrance hall lit by a magnificent Austrian-crystal chandelier before her senses were inundated by the beauty of the chamber in which she found herself. A parquet floor was covered partially by an intricately designed Aubusson rug; ice-blue walls were enhanced by delicately carved white wainscotting and crown molding; beautifully crafted Chippendale furniture was strategically situated, as was an ormolu clock and several Sèvres vases.

Annabelle was placed upon a blue satin settee and barely had time to rearrange the folds of her rust-coloured travelling costume before a tall, stern-faced major-domo by the imposing name of Bajardous appeared at Lady Margaret's behest.

"Your ladyship rang," he intoned in a stentorian voice. Annabelle jumped slightly and then had to refrain from giggling. Bajardous obviously took himself very seriously indeed.

"Please order up tea, and let us know immediately when the doctor arrives," Lady Margaret commanded, not in the least discomfited by her major-domo's grandeur.

"Very good," Bajardous replied with a slight bow. "And may I add that in future my lady should not take herself outside without benefit of a cloak in what promises to be a cold snap of indefinite duration."

Lady Margaret turned very slowly in her chair and fixed Bajardous with a gaze designed to wither even the most hardy of souls. "No, you may not," she said chillingly, giving the major-domo a definite set down. Lady Margaret then turned to her guests. "Bajardous, unfortunately, suffers from the delusion that he's my nursemaid."

Annabelle clapped her hand to her mouth to keep from laughing out loud.

Bajardous sniffed haughtily and exited the chamber, but not before Annabelle saw Lady Margaret rest her hand briefly upon his sleeve. Obviously there was affection between these two despite their difference in rank.

Tea was an enjoyable affair, as Lady Margaret kept her worried guests amused with tales of Bajardous's more outrageous behaviour. Since the major-domo had been with the family for years, he often took it upon himself to make pronouncements which wouldn't have been tolerated from other members of the staff.

The ladies, Aunt Charlotte in particular, had managed to make quite a dent in the little cucumber sandwiches, macaroons, seed-cakes and other delicacies sent up by the cook when the earl burst into the room, his black hair dishev-

elled by the wind, his very presence an anomaly in the otherwise feminine setting.

Annabelle felt her pulse begin to race as Lord Westerbrook sat down. Cam, as his mother called him, was an exceedingly masculine man. The Chippendale chair beneath
him hardly looked as if it could contain his weight.

Lady Margaret poured her son a cup of tea and he accepted it, albeit with a frown. Cam would've preferred
something stronger, but he was too preoccupied to procure
the brandy which he really desired.

Cam addressed himself directly to Aunt Charlotte. "I'm
afraid your carriage won't be fit for travel for quite some
time," he stated bluntly. "Although we managed to remove it from the road, the left front wheel is irreparably
damaged, as is the axle."

Aunt Charlotte just had time to murmur a distracted,
"Oh dear," before Bajardous re-entered the Blue Salon to
announce the arrive of Dr. Aimsbury.

Setting down her empty teacup, Lady Margaret rose to
greet the doctor. With a crook of her finger, she indicated
that Aunt Charlotte should follow. "Dr. Aimsbury, how
nice to see you again," the countess said with a smile. "I just
wish it were under better circumstances. This is Lady Charlotte Greywood. I'm afraid her niece has been injured in a
carriage accident."

As the doctor questioned the ladies, Cam glanced over
and noticed that Annabelle's eyes had grown quite large in
her head and that she was rubbing her hand nervously
against her skirt. Recognizing a skittish colt when he saw
one, Cam poured a small measure of brandy into a Water-
ford snifter. Keeping his back turned to the trio at the door,
he handed the glass to Annabelle. "I find brandy an excellent restorative at times," Cam said with a wink as Annabelle accepted the amber liquid.

She took a small sip and then another before surreptitiously handing the glass back to the earl. "You must think

me a sapskull indeed," Annabelle said with an apologetic smile. "It's just that I'm rather frightened of doctors."

Cam rubbed his chin thoughtfully. "Thus far we have established the fact that you're frightened of both doctors and horses," he remarked. "Tell me, Miss Winthrop, is there anything of which you aren't afraid?"

"Well, I'm not afraid of you," Annabelle retorted, tossing her curls angrily. She was only too aware that on this day she hadn't shown to her best advantage.

Cam laughed and couldn't resist a suggestive leer. "Are you so very sure of that?" he asked, training his eye on Annabelle's well-endowed bosom.

Blushing furiously, Annabelle told Lord Westerbrook in no uncertain terms that he was no gentleman.

"Never said I was, angel," Cam replied, pulling gently on one of her curls.

Annabelle slapped at his hand and tossed her head again, making it clear that she planned to thoroughly ignore the very unsettling Lord Westerbrook. Cam chuckled and casually sauntered away.

At the entrance to the Blue Salon, Lady Margaret's eyebrows rose slightly as she observed her son and the beautiful Miss Winthrop cavort. Lady Charlotte and the doctor were engaged in conversation and so missed the byplay, but not so Cam's mother. Fingering the folds of her gown absent-mindedly, the countess ushered Dr. Aimsbury towards the settee and his decidedly unwilling patient.

"A sprain," Dr. Aimsbury announced some time later as he clicked shut his black bag. "The patient should avoid undue motion or excitement until week's end. I'll be back on Friday to check Miss Winthrop's progress and at that point expect to find the young lady fully recovered. In the meantime, ice—and plenty of it—should be applied to the sprain, as much as she can tolerate."

"We can't possibly impose upon your generosity for a whole week," Aunt Charlotte cried with a worried frown.

Although Annabelle's health came first, she was loath to force either herself or her niece upon what amounted to virtual strangers.

"Of course you must stay," Lady Margaret insisted with surprising ardour. "Camford," she prompted, turning to her son for support.

"I hardly think you've a choice, given the doctor's orders," Cam said to Aunt Charlotte, shrugging his shoulders nonchalantly. "Mother and I don't mind. Besides," he added, "your carriage ought certainly to be repaired by week's end."

Giving way to the earl's logic, and their generosity, Aunt Charlotte nodded her agreement.

Having settled the matter to her satisfaction, the countess called a footman to carry Annabelle to her rooms. Cam disappeared into the library to go over some matters pertaining to the estate. The earl's mother used the opportunity to escort Aunt Charlotte up the stairs personally. "Annabelle is a charming gel," Lady Margaret stated, beginning to lead her guest towards the sensitive topic the countess most wished to explore.

"Yes, Sir William and I both fair dote on her," Aunt Charlotte replied sincerely.

"She ought to do well in London."

"We've high hopes, but would see her happy above all else."

"Naturally, naturally," Lady Margaret murmured, and then very carefully added, "However, she could do worse than to look for... an earl."

Aunt Charlotte understood Lady Margaret's meaning immediately. Keeping her eyes focused ahead as they climbed the stairs, Aunt Charlotte went straight to the heart of the matter. "Although Sir William plans to dower Annabelle handsomely, we've four sons between us who'll inherit the bulk of our estate. Annabelle is by no means an heiress."

Taking a moment to marshal her thoughts, Lady Margaret replied, "When a man is wealthy, and Cam does own considerable property both here and abroad, a dowry isn't of paramount importance. Cam will soon be thirty years of age and has yet to set up his nursery. My daughter has two children of her own, and as precious as they are, they're both female. If Cam fails to produce a son, the title will pass to a distant cousin, a man no one regards with undue fondness. I'd dislike Westhaven to fall into the hands of an abusive landlord."

Squinting at Lady Margaret through her myopic blue eyes, Aunt Charlotte patted the countess on the back sympathetically. "Life doesn't always seem fair, does it? I was blessed with four healthy sons, and yet my heart always ached for a daughter. Thankfully, Annabelle has filled that void and I would see her happy. Since the chit is still very young, it is my duty to push her in the right direction. I believe we can help each other in that regard, Lady Margaret."

Cam's mother smiled briefly, but there remained a troubled pucker on her lips. "On the estate which runs parallel to Westhaven lives a very determined young lady by the name of Lucinda Moresby. For years everyone has assumed that Cam and Lucinda would marry. The addition of Lucinda's acres to our land has always been a point in her favour, as has the gel's passion for horses. Cam is besotted by the creatures, you must know. He breeds them for sale, and quite successfully, I might add. Yet the years pass and Cam fails to act. I begin to doubt he feels more for Lucinda than friendship."

Turning to look the countess in the eye, Aunt Charlotte stated firmly, "I won't see Annabelle hurt. I cannot encourage a match if Lord Westerbrook's affections are elsewhere engaged."

Taking her guest's elbow, Lady Margaret steered the older woman to the door of the rooms she was to occupy. "I un-

derstand your position, but I'm certain that Cam feels
nothing for Lucinda. I shall plan a small dinner party while
you and your niece are here so that you might judge for
yourself. There are no guarantees in any case. Cam and
Annabelle may resist our attempts to throw them together.
Then, too, your Annabelle's a lovely gel. She'll undoubtedly prove a great hit in London, where she'll meet many
young, eligible gentlemen of the ton.''

Aunt Charlotte nodded her head and placed her hand
upon the doorknob. "Only time will tell, I suppose. And
now," she said with a conspiratorial smile, "I bid you good-
night, general.''

"Admiral," the countess replied, executing a formal bow.
"Until the morrow.''

CHAPTER TWO

ANNABELLE AWOKE the next morn feeling extremely rested. At first she was confused by the strangeness of the bed-chamber in which she found herself, but it didn't take long for her to remember the accident, or the pain in her ankle.

Wincing slightly, Annabelle inched her way into a sitting position and pulled on the bell cord which hung adjacent to the bed. Within seconds a full-figured young maid knocked on the door and then entered the chamber, carrying a tray of hot chocolate, toast and a bucket of ice for Annabelle's ankle.

"Morning, miss. My name is Lucy, and I brung you breakfast and ice like the doctor said." Setting down the tray, the maid began her ministrations. "There you go, miss," Lucy said soothingly as she applied the ice to Annabelle's offending ankle. "A few days of this and you'll be right as rain, you will."

Annabelle grimaced, but she couldn't find it in her heart to unleash her frustration on the jolly maid. "I expect you're right, Lucy," she said, sipping the hot chocolate and running her fingers through Mr. Fitzroy's wiry fur as he lay next to her on the bed.

While the maid attended her ankle, Annabelle took the opportunity to survey her bedchamber. She'd been too tired last night to pay much attention to her surroundings. It was a cheery room, the predominant colour being yellow. Delicately flowered chintz curtains and a matching counterpane offset the dark cherry wood furniture. On the wall opposite hung several sketches which the maid revealed to be early works of the Dutch master painter Rembrandt.

"That's got it, then," Lucy said a while later as she finished situating the ice on Annabelle's ankle. "If you be requiring ought else, miss, Lady Margaret said as how I was to look after you during your stay."

"As a matter of fact, I do have something for you to do," Annabelle stated firmly, in the tone of voice which many of the Greywood servants had come to dread. "Just because I'm confined to these dratted rooms all day is no reason why I must fail to be productive. I'm to make my London début, you know, Lucy, and of late I've become most concerned about my complexion. I've it in mind to take a milk bath if you please."

"Blimey! You're gonna soak your whole body in milk, miss?" the maid asked with incredulous eyes.

"That's correct, Lucy dear."

Being very young herself, and relatively unversed in the ways of the Quality, Lucy didn't question this tonnish miss's somewhat eccentric request. Marching below stairs, she quickly enlisted the aid of two footmen. The footmen in turn enlisted the aid of two groomsmen. Unfortunately, in their zeal, none of the servants thought to consult Bajardous. The major-domo was just showing the vicar out the door when his foot landed in a huge puddle of milk right in the middle of the entrance hall. Bajardous grasped ineffectually at the air around him and fell backwards, landing quite soundly on his rather insufficiently padded derrière. The major-domo, despite his rigid code of behaviour, emitted a bellowing howl which echoed throughout the halls of Westhaven.

Several things then happened all at once, so that no one was sure later exactly what had transpired. Lady Margaret and Aunt Charlotte came running from within the Blue Salon, where they'd been enjoying a comfortable coze following the vicar's departure. Cam appeared in the front doorway and announced in scathing tones that, "There's a bloody cow in the stables." Bajardous managed to crawl to his knees, whereupon he began a crablike pursuit of the head footman. The vicar chased after Bajardous, advising the major-domo quite firmly to turn the other cheek.

In the midst of all the confusion, Lucy appeared at the top of the steps. "Miss Annabelle, having finished her milk bath, requests that the noise be kept to a minimum, as she's attempting to take a nap," the maid parroted, having just received a lecture from that selfsame miss on the importance of proper diction.

"Her milk bath!" Cam sputtered, a sea of red swelling before his eyes. Clasping his hands together tightly, the earl looked heavenward as if seeking divine guidance. And then the absurdity of the situation struck him. He dropped his head into his hands and his shoulders began to shake.

"My lord," the vicar gasped, rushing forth to comfort and soothe.

But Cam's reaction wasn't quite what the vicar had envisioned. Dropping his hands, the earl's quiet laughter soon became a roar. Cam's mother joined her son in his hilarity and the two laughed as they hadn't done since the old earl died. Aunt Charlotte herself wasn't able to contain a chuckle or two despite her mortification. Only the vicar, who by nature did not possess a highly developed sense of humour, and Bajardous failed to find the situation amusing.

Picking himself—and his dignity—up off the floor, the major-domo stormed into the kitchens, where he proceeded to vent his spleen on the hapless servants.

Later that night, Annabelle received a stern lecture from Aunt Charlotte on the evils of disrupting an orderly household, particularly a household which didn't belong to them. Annabelle was properly contrite and even managed to spend the entirety of the next day in bed without causing upheaval. On the third day of her confinement, however, Annabelle began to chafe at the inactivity. She had quickly devoured the Gothic novel brought along for the trip to London and had nothing to do. Determined not to spend another day in bed, Annabelle woke early and gently eased herself into an upright position. Although her ankle pained her somewhat when she attempted to put weight on it, the sprain seemed to be healing nicely. A quick pull of the bell cord brought Lucy with Annabelle's morning chocolate.

"Oh, miss, do you think you ought to be up and about yet?" the maid questioned timidly as she saw Annabelle hobbling round.

"Probably not," Annabelle replied with an infectious grin, "but I vow that another day spent abed will surely turn me into a Bedlamite."

Lucy giggled and eyed Annabelle's leftover toast with relish.

"Go on and finish it, Lucy, if you must, but I warn you that men generally appreciate women with less, shall we say, fully developed figures?"

"The second footman likes me just fine the way I am," Lucy retorted with a satisfied smirk, butter running down her ample chin.

"I yield to the opinion of the second footman," Annabelle replied, for she, too, liked Lucy just the way she was. "And now, if you're finished, I would appreciate some help with my toilette."

"Of course, miss," Lucy replied, "and what's it that you'll be wearing today?"

Annabelle frowned. She had nothing with her save the contents of a single portmanteau. The rest had been sent ahead with her maid Betty. That left her with three choices. She could rewear her burgundy travelling costume, she could don an old yet serviceable sprigged muslin, or she could put on the cream silk. Best save the silk for dinner tonight, Annabelle reasoned, directing Lucy to assist her into the muslin.

Annabelle knew that her desire to be in her best looks was in part dictated by the presence of the divinely handsome Lord Westerbrook, whom through Lucy she now knew to be eminently eligible. This knowledge didn't please Annabelle, for she was unsure that she liked the earl even one tiny bit. Far preferable were the lads her own age at home, whom she'd managed to taunt and tease without censure. Yet Lord Westerbrook was more representative of the London dandies with whom she'd soon be sparring. Perhaps it would behoove her to test the waters with the earl. Annabelle was terrified of being branded a country bumpkin by the ton.

Upon realizing just how tight her sprigged muslin had become, especially around the bodice, Annabelle sighed with exasperation. *Oh well, there's no help for it now,* she thought as she tugged against the straining fabric.

Lucy then proved her worth as a future lady's maid by arranging Annabelle's hair into a becoming knot at the nape of her neck. "Well done, Lucy," Annabelle praised, causing the maid to blush and stammer her thanks. "Now run into Aunt Charlotte's rooms and bring me her walking-stick. I've a mind to take myself outside for a stroll."

For a moment Lucy looked as if she might balk at the request. Annabelle was in no condition to be gambolling about.

"Go on now, Lucy," Annabelle chided, giving the maid a small push. "You wouldn't want me to die of boredom, would you?"

Lucy rolled her eyes but obeyed the command none the less.

Thus it was only minutes later that Annabelle had her aunt's walking-stick firmly in hand and was brandishing it about as if it were a veritable sword.

"Blimey, be careful with that thing, miss," Lucy squealed as she jumped out of range.

"Don't be a ninnyhammer," Annabelle replied with perfect calm. "I was merely testing its weight."

Using the stick to pull herself up, Annabelle was able to cross the room quite easily despite a slight tenderness in her afflicted ankle. Not too bad, she mused silently, standing on her good foot while she opened the door. Seeing no one in sight, Annabelle quickly emerged into the hallway and gingerly made her way down the carpet-lined corridor. The marble stairs looked to be somewhat more of a challenge, but, fortuitously, at that moment a footman appeared in the foyer and rushed to her assistance.

By placing most of her weight on the footman's arm, Annabelle was able to descend the stairs one at a time, arriving at the bottom quite triumphantly only to be accosted by Bajardous, who wore an expression best described as one of extreme dislike.

"I wasn't aware that you'd been given permission to leave your bed, miss," Bajardous said disapprovingly, looking down at Annabelle from his great height.

Annabelle blushed profusely. Aunt Charlotte had told her about Bajardous's tumble during the milk-bath incident and she couldn't fault the major-domo his ire. "Oh, but I feel so much better today, Bajardous," Annabelle said, smiling broadly. Then she allowed her eyes to drop. "I felt I just had to make the attempt to come downstairs, if only to apologize to you for whatever discomfort you may have suffered on my behalf." Lifting her large golden-brown eyes, Annabelle stared at Bajardous entreatingly. "Do say you forgive me."

For a second, Bajardous's cool demeanour dropped and he looked as if he might actually smile. But then he coughed and collected himself. "No need to apologize, miss," he said sternly.

"Oh, but there is a need and I do apologize most profusely."

Bajardous nodded slightly and turned his back, indicating with a flick of his wrist for the footman to be about his business. Annabelle couldn't be sure, but she thought she heard Bajardous murmur, "Baggage," under his breath before he made his slow, imperious way down the hall.

In any case, Annabelle's attention was quickly diverted by the sound of loud clapping behind her. She whirled about, only to find Lord Westerbrook braced casually against the wall. "That was quite a performance, my dear. Too bad your birth precludes you from treading the boards. I'm convinced you would make as fine an actress as Sarah Siddons herself."

Annabelle gasped indignantly, but she could find no words to voice her displeasure, for Lord Westerbrook looked so very handsome that he quite took her breath away. His black hair was carefully combed into a style known as the Windswept; his light brown eyes were twinkling merrily above a snowy white cravat which contrasted sharply with his rather ruddy complexion. His broad shoulders were encased in a perfectly cut jacket of brown superfine, and his long yet muscular legs showed to advantage in buckskin breeches and shiny black Hessians.

Fearing he'd think her henwitted, Annabelle turned towards the door. "I'm going for a walk," she announced haughtily over her shoulder.

Cam followed Annabelle outside. "May I join you, Miss Winthrop?" he asked very properly.

Annabelle shot him a quelling glance and said, "If you must."

To her annoyance, Lord Westerbrook chuckled. "Well then, let me lend you my arm, as I see your ankle has not completely healed."

After a moment's hesitation, Annabelle placed her hand on his arm and allowed Lord Westerbrook to lead her forth. Had she not just decided to practice the art of flirtation upon the earl? However, nothing suitably coy struck her immediately and the two walked in silence until in desperation Annabelle finally blurted out, "Tell me, sir, what do you think of the French situation?" She could've bitten her lip after having uttered the words, for Aunt Charlotte had warned her that gentlemen of the ton didn't care for ladies who were overly blue.

Yet Lord Westerbrook seemed to ponder her question most seriously. "Napoleon was a lunatic, of course. It was our responsibility to restore France to benevolent monarchy."

Uncle William's sentiments exactly, but not necessarily her own! "Don't you understand that the people of France yearn for freedom? For centuries they've been abused under the yoke of the nobility. England, too, must ultimately grant her people greater freedom or face similar consequences."

"Do I harbour a revolutionary beneath my roof? For although there's truth to what you say, surely you recognize that changes of such magnitude must evolve slowly if they're to evolve at all."

Annabelle bristled. "The Americans seem to be instituting quite rapidly the changes of which you speak."

"America is new. Americans don't have centuries of tradition with which to contend."

Thinking quickly of an intelligent rejoinder, Annabelle found herself delighting in the debate. In similar fashion she had spoken with her Uncle William. His lively conversation had constituted the greater part of her education—that and the books he insisted she read despite her aunt's objections. "The gel has a quick mind, Charlotte," Uncle William was fond of saying. "Besides, with the boys gone I must have someone with whom to argue."

As Annabelle and Lord Westerbrook strolled along the south lawn and into the formal gardens which existed behind the estate, neither noticed the small shadow which trailed them from the house with such dogged determination.

In fact, Annabelle was discovering Lord Westerbrook to be just as vexing, if not more so, than her uncle, and Cam was finding himself surprised that a woman as angelically beautiful as his companion could also possess such astute intelligence.

Thus it came as somewhat of a surprise to Annabelle when she found herself in the midst of a large, pebbled retreat with sculpted shrubbery, and a marble reflecting pool sporting a statue of Neptune, from which water would ultimately pour forth as the weather improved. As the day was mild, Annabelle let drop her shawl. Looking about, she recognized the roses which would burst forth shortly, and to her delight spotted a small growth of bluebells which had braved the still-harsh spring weather.

"Oh, my lord, are they not lovely?" Annabelle rhapsodized, bending over the bluebells to view them better.

"Truly lovely," Cam agreed, but his eyes were not focused on the flowers. Instead, he was greedily devouring the sight of Annabelle's ample cleavage as she bent over to gaze at the blossoms.

Sensing his change in tone, Annabelle gazed up quickly to ascertain whether Lord Westerbrook was holding her in jest. That didn't seem to be his intent. In fact, the expression on his face caused her heart to beat faster and her breath to come in short, quick gasps.

"And now," the earl said, grasping Annabelle's upper arms to bring her body close to his, "if you've finished inspecting my mind as well as my flowers, I think I should like to kiss you, for I've been planning to do just that ever since I laid eyes on your angel face."

Annabelle couldn't move, couldn't break free as she knew she ought. Lord Westerbrook held her entranced. He was so very handsome, his body hard against her own, his arm like an oaken pillar behind her back. Annabelle's eyes never left his as he traced a finger down her cheek, down her neck, letting it rest against her tightly fitting bodice.

His lips came down on hers gently, as if he sensed her inexperience. Annabelle sighed and melted into what amounted to her first adult kiss, for the pecks she'd received heretofore couldn't begin to compare.

"Put your arms about my neck, angel," Cam said, beginning his instruction. Annabelle's sweetness, her naïveté, were making him wild.

As if drugged, Annabelle slowly ran her hands up Lord Westerbrook's coat, for he was tall, taller even than Bajardous. She interlaced her fingers behind his neck and tentatively pressed her body closer to his.

Cam groaned and tightened his grip. There was nothing gentle about the kiss which descended upon Annabelle's lips this time, and although for a moment the intensity of his passion frightened her just a little, Annabelle found herself responding to him with passion of her own.

Annabelle revelled in the embrace for several seconds before the impropriety of the situation forced her to push hard against Lord Westerbrook's massive chest. Heavens! Should anyone see them, her reputation would be ruined before she even reached London.

Cam felt Annabelle begin to struggle, but the little minx felt so good in his arms that he was loath to release her. Unfortunately, Mr. Fitzroy, who'd trailed his mistress from the house, didn't understand that Lord Westerbrook's intentions were basically honourable. Rushing forth to battle, the dog clamped on to the earl's buckskin breeches with his teeth and growled as menacingly as a fox-terrier is capable of.

"What the deuce?" Cam sputtered, feeling the sudden pressure on his leg.

"Mr. Fitzroy, desist immediately, I tell you!" Annabelle commanded, but the dog, having ascertained that his mistress was no longer in danger, was not above engaging in what he deemed to be a little harmless play. Thus, Mr. Fitzroy only clamped his teeth together more tightly and refused to let go his prey.

Cam shook his leg and then shook it harder. At one point Mr. Fitzroy's short legs actually left the ground, but the dog was nothing if not persistent. "Miss Winthrop, kindly deliver me of this plaguey nuisance!" Cam demanded with a roar as his ruddy complexion grew redder by the moment.

Annabelle stifled a giggle, for the sight of the exceedingly masculine Earl of Westerbrook bested by a small fox-terrier was one for the record books indeed. However, Annabelle was quite certain that Lord Westerbrook wouldn't remain a meek victim indefinitely, so she knelt upon the ground, grabbed Mr. Fitzroy by the nether half of his squirming body and pulled with all her might.

A sudden rent of fabric landed Annabelle on her posterior, left Mr. Fitzroy with a sizeable portion of buckskin between his teeth, and had Lord Westerbrook staring at disbelief at his denuded leg.

"Miss Winthrop, I do believe that trouble seems to follow wherever you lead," Cam stated baldly.

"I'm not deserving of such a scold," Annabelle replied with feeling. Embarrassment prompted her to add angrily, "If you hadn't kissed me, Mr. Fitzroy would never have attached himself to your leg."

"Oh ho, so it's my fault now, is it? Well I suggest, Miss Winthrop, that you make more of an effort to act your years rather than like a child in leading-strings or you're going to make a cake of yourself in London, and deservedly so!" Cam thundered in scathing tones.

"You're a perfectly beastly man," Annabelle retorted, leaning over to pick up Mr. Fitzroy, who had been following the argument with interest. Once she had the dog firmly in hand, Annabelle turned back towards Westhaven.

"Are you mad? You'll never make it back to the house on your ankle carrying that... that *thing*," Cam stated. He grabbed Mr. Fitzroy out of Annabelle's arms before she could protest and strode back towards the house with the fox-terrier squirming in his embrace.

"You and I have a great deal to discuss," Cam said to the dog when Annabelle was well out of earshot.

Mr. Fitzroy's ears went flat and he sighed heavily.

From a window in Westhaven's Blue Salon, Aunt Charlotte and Lady Margaret watched the combatants as they separated. Aunt Charlotte could barely make out the figures on the ground below and thus had to rely on the countess for an accurate account of what was occurring. Lady Margaret obliged happily, leaving out only the fact that her son had kissed Aunt Charlotte's niece. No need to overset the kindly old lady, especially if it all worked out satisfactorily in the end.

"I do believe there's little more to see," Lady Margaret said at last as Cam disappeared from view and Annabelle limped slowly towards the house. "Won't you be seated? I shall ring for tea."

Aunt Charlotte inclined her head and placed herself upon the blue satin settee. "Well, it seems as if our opening gambit has paid off," Aunt Charlotte said, arranging her skirts most contentedly. Annabelle could do worse than to snare an earl.

"Indeed. I think it most prudent to continue to leave Annabelle to her own devices. After all, it's only natural that she and Cam would drift together, given the fact there is little for two such energetic young people to do here at Westhaven."

Dinner that night was a strained affair, at least for two of the four seated at the enormous cherry wood dining-table. Although Aunt Charlotte and Lady Margaret managed to carry on some semblance of conversation, Annabelle and Cam sat mutely.

Thus it was a relief when the ladies rose to leave Cam to his brandy. That gentleman sighed happily when they were gone, but he proceeded to consume much more of the stuff than was his wont, because he was quite frankly confused. His attraction to a chit just out of the schoolroom was not in character, especially since the earl had no intention of marrying anytime soon. Oh, he knew that eventually he had to produce an heir, but that necessity was years away. Someday he'd probably just give over and marry Lucinda Moresby as everyone expected him to do, since he'd no intention of actually falling in love with the woman he took to wife. Too much heartache. Witness the suffering his mother had gone through when his father died.

In any case, Cam still had much too much living to do to think of marriage. He was fervently looking forward to his return to London. He'd stayed away for the past two years for his mother's sake, but was growing ever more restless. He remembered a little opera dancer by the name of Marie.... Cam grinned and snapped his fingers. Obviously his attraction to Annabelle was predicated upon his need to keep company with a woman of refinement. The buxom doxy who worked out of the Lion's Head Pub in Westhaven Village had long since succeeded in boring Cam to death. He wanted a mistress familiar with the ways of society. And in the not-too-distant future, God willing, he'd have one!

Annabelle excused herself shortly after Aunt Charlotte and Lady Margaret had ensconced themselves in the Blue Salon. Pleading a headache, she hobbled to her rooms, where Lucy waited to help her prepare for bed.

Only when the maid had been dismissed and the candle by her bed snuffed out, did Annabelle allow herself to think of Lord Westerbrook, for the topic was one to which she wished to devote her entire attention. Obviously she was attracted to the earl, despite their argument, and just as obviously he was attracted to her. However, Annabelle wasn't such a goose as to believe him in love with her, nor she with him. London lay ahead—exciting, exhilarating London— and the Town was full of eligible bachelors. Annabelle could see no harm in flirting with the earl, but her heart she wasn't ready to give. Furthermore, Lord Westerbrook obviously

thought of her as little more than a child. Had he not said
so? Annabelle sighed, for despite her logic, Westerbrook
was devilish handsome. Sliding down upon the pillows,
Annabelle allowed herself to relive each intoxicating moment of his kisses.

IT WAS RAINING HEAVILY when Annabelle woke the next
morn, so there was no question of her going outside for a
walk. With Lucy's help, however, she did dress, and using
Aunt Charlotte's walking-stick, began a tour of the magnificent manor. Annabelle noted as she strolled down one
corridor after another that Westhaven was certainly large
enough to fulfil even the most vigorous of exercise regi-
mens. At one point she actually became lost and had to re-
trace her steps in order to figure out exactly where she was.
Since Annabelle hadn't the nerve to enter any of the many
chambers she encountered along the way, it was the portrait gallery which held her interest the longest. She was
amused to note that Lord Westerbrook descended from a
long line of overly large men. She also learned, by careful
inspection of his sire's portrait, that the current Earl of
Westerbrook was the sixth to hold the title.

In fact, Annabelle was feeling with her finger the texture
of the painting depicting the former earl when she heard
behind her a *Tsk, Tsk* noise which could only have one
source: Bajardous! Annabelle quickly dropped her hand
and, whirling about, presented the major-domo with her
heavily dimpled smile. In doing so she prevented the scold
which hung on Bajardous's lips.

"Where's everyone got to this morn, I wonder?" Annabelle questioned, meaning of course Lord Westerbrook,
since she'd failed to turn him up during her tour.

"The countess and Lady Charlotte are in the Blue Salon.
Your *dog*—" Bajardous emphasized the word "—is in the
kitchens begging cook for kippers left over from breakfast.
Lord Westerbrook's in the stables where he's been all night.

Apparently a mare gave birth to two foals early this morn and by all accounts had a very difficult time of it.''

Bajardous hadn't even finished speaking before Annabelle was scurrying down the hallway as fast as her tender ankle would allow.

"I don't believe it a fit sight for a young lady, miss," Bajardous called out after her, but Annabelle didn't pay him the slightest heed. A fear of horses she did have, but Annabelle also possessed a genuine love of animals.

Rushing through the kitchens, for they provided the quickest access to the Westhaven stables, Annabelle absent-mindedly noted Mr. Fitzroy, upright on his haunches, accepting small bits of kipper from plump Mrs. Freedly, the cook. Annabelle shook her head slightly, grabbed a cloak off a hook near the door and rushed out into the rain. She was pelted immediately by torrents of water, made all the worse by the frigid March wind. Annabelle shivered and quickened her pace.

The warm air coming from inside the stables was like nirvana as Annabelle entered the first of several wooden structures. Braziers had been lit against the cold and placed strategically so as to provide comfort to the mare and her newborn foals.

Entering a stall towards the end of the row, for Lord Westerbrook had a large complement of horses, Annabelle saw the earl sprawled out in the hay, running a hand fondly over the neck of the new mother, who was still on her side. One of the foals was greedily sucking at its mother's teats; the other was lying off to the side with its eyes closed.

"Is the poor thing dead?" Annabelle whispered, entering the stall reverently.

"No, but close to it. The foal's so weak the mother refuses to nurse her. I'm afraid there's not much we can do," Cam replied, wearily stroking his unshaven face.

Annabelle felt tears begin to well up in her eyes. "Oh, but there must be something we can do, isn't there?" she pleaded, looking at the rejected foal.

"I thought you didn't like horses," Cam scoffed, weariness and frustration causing him to respond more harshly than he had intended.

Tears coursed down Annabelle's face as she inched closer to the rejected foal. "I never said anything about *baby* horses," she replied nonsensically, reaching out to gently caress the newborn. As if sensing a kindred spirit, the foal's eyes fluttered open and she weakly thrashed her hind legs.

Annabelle sat down in the straw, heedless of her gown, and took the foal's head in her lap. As the golden-brown beauty nestled the horse, Jem, the head groomsman, came rushing into the stall with a specially prepared teat.

"Don't know if this'll work, my lord, but if we can get 'er to take it and build 'er up a bit, mayhap the mother'll take 'er on."

"Do it then, Jem," the earl commanded. But the foal refused to take the teat from Jem's gnarled but capable old hands.

"Steady on, young girl," Lord Westerbrook said to the horse, taking the teat from his head groomsman and offering it to the foal himself. The newborn still refused to suck.

"Let me try," Annabelle offered. Rubbing a bit of the sugar water on her finger, she stuck her hand into the foal's mouth to give her the flavour. The ploy seemed to work, for after Annabelle repeated the process patiently four or five times the foal finally began to accept the teat. A collective sigh was heard throughout the stables as the foal responded to Annabelle's ministrations. Annabelle herself felt a growing sense of exhilaration as the newborn's tentative sucking became stronger.

"Don't get your hopes up yet, Miss Winthrop," Cam cautioned, watching the golden-brown beauty feed the foal. "We've no guarantee that the mother will ever accept her."

"Oh, but she will. I know she will. She must," Annabelle cried passionately. "She is, after all, the mother."

Cam chuckled. "That doesn't always signify, angel," he said.

Annabelle felt her face redden. Lord Westerbrook had no business calling her pet names in front of Jem and the other Westhaven groomsmen. She looked up and found the earl smiling at her wickedly. He was well aware of her discomfiture.

"Jem, take over for me here. I must go," Annabelle stated, feeling a sudden urge to escape the stables, and in particular Lord Westerbrook, for his state of déshabillé only added to his allure. Annabelle couldn't keep her eyes from his smooth chest, which showed beneath the ripped and dirty lawn shirt, nor from the lock of black hair which hung down his forehead, giving him the look of a naughty schoolboy.

"Wait," Cam said, chasing after Annabelle as she fled the stall. "I must thank you for your help before you go."

"I really did very little, as you well know, Lord Westerbrook. In any case, I happen to love animals and children. I pray the foal survives."

"Do you want many children then?" Cam asked, locking his light brown eyes with hers.

Annabelle felt her heart quicken at the intensity of the earl's gaze. "Of course, at least four," she said. "Don't you?"

"Well, not at this very second, but perhaps another time, Miss Winthrop."

"You're a perfectly..."

"Beastly man," Cam finished, watching in amusement as Annabelle flounced out of the stables. Feeling in much better spirits now that it seemed the foal might survive, Cam couldn't resist adding as the golden-brown beauty disappeared from sight, "Oh, and may I compliment you on your complexion. It seems that your milk bath, while causing a minor disruption for the rest of the household, has indeed done wonders.''

"Oh!" Annabelle fumed as she struggled through the rain, "I shall never talk to that man again."

So angry was she that she completely ignored Mr. Fitzroy as she stormed through the kitchens and on towards her rooms. Annabelle was so vexed that she ran full tilt into Cam's mother as that good lady was exiting the Blue Salon.

"Why, whatever has overset you, child?" the countess questioned, noting Annabelle's high colour.

"Lady Margaret, I regret to inform you that your son is an ill-bred oaf."

"Annabelle!" Aunt Charlotte chided, emerging from the Blue Salon in time to hear her niece's barb.

Annabelle had the grace to blush. "I'm very sorry for that remark, Lady Margaret, especially since you've been so kind to us."

"Think nothing of it, my dear," the countess said, trying to contain her glee. "Why don't you go along to your rooms now and take a nap. There's a good gel."

Aunt Charlotte apologized profusely for Annabelle once her niece had departed and added, "It's too bad the children can't seem to rub along. I had such high hopes for a match."

"Don't despair yet, my dear," Lady Margaret advised. "Remember, passion is often equal parts love and hate. I'd say things are moving along quite famously."

CHAPTER THREE

THE RARE ROAST BEEF with Worcestershire sauce looked appetizing, but Annabelle was so incensed that she managed only half of what was on her tray. A delighted Mr. Fitzroy found himself the recipient of what his mistress didn't manage to consume.

After the meal had been disposed of, Annabelle placed herself in front of the fire in her sitting-room and propped her feet up on a small embroidered footstool. She sat staring morosely into the flames. Bored, Annabelle wished belatedly that she'd decided to join the others for dinner. Yet she was still furious with Lord Westerbrook and couldn't trust herself to behave with dignity where he was concerned. Thank heavens there was only Lady Margaret's dinner party to get through tomorrow night, and then the next day she and Aunt Charlotte would leave for London.

After an hour or so of feeling inordinately sorry for herself, Annabelle finally decided to go to bed. She wasn't by nature a self-pitying type of person and began after a short while to feel rather foolish. Lord Westerbrook's behaviour was of little concern to her. Very soon she'd be in London—glittering, sparkling London—where she was sure at least some of the young men of the ton managed to conduct themselves with propriety. Annabelle totally ignored the little voice within her head which hinted that men who behaved with propriety might invariably prove dull.

Just before Annabelle snuffed out the candle beside her bed, a tentative knocking sounded on the door to her rooms.

Annabelle pulled the covers up close beneath her chin and called out, "Who's there?"

"I'm sorry if I woke you, miss," answered Lucy, "but I've something here you best be taking a look at."

Feeling strangely disappointed, yet curious, Annabelle pushed back the covers and padded to the door. Lucy then slipped inside, looking for all the world like the cat who has been given the proverbial bowl of cream. "The master done give me this personal," she stated with satisfaction, handing Annabelle a folded piece of heavily bonded paper.

Annabelle's heart skipped a beat as she fingered the expensive stationery, but for Lucy's benefit she managed a look of disdain. "Perhaps I should just toss it into the fire," she announced, moving closer to the flames.

"Sounds best to me, miss," Lucy said, laughing outright at Annabelle's horrified expression. "Go on, open it, then," the maid added, plopping herself down in one of the yellow-and-white striped satin wing-chairs which flanked the fireplace.

Staring pointedly at her chubby companion, Annabelle proclaimed, "You're excused now, Lucy. I wish to be alone."

"Humph" was the answer as the maid pulled herself up and sashayed to the door. "Already know what it says, anyway."

"Impertinent wretch," Annabelle retorted, smiling as she flung a pillow at Lucy's retreating back. The maid was well aware that Annabelle couldn't complain about her service, not in this instance, anyway, given the clandestine nature of Lord Westerbrook's missive. As ridiculous as it seemed, there existed very strict codes of behaviour governing the sanctity of a lady's reputation.

Annabelle seated herself before the fire and opened the note. Much to her disappointment, for Annabelle possessed a romantic turn of mind, the missive in no way threatened her reputation. In it Lord Westerbrook simply apologized for having overset her, and suggested that she might like to visit the newborn foals first thing in the morn. Annabelle smiled and decided that the earl wasn't so bad after all.

Before she went to bed that night, the golden-brown beauty carefully slipped Lord Westerbrook's note into her portmanteau for safe keeping, although she didn't bother to consider why she felt it worth saving.

Bright sunshine filtered through the cheery yellow curtains the next morn as Annabelle yawned and stretched. She was glad the weather had improved, for now Lady Margaret's guests were assured safe passage on their way to Westhaven that night.

Anxious to find Lord Westerbrook and see the foal she'd helped to nurse, Annabelle rang for Lucy and quickly enlisted the maid in helping her dress. The golden-brown beauty turned her nose up at having to don yet again the tight sprigged muslin, but contented herself with the thought that London was only a day away now and soon the modistes would be sewing furiously on her behalf, thanks to Uncle William's largesse.

Practically skipping down the hall, for her ankle had recovered completely, Annabelle flew down the steps and narrowly missed bumping into Bajardous.

"Pardon me," Annabelle gushed breathlessly, "but have you seen Lord Westerbrook? Is he in the stables?"

"My lord returned from seeing to the horses hours ago, miss," Bajardous intoned. "I believe you can find him in the study, if you like."

Annabelle turned to go. "Oh, Bajardous, which way to the study?"

In his long-suffering manner the major-domo explained, "Up the stairs, miss, and turn towards the west wing. To the left at the end of the corridor. You'll see the double doors straight ahead."

Annabelle nodded and was off. Seconds later she was knocking at the doors to Cam's study.

"Come," was the succinct reply from within.

Annabelle grasped the brass door handles and pushed. She was so awestruck at the magnificence of the Westhaven study that for the first several moments she didn't notice Lord Westerbrook's frown of displeasure. The study contained an enormous collection of leather-covered, gold-embossed books which were displayed in ground-to-ceiling cherry wood bookshelves. A crimson leather couch and two matching wing-chairs had been placed before the fireplace, over which hung an original Thomas Gainsborough landscape. Annabelle took several minutes to examine the Gainsborough before she finally swung round and smiled at the earl, who was seated behind a large cherry wood desk.

"How's our young protegée doing?" Annabelle asked, referring to the newborn foal.

"You'd know yourself if you'd come to the stables with me as I requested first thing this morn," Cam replied somewhat tersely. He was damned if he was going to dance on Miss Winthrop's string.

Annabelle stared at Lord Westerbrook in confusion. "But it is first thing in the morn and I'm quite ready to go as you requested."

Cam could only stare at her, mouth agape. He checked the gold watch which hung from a fob on his waistcoat. "Miss Winthrop, it's exactly one hour short of noon. Do you mean to inform me that you regard this as first thing in the morn?"

Annabelle looked at Cam quite innocently. "Well, naturally, Lord Westerbrook. I very rarely quit my rooms any sooner. In fact, I'm up early, but I thought you'd be pleased with my punctuality. You see, I much prefer to keep night hours. I admit I did retire somewhat early last evening, but then I'm so used to my schedule that I find it quite difficult to break."

"You're going to do extraordinarily well in London, Miss Winthrop," Cam stated, shaking his head. "Extraordinarily well. Unfortunately, I'm unable to accompany you at this hour, as I'm expecting my bailiff shortly and must discuss with him several matters pertaining to the tenants. Naturally, I'll provide escort if you prefer to wait until later this afternoon."

Shaking her head, Annabelle replied, "That won't do either, Lord Westerbrook. You see, I promised your mother and my aunt to help them with a few last-minute details before the dinner party tonight."

At that moment a knock sounded on the door. Lord Westerbrook rose and somewhat distractedly faced Annabelle. "That'll be my bailiff. I'm sorry for the confusion, but if you go to the stables, Jem will be happy to inform you as to the well-being of the foal. Until later, Miss Winthrop."

Hiding her disappointment, Annabelle nodded her head and exited the room, passing the somewhat elderly bailiff on her way out. With time on her hands, she went upstairs, collected Mr. Fitzroy and then headed to the stables, where she was happy to discover that the weaker foal had gained some margin of strength. The mare was still refusing to nurse, but Jem was confident that the situation would soon change for the better.

Having received the good news, Annabelle then led Mr. Fitzroy down the south lawn and into the formal gardens behind the estate. She noticed immediately that the roses had begun to sprout buds, and spent an enjoyable interlude strolling about, the small fox-terrier nipping at her heels.

When her stomach began to rumble, for Annabelle had ignored her hot chocolate and toast earlier that morn, much to Lucy's delight, she headed back to the house, entering the small dining-room the family used during the day by way of a set of French doors covered in Belgium lace.

There she found Lady Margaret and Aunt Charlotte enjoying a light repast of shrimp salad. It wouldn't do to overindulge at midday. The dinner party later that night promised to deliver a sumptuous feast of many courses. Annabelle quickly took a seat, placing a white linen napkin in her lap as a hovering footman served her a portion of the salad.

The three ladies then began a discussion of all which remained to be done before the party that night, and it was decided that Annabelle should write out the name cards to be placed before each plate, and that she should arrange the table's centre-piece using fresh flowers from the garden.

Thus Annabelle found herself busily occupied until tea, at which time she accepted only a small cup of Oolong in anticipation of the dinner to come. Although it was the custom for ladies of the ton to pick daintily at their food when in public, the countess had planned so many courses that Annabelle knew she'd get quite full even if she only took one bite from each offering.

Directly after tea, Annabelle, Aunt Charlotte and Lady Margaret withdrew to dress for dinner. Annabelle was greatly vexed that she'd no other choice than the rather plain cream silk she'd already worn every evening that week, but there was no help for it. She certainly couldn't fit into anything Aunt Charlotte might possess, and Lady Margaret's gowns were inappropriate for a young lady directly out of the schoolroom. Thus, Annabelle had to content herself with a rather elaborate coiffure which Lucy happily arranged, and a brilliant Norwich shawl which the countess insisted she borrow.

"You look beautiful, miss," Lucy offered when she was finally satisfied with her charge's appearance.

Annabelle wrinkled her nose and frowned. "This old gown makes me look quite the ape leader," she dramatized. "But I suppose it shall have to do."

The maid sighed heavily. "Yes, miss, I suppose it shall."

"I do believe you delight in bamming me, Lucy. I must remember to ring a peal over your head concerning the evils of servants who fail to remember their stations."

Not in the least discomfited, Lucy began to straighten Annabelle's room. "I'll wait up to help you undress, miss. You'll be wanting to talk, I'm sure." She threw Annabelle a significant look.

Annabelle shook her head. Whatever did Lucy mean by that cryptic remark? In any case, there was no time to drag an explanation out of her. Annabelle was late as it was.

Hurrying down the steps, the golden-brown beauty arrived in the austere, yet magnificently appointed entrance hall just as the rather dour-minded vicar was being shown into the house. Annabelle smiled at the cleric rather sheepishly, for he'd been an eyewitness to the milk-bath incident, and then turned her attention to the resplendent ivory-liveried footman who opened the doors to the Blue Salon and ushered them inside.

Lady Margaret and Aunt Charlotte were holding court with an elderly couple, the Ponfrets, who lived not far from Westhaven. The Ponfrets' only son, Randolph, took one look at Annabelle and made a beeline towards her. Annabelle smiled sweetly despite the fact that she felt no immediate attraction. Although Randolph Ponfret was handsome enough, with his blond hair and blue eyes, he couldn't be much older than herself, and he was such the dandy that she had difficulty containing her amusement. His shirt points were so high he could scarce turn his neck, his cravat so intricately tied that Annabelle knew instinctively it must've taken the better part of the afternoon to create, his waistcoat such a shocking shade of pink that it was almost blinding—a condition enhanced by the number of chains and fobs hanging from his chest.

However, Annabelle allowed the young Mr. Ponfret to sit next to her on the blue satin settee, for his conversation was definitely preferable to that of the vicar, who had a tendency to pontificate upon all matters large and small. Thus, for the next several minutes, Annabelle found herself the recipient of all sorts of delectable on dits concerning people she scarce knew. Still, it was somewhat entertaining to listen to Mr. Ponfret, whose conversation was interspersed with stories of curricle races, gaming hells, White's, Brooks's, Boodle's, and Gentleman Jackson's. In fact, Annabelle was greatly relieved that Mr. Ponfret seemed intent upon carrying on the conversation when Lord Westerbrook entered the room, for the sight of the earl in his elegant black evening attire, set off by the white of his shirt and a magnificent sapphire stud resting in the folds of his cravat, caused Annabelle to momentarily lose track of her surroundings. Mr. Ponfret's words were reduced to so much babble, not that it mattered. Randolph Ponfret was the type of gentleman who enjoyed hearing himself talk to the exclusion of all else.

Maintaining a heavily dimpled smile for her erstwhile suitor, Annabelle nevertheless watched surreptitiously as the earl made his bow to his mother, Aunt Charlotte, the vicar and the older Ponfrets. She felt her heart quicken as he strolled over to where she sat with Randolph and almost giggled when she saw his look of commiseration. Obviously Lord Westerbrook was well used to Randolph Ponfret's mode of conversation. Annabelle sighed as the earl sat himself in a Chippendale chair close to the settee, and for one instant she wished she had her aunt's walking-stick with which to brain Mr. Ponfret. Would the man never cease talking? Annabelle was of a mind to expand the conversation to include the earl.

Still, Lord Westerbrook was close, and Annabelle delighted in the opportunity to observe him as he ordered a drink from a passing footman. In fact, she was staring at him intently when the door to the Blue Salon opened to admit the last of Lady Margaret's guests, and she was thus privy to the look of appreciation which crossed the earl's face as Squire Moresby and his daughter Lucinda were announced.

Annabelle quickly noted Lucinda's beauty, and struggled to overcome the instantaneous feeling of dislike with which she was assailed. Tall, possessed of golden hair, clear, lovely green eyes above a smile which lit the room: Lucinda was everything Annabelle wasn't. Annabelle fingered her brown locks distractedly as every male eye turned towards the vision in pink. Lucinda was dressed in a gauze evening gown which fell perfectly over a simple yet elegant satin slip. Her diamond necklace was perhaps a bit inappropriate for an unmarried lady, yet Lucinda was hardly a girl and the necklace was a sublime compliment to the delicately lovely gown. The stunning blonde was clearly the type of woman who'd be first noticed in any gathering, even if her features weren't perfectly matched. She was mesmerizing.

Annabelle watched intently as Lucinda walked purposefully towards Lord Westerbrook. For such a beautiful female, she had a decidedly masculine stride which Annabelle couldn't help but notice and applaud. The icon was not without fault.

"Cam, it's been an age," Lucinda cried in a loud, jarring voice which was also oddly incongruous with her delicate appearance.

She calls him Cam, Annabelle thought to herself miserably.

"Yes, it has been," the earl replied, quickly turning the stunning blonde towards Annabelle and Randolph Ponfret as if hesitant to pursue that line of conversation. "Lucinda, you know Randolph, of course. And this is one of our house guests, Miss Annabelle Winthrop. She and her aunt were involved in an accident on their way to London and have been staying with us until their carriage is fit to travel. Miss Winthrop was slightly injured, but I believe she's since recovered completely."

At Lord Westerbrook's raised eyebrow, Annabelle replied, "Yes, I'm feeling fine now. It's a pleasure to meet you, Miss Moresby," she added diplomatically, although pleasure wasn't by any means the emotion she was currently experiencing.

"When do you go on to London, Miss Winthrop?" Lucinda questioned sharply, not liking at all the looks of the little chit who sat so comfortably in Lady Margaret's elegant Blue Salon.

"We leave on the morrow," Annabelle replied, unsure why she seemed to have incurred Lucinda's enmity. A stunning beauty such as Miss Moresby could hardly fear someone like her.

"Too bad," Lucinda replied in her brusque manner, although she didn't really seem in the least disappointed. "You'll miss the Founders Day Race. Cam is sure to supply the winner just like he does every year, although this time we're entering a horse which I believe might surprise everyone."

"The Founders Day Race?" Annabelle questioned.

Mr. Ponfret, who looked to be turning red in the face from having been ignored so long, lost no time in explaining to Annabelle that the Founders Day Race was an annual event held to judge the potential of area one-year-olds for races farther afield. Annabelle nodded her understanding but was quite left out of the conversation as Lord Westerbrook, Mr. Ponfret and Lucinda engaged in a lengthy discourse about past winners, training methods and breeding strategies.

Annabelle's attention had begun to wander when it was jerked abruptly back by Lucinda. "What's this I hear about you trying to save a foal too weak to nurse? That horse will never be good for anything, Cam. It ought to be destroyed."

"No!" Annabelle cried vehemently, colour leaping into her cheeks. "That is to say," she began more reasonably, "I'm sure the horse can be used for some future purpose."

"Thoroughbreds don't plow fields, Miss Winthrop. It's best to be realistic. Cam is simply wasting time and money on what can only in the end prove to be a bad investment."

"I don't believe the saving of a life, any life, can be couched in terms of investment. That foal's in need of assistance and I think it should be given her. She's so small and helpless and so very adorable...." Here Annabelle stopped, for Lucinda was staring at her with a superior air which quite rankled.

"Emotion can serve no purpose in business, Miss Winthrop," Lucinda remarked, looking directly at Cam.

It was Mr. Ponfret, however, who came to Lucinda's defence. "Your womanly sentiments are admirable, Miss Winthrop, and to be expected, but Miss Moresby has a point. Sentiment has no place in business," he proclaimed, patting Annabelle on the hand as if she were directly related to Mr. Fitzroy.

"Sentiment and cruelty are two separate issues," Annabelle argued heatedly, jerking her hand away from Mr. Ponfret. If there was one thing she couldn't stand it was male condescension.

Cam felt a sudden need to reassure Annabelle that the foal would indeed be taken care of. He understood well the point Lucinda and Ponfret were trying to make, but Cam loved horses too well to destroy one unless it was absolutely necessary. The earl raised his hand. "The foal will be given every opportunity to survive. And now I see Bajardous in the doorway. Dinner is served."

True to Annabelle's expectations, the meal ordered by Lady Margaret was every bit as elaborate as that which befitted an earl. The meal began with salmon in wine sauce, progressed to lamb served with snow peas, and continued through rarebit, roast beef, and capon. Throughout the meal, Squire Moresby maintained a running discourse designed to highlight his daughter's many and varied accomplishments. It was obvious that he was a doting parent, and it became equally obvious that he regarded Lucinda and Cam as practically engaged. This knowledge, whether true or not, caused Annabelle's appetite to flee and made her much quieter than was her norm. In fact, Annabelle thought that if she had to listen to stories concerning Lucinda much longer she was going to be acutely ill.

"Tell me, Miss Winthrop, of what accomplishments can you boast?" Squire Moresby asked at length, no doubt sensing that his audience was beginning to tire.

"None," Annabelle said emphatically and then added with a sense of mischievousness she couldn't control, "I've no accomplishments." Now this was blatantly untrue, as Annabelle was not too inferior at the piano and could paint a passable water-colour. But she had had more than enough of the Moresbys. "In fact, in terms of a true business investment, I suppose I ought to be destroyed."

Cam choked on his capon and as he did so emitted a strange snort which sounded suspiciously like a laugh. Randolph Ponfret wasn't so restrained. He threw back his head and roared as his parents, the vicar, Lady Margaret, the Moresbys, and Aunt Charlotte in particular, looked on aghast. When he was able, Ponfret gazed at Annabelle with renewed appreciation, obviously beginning to sense that she was no ordinary schoolroom miss, but was in fact a diamond in the rough, one he looked forward to being credited with discovering.

"Truly, Miss Winthrop—a marvellous hit," he crowed. "You must allow me to call upon you and your aunt just as soon as I arrive in London."

"You go to Town as well?" Annabelle questioned, eager to have at least one available escort at the ready.

"As soon as I can get away," was his impassioned response.

Ponfret's obvious adoration of Annabelle drew a frown from Lord Westerbrook, which no one noticed save Lucinda. The other guests were too busy wondering what in heavens the seemingly highly strung Miss Winthrop had meant by her extraordinary remark.

Annabelle was relieved when Lady Margaret finally rose to lead the ladies from the dining-room. She was full to bursting and was looking forward to walking off some of the sumptuous repast. In fact, Annabelle would've loved to slip away from the party and take a lengthy stroll about the gardens, but she knew that she couldn't be so rude. Aunt Charlotte was sure to scold, was probably planning to do so anyway, because of her scandalous remark at dinner. Annabelle was reluctant to provoke her aunt further.

Cam sat back in his chair and signalled the footman to bring forth the port. Bajardous was already passing out fine cigars which contained imported Haitian tobacco. Usually Cam enjoyed this ritual, but tonight he found himself anxious to join the ladies. One never knew what the engaging Miss Winthrop was about and Cam found the anticipation quite intoxicating. Annabelle was never boring like...like Lucinda, he forced himself to acknowledge. Cam experienced a pang of guilt. For years he'd in so many ways led Lucinda to believe that they'd marry. After all, her estate marched parallel to his; she was enthralled by horses; she rose early in the morn; she had little use for lap-dogs; and she was as beautiful a woman as any man could want. Cam sighed. He'd marry Lucinda as he'd long planned to do. It really was the only prudent course to follow in order to ensure a marriage of convenience. Why then did the thought of marrying the stunning blonde leave him cold? Cam shrugged and forced himself to listen to a ribald story being told by Squire Moresby. There was plenty of time to think of marriage...later. After all, he did plan to return to London one day—when his mother was fully recovered— and all the decadence that went with a life in Town.

When the men finally rejoined the ladies, who'd repaired to the music room, Lucinda was already seated at the piano running scales. *Apparently, she's not only an accomplished horsewoman, but also a gifted pianist,* Annabelle thought miserably. In fact, Lucinda did play the piano well, her long, slender fingers lending themselves aptly to the needs of that particular instrument. Clearly she was enjoying the attention and obviously felt it was her due. There was no doubt that Lucinda was not about to abandon her plan to become the next Countess of Westerbrook.

Lucinda played Mozart with technical perfection. Her fingers fairly flew across the keys, but unfortunately her ability was somewhat lacking because she was unable to imbue the music with any true feeling. Annabelle wasn't surprised, for Lucinda's music seemed to mirror her rather cold and haughty personality. Smothering her feelings of exultation at Lucinda's lack of ability, Annabelle stifled a yawn as the blonde continued to play. She found her attention wandering to the elaborate rococo decoration of the music room. Portions of the ornately carved walls and ceiling had been gilded in gold, providing a stately air. An enormous tapestry on the far wall, as well as several smaller ones elsewhere, further added to the room's grandeur.

As Lucinda finished her piece and the guests joined in a round of polite applause, led of course by Squire Moresby, the stunning blonde rose from the piano and indicated with a flick of her wrist that Annabelle was now free to entertain. From the smug expression on Lucinda's face, Annabelle guessed that she thought her incapable of topping such a stellar performance.

Annabelle tossed her golden-brown curls and sat down at the piano. She'd decided to play a set piece of Bach that she'd long since memorized for just such occasions. But Lucinda's smug expression rose up in her mind and Annabelle experienced a change of heart. She, too, was no musical genius, although she liked to think her playing better than Lucinda's. But would the guests be able to distinguish between two relatively uninspired performances? Annabelle thought not. Recalling last Christmas, when all the Greywood boys had returned home to Brierly and got absolutely bosky, Annabelle proceeded to play a little ditty she'd heard them sing:

> Prinny sits in Brighton town
> As Regent he's denied the crown
> Instead he builds wonders fair
> Criticize, no one would dare
> Of Caroline to whom he's wed
> It's said she'll not share his bed
> Both their pleasures elsewhere seek
> Though Prinny's girth doth make him weak

Mr. Ponfret could contain himself no longer. Apparently the tune had made the rounds amongst the London bloods and he jumped up to join Annabelle in song as she went through several more verses. The reaction of the other guests was somewhat more mixed. Squire Moresby, a man with a somewhat off-colour sense of humour, found himself tapping his foot quite automatically. Lucinda simply glared. How could her own father encourage such outrageousness? The older Ponfrets didn't seem to know how to react, although the obvious enjoyment of their son seemed to mollify their natural inclination to disapprove. Lady Margaret and Cam stared at each other, trying very hard not to laugh. Annabelle's song was, after all, treasonous, and completely inappropriate coming from the mouth of a schoolroom miss. The vicar sat with pursed lips, scarcely able to countenance such unseemly behaviour. Yet if the earl and countess didn't object, who was he to question his betters? It was Aunt Charlotte who had the most extreme reaction, and unfortunately for her niece, she wasn't pleased.

When Annabelle finished, Mr. Ponfret exclaimed excitedly, "Oh, I say, that was simply brilliant, Miss Winthrop. Play another, do!"

Aunt Charlotte chose that particular moment to call a halt to the proceedings, before the situation got totally out of hand. "I'm afraid Annabelle and I must say our goodnights. It's been a most enjoyable evening, but we leave early tomorrow morn and should get some rest."

"But, Auntie, we're to play piquet later," Annabelle protested, forming her perfect pink lips into an artful pout.

"I'm sorry, my dear, but I really must insist," Aunt Charlotte said mildly. Her expression, however, brooked no disobedience.

Annabelle knew when to give in gracefully, so with a somewhat sorrowful sigh, she rose from the piano bench and dipped a small curtsy to the assembled guests. Upon exiting the music room, Annabelle noted Aunt Charlotte's ramrod bearing and knew that she was about to suffer a monumental scold.

Annabelle was correct. It started just as soon as the footman had closed the doors behind them. "Well, my gel, whatever were you about to embarrass me in such fashion?"

"But, Auntie," Annabelle pleaded, "Uncle William and the boys sang that song at Christmas...."

She got no further. "Use some sense, gel. That song was sung by a group of drunken men, in the privacy of our own home. It wasn't meant for your ears, and was hardly appropriate for you to perform."

"Yes, Auntie," Annabelle said dolefully, casting her enormous, golden-brown eyes to the floor.

Aunt Charlotte wasn't mollified. "You'd best attend me, gel, else your London days will end in ruin. Men may appreciate that kind of entertainment from a certain sort of woman, but they don't appreciate it from a young lady looking to be a wife and mother. Your impulsiveness may very well spell disaster, Annabelle. So far you've failed to embroil yourself in any real trouble, but then we're in the country, far removed from the dictates of London Society. Do what you just did in a London drawing-room and you shan't be received—anywhere!''

Red splotches appeared on Annabelle's cheeks and she felt truly humiliated. She had no desire to make a cake of herself, or ruin her chances at marriage.

Seeing her niece's contrite expression, Aunt Charlotte relented somewhat. ''I only want what's best for you,'' she said, taking Annabelle by the arm as the two proceeded to their rooms. ''Your high spirits will stand you well in London, but you must ever be on guard against excessive behaviour. You're young and prone to foolishness. I trust you'll come to me when you're in need of guidance, and will rely upon me to make the right decisions?'' As her niece nodded her head eagerly, Aunt Charlotte sighed. Would Annabelle truly heed her advice? ''Let us review then the tragedy of Caro Lamb,'' she said, newly inspired.

It took Annabelle a long time to reach her rooms that night. Aunt Charlotte detained her for upwards of an hour. When she finally did arrive, she'd forgotten about Lucy and the maid's promise to wait up. Suddenly, though, Annabelle knew exactly why Lucy had been so insistent upon waiting.

''She's a cold one, she is, but beautiful, what?'' the maid asked, helping her mistress out of the cream silk gown.

Annabelle knew that as a young lady of Quality she shouldn't engage in gossip with servants, but this was one instance when she had absolutely no intention of obeying that stricture. ''Does Lord Westerbrook plan to marry Lucinda?'' Annabelle asked quietly.

''The idea's been bandied about some,'' Lucy granted, taking down her mistress's hair. ''But if you ask me it'll never happen. It's plain as the nose on yer face that he don't love 'er. And in all these years he ain't never asked 'er.''

Sighing heavily, Annabelle turned to the maid and, surprisingly, before she could stop herself, burst into tears. It hadn't been a good night. She'd met the beautiful woman Lord Westerbrook undoubtedly planned to marry, no matter what Lucy said, and the idea upset her far more than she was consciously willing to admit. Furthermore, she'd embarrassed herself in front of strangers and earned Aunt Charlotte's censure in the process. Most importantly, tomorrow she left for London despite the fact that now all she really wanted to do was remain at Westhaven.

Lucy comforted her mistress as best she could and put her to bed. Despite an initial period of restlessness, Annabelle eventually slept soundly and in the morn felt much better. Yawning, for she didn't normally awaken at such an early hour, she allowed Lucy to help her into her burgundy-coloured travelling costume once more.

While Annabelle dressed, the countess sat with Aunt Charlotte in the small dining-room sharing one final coze.

"I apologize for retiring early last night, but Annabelle's conduct was most inappropriate," Aunt Charlotte said, peering myopically at Lady Margaret.

The younger woman smiled and waved her hand. "It doesn't signify, for my objective was accomplished. It's obvious my son doesn't harbour a serious tendre for Lucinda Moresby. Why, after your niece retired, Cam and young Mr. Ponfret were both most restless."

Aunt Charlotte smiled. "I too am convinced that Cam is attracted to Annabelle and she to him. Why, my gel has hardly mentioned London since we've been here and she used to talk of nothing else. Yet how do we further relations between the two with Annabelle in London and your son here at Westhaven?"

"Admiral, I shall send Cam to you at the first opportunity," Lady Margaret promised with a wink.

"That sounds a fine plan, general. I'll be sure to keep you informed."

The newly repaired Greywood coach-and-four was packed and ready to go; the Greywood outriders mounted and armed. As the countess and Aunt Charlotte hugged, for the two women had grown enormously fond of each other, Cam appeared next to the carriage and took Annabelle aside.

"I've enjoyed having you here, angel. I almost wish you didn't have to leave. Be good in London and be sure to save me a waltz at Almack's."

"Why, Lord Westerbrook, I'd think the infamous marriage mart beneath an obvious Corinthian such as yourself," Annabelle bandied, her confidence as usual fully restored.

"On second thought it's probably best that you are leaving, because when you're near I've an almost constant, uncontrollable urge to turn you over my knee," Cam stated, his light brown eyes twinkling merrily.

"You wouldn't dare," Annabelle replied in a scandalized tone, but she smiled as she bent her head over Mr. Fitzroy, who was busily squirming in her arms.

"Say goodbye to Lord Westerbrook, pet," Annabelle coaxed, fully expecting the dog, now considerably fatter thanks to the Westhaven cook, to growl and bare his teeth. Much to her vexation, Mr. Fitzroy licked Lord Westerbrook's hand.

Cam laughed. "I'm quite good at taming unruly creatures," he said smugly.

"Balderdash!" Annabelle sputtered and flounced away, allowing herself to be helped into the carriage. She refused to give Lord Westerbrook the satisfaction of waving goodbye, but felt quite miserable as the carriage began to roll down the long, willow-lined drive.

Cam stood beside his mother as the carriage disappeared, a bland expression on his handsome face. But Lady

Margaret noted the way his fist tightened on his riding crop. As they re-entered the house, the countess was unable to contain her glee and spent the remainder of the day with a secret smile plastered on her still-youthful face.

CHAPTER FOUR

LONDON! Despite plaguing thoughts of the earl and West-haven, Annabelle felt her spirits rise the nearer the Greywood carriage came to the sprawling metropolis. She bounced back and forth anxiously between the windows on either side of the vehicle as Aunt Charlotte watched with amused tolerance. One's first sight of Town was always special, the elderly lady knew.

"Why, Auntie, there's so much traffic I don't see how anybody manages to pass," Annabelle exclaimed, watching the post-chaises and carriages and phaetons and curricles all vying for position. "And, Auntie, it smells most dreadfully, and listen to the noise. Why, however shall we sleep amidst the clamour? Oh, and look, there's the Tower. I can't wait to tour it. You know I've always been most partial to poor Anne Boleyn. And over there's an open market. They're hawking bunches of violets and meat pasties and all manner of items."

Having seen the sights many times before, Aunt Charlotte sat back and let Annabelle ramble. Her thoughts were preoccupied with the work which awaited her when they arrived. There was the hiring of additional servants to be done, the planning of Annabelle's ball, the shopping for new clothes, the invitations to sort through—for she'd written to several old friends that they were coming. There were the balls and parties and routs to chaperon.... Suddenly Aunt Charlotte smiled. She hadn't felt this alive in years. Perhaps she and William were too buried in the country. From now on she would make more of an effort to get to Town.

By the time John Coachman had managed to manoeuvre the Greywood carriage into the West End towards Berkeley Square, some of Annabelle's exuberance had faded. It was starting to darken outside and she was tired. Annabelle listened to the clip clop of the horses' feet against the cobblestones and closed her eyes. At long last she was in London! But why, oh why had she ever been forced to set eyes upon Westhaven and its magnificent master?

The Greywood townhouse was smaller in comparison to most of the other residences in fashionable Berkeley Square. The property had been purchased long before the address had become such an exclusive one. Nevertheless, Aunt Charlotte had managed to imbue the house with an air of elegance hard to deny. The Greywoods need never fear censure on that score. And to Annabelle's way of thinking, no place could've been more perfect from which to launch her début.

The following weeks were busy ones for the golden-brown beauty and she was glad of it, for she found herself with little time to pine over the Earl of Westerbrook. In fact, it wasn't long before she began to wonder if her feelings for the handsome Camford Singletary weren't little more than a young girl's infatuation. With typical enthusiasm, Annabelle threw herself into fittings, and into making new friends. She met several girls who were also in London for the first time, and together they shared long walks properly chaperoned by their maids, carriage rides through Hyde Park, numerous discussions about everything from the latest scandals to the fashions of the day, and many other pursuits especially recommended for young ladies of the ton.

Aunt Charlotte had limited their acceptance of invitations to small gatherings, waiting upon such time as Annabelle's new wardrobe was complete. Then too, knowing her niece's propensity for impulse, Aunt Charlotte had determined to introduce Annabelle to London slowly. Let the gel absorb as much as possible before she was thrust into the full social whirl of the Season.

After two weeks, however, Annabelle began to chafe at the restriction. All her new friends had already attended Almack's and were busy with a full schedule of social engagements. Annabelle launched an all-out attack on Aunt Charlotte and was rewarded with that lady's begrudging capitulation. On Wednesday, Annabelle would finally be allowed to attend London's infamous marriage mart, after which they'd begin to accept invitations to larger, more sophisticated gatherings.

When Wednesday finally arrived, Annabelle's excitement knew no bounds. She awoke that morn much earlier than was her wont and found herself snapping at Mr. Fitzroy for no good reason. She refused to accompany her aunt on morning calls, feeling that her air of distraction might be misinterpreted as boredom. Annabelle soon came to regret her decision, however, as time weighed heavily on her hands. She tried to read a book, but her eyes continually strayed from the page. With nothing better to do, she wandered down to the kitchen, but the servants didn't appreciate her presence as they might have done at Brierly. Here she was a stranger.

Somehow, however, Annabelle contrived to get through the day until at last it was time to dress. She chose her gown with care, wishing that it were Lucy helping her and not the ever-pessimistic Betty.

"It's no use worrying overmuch about your appearance, miss," the maid intoned as she was fixing Annabelle's hair. "It's likely to rain in any case and all our work will be for naught."

Annabelle stared at Betty in the mirror and sighed. Though a cut above the usual servant, she was skinny to the point of looking starved and wore her prematurely grey hair pulled back tightly into a chignon. Annabelle rather liked the maid, for Betty had been with her for two years now, but she sometimes wished the woman would learn to look at life a little more optimistically.

"Whether it rains or not this is my first appearance at Almack's and quite naturally I'd like to look my best," Annabelle chided mildly.

"Why any sensible woman would fuss about looking nice just to catch a husband is quite beyond me, miss, but I expect that's your business."

"What's wrong with getting married?" Annabelle asked fatalistically, even though she knew she ought not. Tonight was special. Why ruin it by listening to Betty's predictions of doom and gloom?

"Men have all the say in marriage," Betty explained, her mouth full of hairpins. "Get a bad one and your life won't be worth living."

"But Betty, I'm fortunate in that my aunt and uncle plan to allow me to choose my own husband, within reason, of course," she added, knowing that they'd hardly allow her to marry just anyone.

"Never can tell about men first met, miss. Some of them take years to show their spots."

"Yes, well, ah, thank you, Betty, for your advice," Annabelle said, having heard enough. Seeing that the maid had finished her hair, the golden-brown beauty got up to look in the mirror and had to admit that she was extremely pleased with the results. A pessimist she might be, but Betty was also well worth her weight in gold as a lady's maid. Taking the velvet cloak, ivory fan and silk reticule which Betty held out to her, Annabelle flashed the maid her heavily dimpled smile and rushed out the door. At the top of the steps she paused for dramatic effect, seeing that her aunt awaited her in the entrance hall below. She then proceeded down the steps very slowly.

Through her newly purchased quizzing glass Aunt Charlotte watched her niece descend the steps, for once taking them as a young lady ought, and felt the tears well up in her eyes. Would that the gel's parents had lived to see this night. They would've been so proud, for Annabelle had inherited from them the very best of their combined good looks. Her head seemed to shimmer like a halo with her golden-brown curls piled high, augmented by a spatter of pearl pins. Her matching brown eyes twinkled excitedly and her cheekbones were bright with natural colour. A simple strand of pearls encircled her long, swanlike neck and matched the pearl bracelet upon her wrist. The white jaconet muslin gown worn over a sarsenet slip (which was also trimmed at the bottom with pearls) made Annabelle's complexion literally glow.

"You look lovely," Aunt Charlotte complimented as Annabelle glided close. She gave her niece a gentle squeeze.

"Thanks to you, Auntie," Annabelle replied, returning the hug.

"Well, enough of this sentimental nonsense. We'd best leave if we have any hope of avoiding the crush."

Their timely departure availed them naught. Awaiting access to the Assembly Rooms, carriages were lined up on King Street as far as the eye could see. "Blast, I'd forgotten just how bad it gets," Aunt Charlotte remarked, using a rare expletive. Annabelle hardly noticed as she sat stiffly on the seat opposite, her foot beating a rhythmic tattoo. The ladies were nervous, as they both had high hopes for Annabelle's success. Although it seemed unlikely she'd be relegated to the ranks of wallflower, the possibility loomed large in both their minds. Annabelle had looks aplenty, but she didn't possess an enormous fortune and she had a tendency towards the impulsive.

About a half-hour later the Greywood carriage finally pulled up to Almack's. Annabelle seemed incapable of movement as she stared at her aunt with large frightened eyes.

Aunt Charlotte knew she had to appear confident for her niece's sake. "Chin up, my gel. And don't forget to act with decorum."

That brought Annabelle round, for if there was one thing she couldn't stand it was an unnecessary scold. "I shall be the perfect lady," she announced, slightly miffed, allowing the footman to hand her down from the carriage.

"We'll see," Aunt Charlotte muttered under her breath, following her niece into line.

The physical reality of the Assembly Rooms was a great disappointment to Annabelle. Considering the fact that Almack's was a veritable institution amongst the ton, she couldn't credit the plainness of the décor, nor the unappetizing fare.

It wasn't long, however, before Annabelle began to regard Almack's as an almost magical place. Within seconds of her arrival, Annabelle had spotted one of her new friends, an engaging redhead who couldn't be acknowledged a beauty, but who possessed a fortune which had already ensured her success. Lady Violet Silverton, daughter to the Duke of Montvale, saw Annabelle at precisely the same moment and waved excitedly. It wasn't long before both the girls were surrounded by a sea of men, for Lady Violet's inheritance was the stuff of legends and Annabelle's beauty was quite fearsome. In the distance, Aunt Charlotte noted the mêlée and breathed a huge sigh of relief. Now she could retire with the turbaned Mrs. Arthur Johnstone for a lengthy gossip.

Annabelle laughed happily as she busily scribbled names onto her dance card. She promised the first dance to Randolph Ponfret, who seemed to have appeared out of nowhere. As the set formed, Annabelle gave the blond dandy her hand and allowed him to lead her forth.

"You look perfectly beautiful this evening, Miss Winthrop," Ponfret gushed as he took in Annabelle's glowing golden beauty.

Annabelle had long since taken Ponfret's measure. He didn't confuse her the way Lord Westerbrook did. Randolph Ponfret was an egotist, overly concerned with the opinions of others. Still, he was young and fun and Annabelle felt on top of the world. She didn't hesitate to flirt shamelessly. "If I'm indeed as beautiful as you say, Mr. Ponfret, why is it then that you've yet to call?"

Randolph actually blushed and his blue eyes stared beseechingly into her own. "Miss Winthrop, I'm only recently come to Town. In fact, my father insists I return for the Founders Day Race. We've several entries, you know, though none expected to do as well as Westerbrook's horse. I'm in Town only to look at some prime goers for my father at Tatt's tomorrow. Then it's back to Sussex until after the race on Saturday."

Nodding her understanding, Annabelle listened with half an ear as young Ponfret continued with a diatribe on the necessity of obeying one's parents. Perhaps Lord Westerbrook would come to Town after the race as well, Annabelle surmised. After all, he'd promised to partner her at Almack's. That had to mean he intended to visit London sometime during the Season, didn't it? Or would he keep himself confined at Westhaven for Lady Margaret's sake?

"...Don't you agree, Miss Winthrop?"

Annabelle looked up at Randolph Ponfret blankly. She hadn't the foggiest notion to what he was referring. But she smiled, nodded her head and stated, "Oh, undoubtedly, undoubtedly."

Her remark seemed to satisfy Ponfret, for he was most reluctant to relinquish Annabelle to her next partner. Finding her card completely full, a fact which prevented him from claiming another dance, Randolph squeezed the golden-brown beauty's hand tightly and promised to call when next he came to Town.

Using her heavily dimpled smile to full effect, Annabelle tossed her curls and said she looked forward to seeing him again, but in truth Randolph Ponfret was already forgotten as she floated away on the arm of a Major Jack Sprawlings.

Swaggering into the card-room, for Randolph hadn't missed the envious glances thrown his way by those young bucks not fortunate enough to have secured a dance with the lovely Miss Winthrop, Randolph grabbed a full bottle of champagne from a passing footman and proceeded to get himself totally bosky. With only one night in Town, he had to enjoy his pleasures to the fullest. Furthermore, Randolph felt the need to celebrate. The swath which Miss Winthrop—Annabelle, he corrected himself—was cutting had quite convinced him that he wanted her for his very own. He'd marry the chit, by Jove, fortune be damned! Annabelle might not be an heiress, but she was the prettiest little thing he'd ever seen and popular, as well. Being the somewhat self-centred gentleman that he was, Randolph never considered the fact that Annabelle might not return his high regard. He was young, he was rich and he was tolerably handsome. The only thing he didn't possess was a title. And considering his other attributes, Randolph felt this one small lack to be quite minor. Simply put, Annabelle could do no better.

The object of Randolph Ponfret's affection was at that moment swirling about the dance floor with her latest partner of the evening, a rather portly yet amusing young man by the name of Freddy Merryweather. Sally Jersey had unexpectedly given Annabelle permission to waltz straight off, and although she could've wished for a more romantic partner during her first waltz at Almack's, she found that she liked Freddy Merryweather a great deal. He was a refreshing change from the gentlemen she'd danced with thus far this evening. The others had been self-centred dandies like Randolph Ponfret, or men who seemed almost too shy to speak, like Major Sprawlings. At least Mr. Merryweather treated her like a person, not like a pretty doll.

Annabelle found herself inordinately glad that the portly young sprig had bespoken her company for the refreshment room.

"You move divinely, Miss Winthrop," Freddy ventured with a certain dramatic flair popular amongst the younger members of the ton. "In fact, I predict that you will take our set quite by storm. Too bad, really."

"And why is that, Mr. Merryweather?" Annabelle enquired, peeping up at her partner through lushly fringed, golden-brown eyes.

Freddy Merryweather resisted the urge to sigh. *So beautiful,* he thought to himself. "Because, Miss Winthrop, I don't stand a chance, that's why, for all that I shall be a viscount one day."

Annabelle giggled merrily. "Nonsense, Mr. Merryweather. You're trying to make me feel sorry for you and thus further your suit. Most original, I'll grant you that."

Freddy sighed theatrically. "You've found me out, Miss Winthrop. You've discovered my most effective ploy: self-belittlement. Most women simply can't resist the urge to comfort and soothe. Promise you won't tell."

Laughing outright, Annabelle strove to match his dramatic bent when she said, "I shall keep your dreadful secret providing you share with me every on dit you know. You see, I'm new to Town and thus far have only been privy to information considered acceptable for the ears of a young lady."

"In other words, you want the truth."

Annabelle nodded vigorously at Mr. Merryweather as he took her elbow and began to lead her into the refreshment room. She hardly touched the rather stale-looking cakes which he placed upon her plate, and watched in amazement as he quickly polished off four or five himself. "Famished, you know," Merryweather proclaimed somewhat apologetically, but he winked upon the completion of his repast and began to comply with Annabelle's request for information. "Do you see Lady Mannerly over there? The one with the gold turban."

Annabelle quickly spotted the woman of whom he spoke. "I know that she's somehow considered beyond the pale despite the fact that she isn't a social outcast."

"My dear, how can she be when it's said that she's slept with almost every high-ranking member of Parliament except her husband, poor man."

"Do tell," Annabelle encouraged with widely rounded eyes. Who would suspect it of the rather dumpy-looking Lady Mannerly?

"Then there's Sir Rathmore," Freddy continued, pointing unobtrusively at an older gentleman who was possessed unfortunately of a rather strange facial tick.

"Oh, what about him?" Annabelle prompted, for she'd heard nothing of this unfortunate gentleman.

"Deep in dun territory," Freddy replied, shaking his head. "About to lose everything for all that he's got a wife and four children."

"Scandalous," Annabelle replied breathlessly, feeling somewhat guilty that they were discussing these people so. Unfortunately, she'd always been inordinately fond of gossip and found that she couldn't stop. "What else?" Annabelle demanded, pulling on her companion's sleeve impatiently.

Freddy looked amused. "Just one more titbit, my dear, and then you must wait for Princess Esterhazy's rout before I tell you more. That way you'll have no choice but to dance with me."

"Silly. I'd dance with you in any case. You're by far the most interesting gentleman I've met this evening."

"Does this mean I've reason to hope?" Freddy enquired, getting down on bended knee.

"Oh, do get up," Annabelle entreated, realizing that they'd become the centre of attention.

Freddy complied with a laugh, but quickly yelped as Annabelle struck him with her fan. "Very well," he conceded, rubbing his shoulder. "Do you see that rather good-looking gentleman at the second table? The one surrounded by all the women?"

"The Marquis de Dambere? He's a rake. Everyone knows that."

Freddy gave Annabelle a superior look. "Perhaps I shouldn't be telling you this, but forewarned is forearmed, I always say. It's well known in most circles that de Dambere is responsible for ruining several young ladies of good name. He doesn't confine himself to lightskirts, nor even to married women, but prefers young innocents such as yourself."

Annabelle gasped. "Why then is he permitted in Almack's?"

"Each incident has been carefully kept quiet, each girl married off at the earliest opportunity."

"How do you know that?"

"One of his victims is a distant cousin of mine."

"So sorry."

"Don't be. I wasn't particularly fond of her. In any case, I hear the musicians beginning to play, and if I don't miss my guess, I see another one of your eager swains approaching to claim your hand for the next dance. I've quite enjoyed talking with you, Miss Winthrop, and look forward to seeing you again," Freddy proclaimed as he made his bow and moved on.

Although Annabelle was by this time extremely tired, she gave her hand to Major Jack Sprawlings, who'd indeed come to claim her for the last set. In fact, they were just ready to take the floor when to Annabelle's horror she saw none other than the infamous Marquis de Dambere heading straight towards her, even as the rather shy Major Sprawlings held her lightly by the elbow.

"Pardon, young man," the marquis commanded in a tone of voice which indicated that he was used to getting his way. "I simply must dance with this ravishing creature. You don't mind, do you? After all, you've already danced with her once this evening."

Major Sprawlings began to stammer, but it was obvious from the redness in his cheeks and from his timid manner that the marquis was indeed going to get his way. And in fact, had Freddy Merryweather not warned her about the marquis, Annabelle herself would've felt flattered by de Dambere's attention and challenged by the prospect of a more entertaining partner. As it was, she had absolutely no intention of spending any time at all with such an odious man.

Moving quickly, Annabelle thrust her arm through Major Sprawlings's and, looking directly at the marquis, who was a swarthy yet handsome man, told him in no uncertain terms that she intended to honour the commitment according to her dance card.

The marquis immediately stiffened at the set down and turned a frosty glare upon the major, who looked as if he might actually come to the impertinent chit's defence. "Oh, but I insist, Miss Winthrop. It is Miss Winthrop, is it not? I shan't be able to sleep tonight lest you grant me a dance," he importuned, in as suave a manner as possible given his irritation.

"I fear then that you shall have a very restless night," Annabelle retorted, poking the major in the ribs to speak in her defence.

"Yes, um, quite," Major Sprawlings stammered, much to Annabelle's disgust. God protect England if all her soldiers were as spineless as this one!

The marquis laughed outright at the major and grabbed Annabelle by the hand. She would've struck him with her reticule had she not noticed that they were beginning to attract quite a bit of attention.

Instead, Annabelle stood up on her tiptoes and whispered furiously in the marquis's ear, "You would oblige me by going straight to the devil, sir."

The marquis dropped Annabelle's hand instantly and stared at her as if she'd gone stark raving mad.

Annabelle had an insane urge to laugh, but instead took advantage of the marquis's stupefaction and propelled Major Sprawlings onto the dance floor.

The marquis recovered his composure a few moments later, but instead of being angry, he found himself vastly amused. The virgins he preferred were all too often boring, insipid creatures easily cozened into betraying their gentle upbringing. Here was a chit with fire. Unfortunately, someone had been whispering in her ear and the marquis was willing to bet that it was that rotund Freddy Merryweather.

"I see the lovely Miss Winthrop didn't fall into your arms quite as easily as you imagined," teased Lady Jersey, who'd come up on the marquis from behind. "The whole room is whispering about it, you know," the patroness added with a malicious zeal.

De Dambere would have taken her to task, but he knew he was in no position to do so, his reputation being very close to irreparably damaged. Lady Jersey could easily bar him from Almack's, thereby removing the marquis from one of his prime hunting-grounds, and a testy rejoinder was not worth the risk.

"My dear countess," the marquis replied, lifting Lady Jersey's hand to his lips briefly, "who would've dreamed the angel could be so wayward? Still, I'll continue to hope that in time she'll come to look upon me in a more favourable light."

"God help her if she does," the patroness retorted, snatching her hand away. Although she had a well-deserved reputation for gossip among the ton, she was not known to be a mean-spirited creature who would enjoying witnessing a young girl's ruin.

Annabelle didn't suffer the scold which she'd expected from Aunt Charlotte when the two were safely seated inside the carriage on the way home. Instead, Aunt Charlotte carefully pursed her lips when Annabelle dared to mention the marquis's name, signalling to her niece that the topic wasn't one which she cared to discuss; that the man wasn't one of whom she'd approve. Obviously Aunt Charlotte had heard something of de Dambere's unsavoury reputation. Thus Annabelle was able to enjoy a sound sleep that night, and in fact didn't make her appearance below stairs until well past noon the following day.

It was a good thing Annabelle enjoyed her rest, because she found her Aunt Charlotte pacing the floor in the large drawing-room with a look upon her face which didn't bode well for sleeping soundly on any night to come.

"Why, Auntie, whatever is the matter?" Annabelle questioned anxiously, seating herself with trepidation on the pink-and-white striped satin settee. She couldn't think of any infraction she'd committed lately which warranted this kind of agitation.

"Just look at this tripe," Aunt Charlotte roared in her best imitation of Uncle William, brandishing a newspaper high overhead. "You're famous, my gel! Wayward Angel indeed! I've it in mind to call upon the publisher of this rubbish and demand satisfaction."

Totally mystified, Annabelle nevertheless managed to pry the *Gazette* from between her Aunt Charlotte's fingers in order to peruse the story which had the older woman so upset:

Just up from the country a new beauty known by the name Wayward Angel! This golden-eyed, golden-haired young lady, while undoubtedly a hit with many members of the ton, didn't fare as well with a certain dark-haired peer. The two were seen arguing heatedly. Can it be love?

"Love!" Annabelle exclaimed in horror. As if she'd ever view the Marquis de Dambere with anything less than loathing. But then the golden-brown beauty began to see the humour in the situation, especially when she read an article farther down which referred quite blatantly to the large fortune possessed by her friend Lady Violet Silverton. "It's all right, Auntie, really," Annabelle said at last, chuckling. "I doubt anyone takes this tripe very much to heart."

"Perhaps not, my gel, but you'd better get used to the fact that from now on you're going to be known as the Wayward Angel."

Annabelle appeared reflective. "Well you know, Auntie," she mused, "I am rather wayward when you come down to it. I don't think I mind so terribly much."

"I suppose it's not so bad," Aunt Charlotte agreed finally, fingering the stem of her quizzing glass. "After all, the important thing is that you were mentioned in a prestigious newspaper, and quite prominently, too. You're a hit, my gel. A hit."

"Oh, Auntie," Annabelle chided, yet she couldn't hide the blush of pleasure which suffused her face, nor the smile which dimpled her cheeks.

A FEW DAYS LATER, given the fact that the post brought news late to the country, Lady Margaret Singletary, Countess of Westerbrook, was reading the same article which had so overset Aunt Charlotte. Her reaction, however, was quite different. "Hurrah!" Lady Margaret fairly shouted, so startling the major-domo Bajardous that he almost dropped the tea-tray which he was at that moment carrying into the Blue Salon.

"Good news, no doubt," Bajardous intoned with just a touch of sarcasm as he wiped a bit of clotted cream off his immaculately starched uniform.

"The best, Bajardous, the best," Lady Margaret replied, keeping her own counsel. For weeks she'd been thinking of ways to get her son to London following the Founders Day Race, and now she had just the ammunition she required.

It was at dinner that night when Lady Margaret began her campaign. Both she and Cam were seated at table enjoying a sumptuous repast prepared by Mrs. Freedly. Cam, however, hardly noticed the food which he put into his mouth, so preoccupied was he with the upcoming race.

"Will we win?" Lady Margaret asked, although she already knew the answer. Cam's horse always won the Founders Day Race because her son had far more resources at his disposal than any other landowner in Sussex County, and also because Cam genuinely knew what he was about. He was talented with horses, more so than any other family member of recent history.

"Of course," Cam responded, although his eyes were staring off into the distance.

"Good. And as a treat for your victory, I think you must take yourself off to London for a bit after the race. You're much too young to bury yourself in the country."

That got his attention. Cam's light brown eyes focused sharply on his mother. "But you'll be all alone," he said quickly, without thinking. Then his eyes dropped to the white Irish linen tablecloth. "That is to say, with father's death and all..."

Lady Margaret rose from her seat and walked over to her son. She placed a hand on his shoulder. "I'm eighteen years your senior, Cam. I'm quite capable of making do. For the past two years we've been buried here at Westhaven. I've needed the time and I'm not sorry for having taken it. Your presence, of course, has made it all so much easier. But life does go on. Your father's dead. I've accepted it and I've mourned him. Now I think I'm ready to start getting about a bit more and I know that you are as well. Go to London, Cam. Enjoy yourself. Open the townhouse. Who knows, I may join you myself for a few weeks later this Season.''

Cam patted his mother's hand and then watched as she resumed her seat. He ate a piece of roast beef and shook his head. "I don't know," he began, but again his mother intervened.

"I have another, more selfish reason for wanting you to go to London. It seems that our Miss Winthrop, whom you know I'm exceedingly fond of, has cut quite a swath amongst the ton. But I'm worried, Cam. She's so, well, so headstrong. Who knows what kind of mischief she's got herself into? Lady Charlotte isn't that young any longer. Annabelle is quite capable of getting round her. Someone should check on them and see how they go on.''

"You're doing it a bit brown aren't you, Mother? Lady Charlotte seems more than able to rein in her young niece. Besides, it isn't as if we're related to them. They may resent the interference.''

"I suppose you're right, my dear. I just want Annabelle to do well. That silly article in the *Gazette* paints her as such a forward creature, which we know of course she isn't.''

"What article?" Cam demanded, bringing his knife down with a clatter.

"In the *Gazette*. Beside your plate, my dear," Lady Margaret replied, the picture of innocence.

Cam turned quickly to the Society page and scanned the contents. "Why, you mean this ridiculous reference to the Wayward Angel? We don't even know if it is she.''

"The article mentions golden hair and golden eyes. Who else but Annabelle? Furthermore, you know as well as I that she's possessed of an angel's face. There can be no doubt. The question is, who's the dark-haired peer?''

"I'll find out, don't you worry," Cam stated querulously before he realized where he was and to whom he was speaking. "That is, I think it best if I do go up to London for a bit. There are certain matters which must be attended to. Estate matters, of course."

"Oh, of course," Lady Margaret agreed, keeping her attention carefully focused on her plate.

Cam watched his mother carefully for several seconds before he continued with his meal. Then suddenly he pounced. "Madam, I hope you aren't trying to gammon me. I think you've got yourself up to a bit of matchmaking. You know I'm not ready to wed, not for a long time."

Lady Margaret looked directly at her son. "Well, I certainly do hope you change your mind about marriage, because privilege unfortunately entails responsibility. I for one would dislike Westhaven to go to Cousin Edward. And," she added cleverly, "Lucinda won't wait forever."

That last part confused him, she could tell. "No, I don't suppose she will," Cam agreed before shaking his head as if to clear the cobwebs. "Dash it, Mother, you know I don't like talking about this. Let's change the topic, shall we?"

"Certainly, my dear," Lady Margaret agreed most solicitously. After all, she'd accomplished her purpose, in the same manner she'd more often than not employed with Cam's father. Men were easily led, providing one knew how to lead them, and providing they never for a second suspected that they were being led. Lady Margaret sighed imperceptibly.

THE NEXT MORN, SATURDAY, dawned as fair as any spring day could dawn. The sky was cerulean blue, the temperature warm but not overly hot, the trees and grass lushly green.

Cam inhaled deeply, savouring the scents indigenous to the warmer months. He sat atop Merlin, holding the reins of the horse he planned to enter in the Founders Day Race. The earl had begun the journey at dawn with his head groom Jem and two of Jem's assistants. Chatham Fields, the site of the race, was a good hour away. As the five horses trotted briskly forward, although not too briskly, for Cam didn't want his latest thoroughbred winded, birds chirped loudly overhead and butterflies floated past, lending their glorious colour to an absolutely perfect day.

Soon enough the Westerbrook party had Chatham Fields in sight, and what a sight it was! Multicoloured banners flapped in the wind high atop the Chatham Fields tower. Heraldic trumpeters had been stationed round the track. Clowns and jugglers wandered at will throughout the crowd. The medieval pageantry brought forth for the race never failed to impress Cam. He could almost picture himself outfitted in a suit of armour rather than his bottle-green riding coat. Cam held back a laugh. Medieval armour was said to have been extremely uncomfortable at best. He was glad to be the sixth Earl of Westerbrook rather than the first!

Once Cam and his group reached the paddock, however, all thoughts of pageantry vanished as they prepared for the race. The horse was put through his paces, the smaller of Jem's groomsmen outfitted to ride. Thus by noon, when the horses took to the field, Cam and his men had already put in a full day's labour.

The earl was keeping a careful eye on the gatepost when Lucinda Moresby breezed into his box, looking cool and delicious in an apricot-coloured frock and matching bonnet. "I came to watch the race with you, and to wish you good luck," Lucinda said in her brusque manner, eyeing her intended with appreciation. That he was handsome made the fact that he was an earl all the more inviting.

"Thank you, Lucinda, the same to you. Where might your father be?" Cam asked politely, wishing irrationally for a split second that the face looking up at his was possessed of a pair of golden-brown eyes rather than the green ones the stunning blond beauty boasted.

"In the paddock taking care of some last-minute business," Lucinda replied. "He should be along shortly."

Cam nodded distractedly, waiting for the start of the race.

"Do you go to London this Season?" Lucinda questioned after a few moments of silence. She never knew exactly what to say to this man, despite the fact that they had so much in common.

"What's that?" Cam asked and then coughed in embarrassment. "Ah yes, London. I do believe I shall go up for a while this year. Mother's feeling a great deal better and may even join me."

"You're to be commended for looking after the countess so solicitously," Lucinda replied. "Children can indeed be a great comfort."

Cam turned to Lucinda and startled her by taking her hands in his. "And do you want children, my dear?" he asked, staring at her intently.

Lucinda sucked in her breath. She was aware that her answer was important. Just what did he want to hear? "It is of course the duty of all women to provide their husbands with an heir. I shan't be remiss in my duty."

Cam squeezed her hands, but then quickly dropped them as he turned towards the gatepost. Lucinda was so stuffy, so intent upon doing perfectly all the things she was expected to do that something was always lost in the effort.

Aware that she'd somehow displeased him, as she usually managed to do, Lucinda was subdued throughout the race, even though her horse and Cam's ran neck and neck until the final stretch, when his stallion managed to pull away and win.

Sensing her despondency, but mistaking it for disappointment in the outcome, Cam grabbed Lucinda's hand and squeezed it encouragingly. "First and second. We both won," he shouted, his engaging grin making him look quite the little boy.

"So we did," Lucinda replied, returning his smile, but her hands were cold and so was her heart.

CHAPTER FIVE

ANNABELLE WAS disappointed with her London Season. Although she enjoyed outings to see such sights as Westminster Abbey, the Tower of London, the Elgin Marbles and Kew Gardens, she quickly grew tired of the endless round of parties and social engagements. Not by nature a vapid person, Annabelle found she was required to be just that amongst the ton. On the few occasions when she did attempt to join an intellectual discussion, her comments were invariably rejected, and once actually ridiculed. And although she loved to dance, Annabelle found that her partners were usually tedious, unwilling to believe that she had a brain in her head. She was bored with hearing platitudes concerning the stars which shone forth from her eyes and other such nonsense. She longed for more men like Freddy Merryweather, with whom one could at least have a measure of fun.

Annabelle's life felt oddly flat; she seemed to be suffering from a strange kind of ennui which had never affected her before. Always lively, Annabelle now found that even the prospect of a new frock could not lift her out of her stupor. Fortunately, it was considered quite tonnish to affect boredom—real or not. If anything, Annabelle's popularity only increased.

''It's all so meaningless,'' the golden-brown beauty complained to her friend Lady Violet Silverton one afternoon as the two sat in Violet's enormous bedroom, examining the fashion plates contained within the pages of *Le Beau Monde*. "I wish something truly exciting would happen."

"Oh, pish," Violet teased, patting her red hair with satisfaction. Her maid had spent upwards of two hours that morn creating a style with which Violet was inordinately pleased. "One would think you'd been relegated to the ranks of wallflower or some such nonsense. You're the Belle of the Season. Your drawing-room is full of flowers sent by admirers and I've never seen your dance card anything but full. You're invited to the theatre, the opera, you're on everyone's guest list, and you've already received one proposal of marriage. How much more excitement could you possibly wish?"

"I hardly consider Major Jack Sprawlings an ideal candidate for matrimony," Annabelle retorted, suppressing a giggle. Poor Major Sprawlings. She'd felt very sorry for him, really, when she'd rejected his offer of marriage, but how could he have presumed to think they would suit? Why, she would've dominated the poor man all the days of his life. "It's just that all the parties seem so routine. We see the same people, we discuss the same topics," Annabelle added, trying to give voice to her feelings of listlessness.

Violet gave her friend a knowing look as if she were much older than Annabelle, although the two were in fact separated by a mere two months. "It's not that you're bored with London, my gel, or even with the ton, although I do admit that they both can be tiresome at times. The fact of the matter is that you're bored because you're not in love. Think of how much more exciting the parties would seem if you had someone to look for, someone special with whom to dance and flirt."

Annabelle gaped. "Violet Silverton," (for Violet had insisted Annabelle drop her title almost from the start) "what a Banbury Tale you weave," she sputtered, although her eyes were carefully focused on the sprigged bed curtain and not on the red-haired young lady who sat by her side.

"Or is it that you *are* in love," Violet guessed with sudden insight, "but the man you desire is not attainable?"

"I wouldn't go so far as to say that," Annabelle shot back before she realized the truth of her lamentable words. Why had she refused to admit it to herself before? The fact of the matter was that she was hopelessly besotted with Lord Camford Singletary, Earl of Westerbrook. None of the men she'd met in London thus far could begin to compare, and although she had forced herself to keep her thoughts on other matters, Lord Westerbrook had been in the back of her mind all the time, plaguing her, keeping her from truly enjoying her come-out Season.

Violet squealed. "Do tell who he is," she insisted, grabbing Annabelle by the hand.

The golden-brown beauty's expression took on a dreamy countenance and her cheeks flooded with colour. "I met him on the way to London. He's the most handsome man, Violet, although he can be rather vexing at times. He's tall and broad-shouldered and he has the most unusual light brown eyes. His hair is black and—"

"Yes, yes, I concede that he's Adonis personified, but who is he?" Violet interrupted eagerly.

"Lord Camford Singletary, Earl of Westerbrook."

Violet's eyes all but popped out of her head. "Cam Singletary! You cannot be serious. Trust you to fix your interest on a man no one has come close to bringing up to scratch, though it's rumoured he has an understanding with that pompous Lucinda Moresby. Furthermore, I had it from my second cousin who had it from her maid's sister that Westerbrook has over the years supported an inordinate number of women who can't exactly be described as ladies, if you take my meaning. I'm afraid he's somewhat of a rake, Annabelle," Violet concluded, shaking her head sympathetically.

"I know it's ridiculous," Annabelle replied softly, "but one can't help where one loses one's heart. At first I thought my feelings for him nothing more than a tiny tendre. But in truth, I've been miserable for weeks.''

"Well, if anyone can bring him to heel, it's you!" Violet declared emphatically, trying to console her newfound friend.

"I truly wish that that were the case, but I'm afraid I haven't a chance," Annabelle replied morosely. "If only I'd fallen in love with someone like, well, someone like Freddy Merryweather. I'm sure I could bring him round quite easily."

"I'm sure you could," Violet answered in a tight-lipped manner, which marked a sudden departure from her usual cheerful disposition.

Annabelle didn't miss her friend's substantial change in demeanour. "Freddy?" Annabelle asked.

Violet shook her head ruefully. "I know he isn't the most handsome of men, but he makes me laugh. I adore his wit. In any case, you and I are quite the pair—both in love with men who obviously do not return our regard."

"But Violet, Freddy is quite fond of you. He always invites you to dance, sometimes more than once. I'd say you have a definite chance in that quarter."

"You ninny. Freddy asks me to dance because he knows we're friends. Most of our conversations revolve round you. There's even a bet on at White's that Freddy will offer for you before the close of the Season."

"How do you know that?" Annabelle asked in amazement. "No, don't tell me," she said with a wave of her hand, "your second cousin's maid's sister."

Violet chuckled. "Something like that."

"Well," Annabelle replied airily, "I simply don't believe it and you shouldn't, either. Who'd wager on such a ridiculous thing?"

"My dear girl, men will wager on just about anything. I'm quite positive the bet exists, although I'm not sure how I can prove it to you. I suppose we could ask someone who has direct access to such matters, but I'm not sure that would be considered good ton."

Annabelle jumped off of the bed and began to pace round the room, some of her old animation apparent in her jaunty stride. "There's only one way to prove the bet exists or not, and that's to see for ourselves. If it's a legitimate wager, it will have been logged in White's infamous betting book."

Violet collapsed heavily onto her bed, only to immediately spring back up. "I do begin to believe you're mad! White's does not admit females. How do you propose we get in?"

"We shall simply disguise ourselves, my friend. It shouldn't be too difficult to obtain men's evening wear. I can borrow something from my uncle William—he always has garments in the townhouse even when he isn't in residence—and you can remove something suitable from your father's wardrobe."

"And how do you think it best I do that? Mayhap I should just tell my mother that I plan to visit White's with my Bedlamite friend, Annabelle Winthrop. I'm sure she'd fall in with the plan quite nicely."

"I leave it to you to use your imagination," Annabelle stated firmly, earning a withering stare from her red-haired friend. "As to the manner of our escape, we shall simply plead the headache in order to remain home on the appointed evening. A hackney will deliver us to White's. You can leave that part to me."

"Generous of you, I'm sure," Violet muttered under her breath.

Annabelle rushed over to where her friend sat upon the bed and plopped down beside her. "Is it agreed, then? Do say you'll go along. After all, you must admit that such an adventure would add excitement to our rather loveless lives."

Violet eyed Annabelle speculatively. "Oh, most assuredly, yet I fail to see how this madcap scheme of yours will help either one of us garner the attention of the men we love."

"Well, if we learn the wager does exist, then we'll simply devise a way to make sure Freddy never offers for me," Annabelle temporized. "For I do like him and should hate to see his feelings hurt as the result of such a bramble. Furthermore, if he does offer for me and I reject him, he might decide to avoid both of us. That would prove disastrous to your interests. At least one of us deserves to be happy. So, are we in agreement—or not?"

"Under one condition," Violet said slowly, struggling to contain her mirth. "If the wager is in the book, then you must kiss your canine friend Mr. Fitzroy straight upon the lips."

"And if it isn't?"

"Then I shall kiss him," Violet shrieked, exploding with laughter.

"How utterly disgusting—for Mr. Fitzroy, that is," Annabelle shouted between giggles. "But I accept your terms!"

As Annabelle and Violet squealed with laughter, the door to the bedroom slowly opened, admitting the regal presence of the Duchess of Montvale, Violet's mother. "Young ladies," the duchess proclaimed, clapping her hands together loudly, "a little decorum, if you please. I don't wish to disrupt your fun, but you must promise to be good."

"We promise," Violet agreed tremulously, but after the duchess had departed, both she and Annabelle fell against the pillows of the bed as they vented their continued hilarity. *Promise to be good indeed!* If only the duchess knew just how bad Annabelle and Violet planned to be.

THE NIGHT OF THE SORTIE to White's proved so miserable, both Annabelle and Violet had second thoughts about their dubious scheme. A treacherous fog had slipped over the entire city like a second skin. Yet the hackney had been procured, their disguises obtained; there seemed no real reason to demur.

"Do be careful, miss," the dour-faced Betty admonished as Annabelle slipped into her uncle's grey silk waistcoat. "You could be killed, you know."

Annabelle turned towards her maid with open-mouthed wonder. "I think that's doing it a bit brown, Betty, but yes, I shall be careful," she replied, regretting the necessity of dragging her ever-pessimistic maid into her schemes. Yet who else could've procured the hackney, and helped her to temporarily alter Uncle William's evening attire? Slipping into the man's coat, Annabelle added, "Now, not a word to Aunt Charlotte. She's already left to play cards at Mrs. Arthur Johnstone's, in any case. I should be back well before she is."

"Very good, miss," Betty said with an audible sigh. The maid wasn't at all pleased with Annabelle's latest start, yet who was she to question the antics of her betters? "Be careful," she repeated somewhat shrilly as Annabelle disappeared down the staircase and out the door.

Annabelle manoeuvred through the fog until she found the hackney waiting beside the townhouse, just as Betty had promised it would be. Quickly she clambered inside, after giving the coachman directions to the home of the Duke of Montvale. Once she arrived, Annabelle was a study of nervousness until at long last the hackney door was jerked open and Violet stepped inside.

"You look ridiculous," were the redhead's first words, and she meant them. "We'll never get away with this."

"We'll be in and out so fast no one will have time to question our appearance," Annabelle proclaimed, although she wasn't really certain about the validity of such a statement. Violet didn't look especially masculine, even in her father's clothing, and Annabelle knew she didn't, either. Drastic circumstances required drastic action. "Here," she said, handing a small, fuzzy object to Violet, being careful not to touch the back side, which she'd coated heavily with glue.

"What the deuce?" Violet asked, staring at the thing in her hand.

"It's a moustache. Put it on," Annabelle commanded, sticking her own above her lip. "I snipped a little hair from Mr. Fitzroy's underbelly. I decided we needed it more than he did."

Violet attached the strange-looking object to her lip, giggling as she did so. "Well, if this isn't the outside of enough," the redhead remarked. "Here I am on a foggy night in a strange and I may say shabby coach, as these public conveyances inevitably are, wearing my father's clothing with dog hair stuck to my upper lip."

"Exciting, is it not?" Annabelle replied, giggling herself. She then rapped upon the roof of the vehicle with Uncle William's ivory-embossed walking-stick and instructed the coachman to stop directly across from White's. When the hackney arrived, both young ladies descended, whereupon Annabelle handed the coachman a small purse of money. "Wait for us," she ordered with the authority of one long used to commanding servants. The coachman nodded his understanding, too happy with his unforeseen windfall to comment upon the strange appearance of his passengers.

Annabelle and Violet faced each other nervously. Annabelle pushed a stray red curl back inside her friend's hat and then took a deep breath. "Are you ready, Victor?"

Violet looked as if she might have apoplexy right then and there, but she squared her shoulders and replied, "Onward, Alexander."

The doorman at White's had been trained to keep his expression carefully schooled, yet when two short, strange-looking gentlemen entered the sacred portal to London's most exclusive men's club, he almost laughed out loud. His next reaction was to stop what obviously had to be a pair of schoolgirls up to no good, yet the fine cut of their clothing forestalled his better instincts. Let his superiors see to this problem. He wasn't of a mind to lose his job due to a situation he had no idea how to approach.

Once inside, Annabelle knew that it wouldn't do to stand idly about. They were sure to be challenged before long. The most important thing was to locate the infamous betting book and have done. Moving quickly, neither Annabelle nor Violet took time to investigate their surroundings, noting only surreptitiously the rich and obviously expensive masculine décor.

It wasn't long before they'd located the betting book. Skimming back to the start of the Season, they began to examine the pages. Annabelle felt her heart pounding most alarmingly. Her palms were decidedly damp. Yet some of the bets that she and Violet noted were enough to make her forget her nervousness. Violet was right. It seemed that the gentlemen saw fit to bet on just about anything. Why, there were wagers concerning the size of dog litters and happenings abroad, as well as more scintillating ones concerning, for example, the number of men a currently well-known actress had slept with in a single night. Heavens!

And then they saw it. Someone had bet that Mr. Freddy Merryweather would offer for Miss Annabelle Winthrop by Season's end. Violet threw Annabelle a triumphant look which rapidly turned to one of sadness. Annabelle sighed and motioned that they should leave. Unfortunately, at that precise moment Annabelle and Violet were frozen in their tracks, as the Marquis de Dambere stepped directly in front of them, blocking their retreat.

"Going somewhere, ladies?" he asked slyly, earning two extremely fearful glances.

"So you've found us out, my lord," Annabelle replied, trying hard to regain some semblance of control. "Just what do you plan to do about it?" she challenged quite audaciously.

"Why, nothing, my dear Miss Winthrop," he said, his dark eyes dancing merrily. "In fact, I plan to make certain that you both are returned home safely. First I shall take Lady Violet, and then I shall see to you."

The marquis's plainly seductive leer left no doubt in Annabelle's mind as to what would occur should she be forced to ride home with him alone. Yet what was the alternative? If he exposed them, they'd have to leave London in disgrace. The scandal wouldn't be one of enormous proportions, but a scandal it'd be none the less. She and Violet would be branded wicked hoydens unmindful of duty or position.

Annabelle's fists clenched tightly at her side, but she remained momentarily mute. There seemed no acceptable alternative.

"I'm afraid your offer of escort is quite out of the question," Violet stated bravely, jumping into the fray. She was well aware, having been informed by Annabelle, of the marquis's unsavoury reputation.

Turning to Violet, Annabelle whispered, "I don't see that we have much choice."

"Do take all night to come to a decision, ladies," the marquis said suavely as he indulged in a pinch of snuff. "It seems that we've drawn a certain amount of attention already and in a matter of seconds my offer may well be moot."

Annabelle and Violet simply stared at each other, horrified looks upon their faces as yet another man strolled casually over. Annabelle's expression, however, turned quickly to rapture as she recognized the Earl of Westerbrook. Immediately, she experienced the same weak-kneed sensation she'd felt when first they'd met.

"And what have we here?" Cam asked, turning his broad back to the room so as to minimize Annabelle's exposure.

"Do leave off, old boy," the marquis stated jovially. "It seems that two of our more adventurous young ladies have got themselves up to a small lark. But we've agreed that I shall convey them home and no one need be the wiser.''

"I shall escort the young ladies home,'' Cam stated firmly, giving the marquis such a cold look that the dark-haired peer immediately fell back. The Earl of Westerbrook was known to be a crack shot, having served as an officer in the light brigade until shortly after the Battle of Waterloo.

Annabelle offered Lord Westerbrook a look of gratitude as he grabbed her arm with one hand and Violet's with the other. However, the earl didn't deign to return her favour. In fact, the expression on his face was one which distinctly didn't invite approach. Moving rather rapidly, so fast, in fact, that both girls had to run to keep up, Cam had them out of White's and onto the pavement outside so quickly that none of the other members had time to investigate the strange goings-on.

Inside the famous gentleman's club, the Marquis de Dambere was besieged with questions from eager members sensing the makings of a scandal. However, the marquis, remembering the earl's expression, wasn't so foolhardy as to risk his life and member. Instead, "To the book,'' he roared, having drunk enough that night to be more than a little bosky. "I wager that the Earl of Westerbrook offers for the Wayward Angel before Season's end.''

"Are you referring to Greywood's niece?'' one of the gentlemen enquired. "The little beauty who has all the young bloods in such a pother? Are you suggesting that Westerbrook is also vying for her hand?''

A hearty chorus of denials resounded throughout the room.

"Westerbrook? Nonsense. He's much too sly to be taken in by some young chit's lures, no matter how angelic.''

"Besides, he's promised to the Moresby gel,'' another of the gentlemen proclaimed.

"Place your bets,'' the marquis replied.

Outside the club, Cam quickly dismissed the waiting hackney, but not before further enriching that lucky coachman's purse to ensure the man's silence. Then Cam ushered Annabelle and Violet into his waiting coach-and-four.

Annabelle remembered the richly appointed brown velvet interior and was about to commend Lord Singletary on the comfort of his conveyance as she leaned back against the luxurious squabs. She thought better of the notion upon taking a closer look at the earl's face. That he was furious was apparent from the fact that his normally ruddy complexion had grown that much redder. Then, too, his eyebrows were drawn tautly together and his lips were pursed, much as they'd been that first day when he had carried Annabelle from the wrecked Greywood carriage. Instead, the golden-brown beauty ventured a glance at Violet, only to observe that young lady's guilt-ridden expression. Knowing that the plan had been hers in the first place, Annabelle felt compelled to speak.

"You don't mean to tell Violet's parents about this unfortunate little incident, do you?" Annabelle asked in a small voice, glancing up at the earl through her heavily lashed, golden-brown eyes.

"I ought to, simply to forestall you both from engaging in any further nonsense," Cam replied icily. "Do you, either one of you, realize just how much trouble you could've caused by entering White's in such a ridiculous manner?" Cam's voice grew in intensity until the last was virtually shouted. For although he did feel both ladies had acted in a hoydenish way which may well have damaged not only them but the reputations of both their families, his real fury stemmed from the possibility that Annabelle had formed a tendre for the reprehensible Marquis de Dambere. Obviously, de Dambere was the dark-haired peer referred to by the *Gazette* in the notice concerning the Wayward Angel.

"Please don't ring a peal over us, my lord. It was a foolish thing to do—I think we both realize that now—but I can't help but feel you're reacting a bit too strongly," Annabelle ventured bravely, despite the fact that she was quite unable to look directly at the earl. How very humiliating to be lectured like a child by the man with whom one was in love.

"Annabelle..." Violet warned, but she was abruptly cut off by Lord Westerbrook.

"And I suppose had you lost your virtue this night you would've counted it nothing more than the result of a foolish escapade?" Cam asked in scathing tones.

Annabelle gasped and could find no suitable reply. He was right, of course, although she found it incredible that he could refer to the possibility so blithely.

"This incident is just the sort of ramshackle behaviour of which your Aunt Charlotte warned. How do you think that good lady would feel if she got wind of this night's work?" Cam demanded, castigating them soundly.

By now both Annabelle and Violet were thoroughly cowed, thoroughly ashamed of their actions.

"I...we apologize most profusely, my lord," Violet stammered quietly as the carriage rambled up to the Montvale mansion. "We're most grateful for your intervention. The situation could indeed have become most disastrous had you not happened upon the scene."

"There's no need to apologize to me," Cam stated firmly, moving to open the door of the carriage for Violet. "However, let this be a lesson to both of you. Although the rules of Society can sometimes seem most confining, especially to young ladies, they exist for a reason."

"Yes, my lord, and thank you again," Violet muttered just before she leapt from the carriage quite unassisted, although the earl's tiger had jumped down from his position to lend the unusually dressed young lady a hand. Obviously, Violet was anxious to be away from the vexed earl and safely ensconced in her own bed.

Lord Westerbrook and Annabelle sat patiently as Violet made her way round to the kitchens, where her anxious maid waited to let her in. Although the fog made it somewhat difficult to see exactly what was happening, the sudden slam of a door indicated that the girl was safely inside. Cam signalled his coachman to be under way.

An extremely uncomfortable silence ensued as the earl's carriage progressed down the cobblestone streets. Annabelle was quite at a loss as to how she should proceed, knowing that an apology was due yet unsure how to frame it. Similarly, the earl was also plagued by worry, albeit of a different nature. Finally it was he who broke the silence. "De Dambere is not a suitable companion, you know," he mentioned at last, searching Annabelle's face for her reaction.

"Well, of course he isn't," the golden-brown beauty replied with distaste.

Cam's relief was almost palpable. So Annabelle wasn't in love with the dark-haired peer. More likely than not de Dambere had marked her as his next victim. The situation was one that certainly bore watching, yet if Annabelle behaved herself, it was Cam's guess that de Dambere would eventually lose interest and move on to more fertile ground. Therein, however, lay the rub. Annabelle couldn't be counted on to behave herself. His first night in Town and he'd already caught her out in an outrageous scheme. How right his mother had been about the gel. Annabelle was incapable of conducting herself with decorum. She risked being branded an Incorrigible or worse. And Cam certainly didn't have the time to follow the chit all hours of the day and night. Having only recently come to Town himself, he was anxious to pursue certain interests which had been seriously curtailed in the country.

"Now look here, my gel," Cam began, his voice once again returned to normal. "You're just going to have to make more effort to behave yourself. This kind of thing won't do at all, you know.''

Annabelle was overjoyed that the earl seemed once again in control of his anger. "I know it won't," she said earnestly. "And I promise to think things through a bit more thoroughly in future," the golden-brown beauty added by way of an apology.

Cam raised his eyebrows as if he seriously doubted her declaration and picked that unfortunate moment to laugh.

"Do you doubt me, sir?" Annabelle asked, most offended.

"Of course I do," Cam replied and added, "not only because it seems most unlikely, given your nature, but also because it's exceedingly difficult to take seriously the word of a woman who has hair glued to her upper lip. Or is the moustache natural, my dear?"

"It is not!" Annabelle shrieked, ripping the offending article from her skin. "Ouch!" she yelped, rubbing furiously the spot where only seconds before had resided a small bit of Mr. Fitzroy. In all the confusion, Annabelle hadn't given the slightest thought to her appearance. Now she found herself mortified by the way she must look, especially since Lord Westerbrook appeared so devastatingly handsome in his evening attire.

Cam noted Annabelle's blush even in the darkened interior of his carriage, and moving to sit next to her, he took one of her small hands in his own and said, "Even in men's clothing you look charming my dear. I've missed you, angel."

Annabelle peeped up at him through lowered lashes to see if he was serious. Although there was a definite twinkle in his eye, he didn't appear to be laughing. "I missed you, too," she admitted finally, sounding, however, none too pleased, given the disadvantage of her current situation.

"How sincere you sound, *Mr.* Winthrop," Cam remarked, no longer able to contain his amusement. Annabelle looked too ridiculous, dressed as she was in men's clothing.

The golden-brown beauty rounded on him like a hound come upon a fox. With fists clenched, she peppered his thighs and his arms with a series of frustrated blows. Cam withstood the pummelling, laughing all the while, until Annabelle's fists grew more deadly, and then quick as lightning he bundled her up into his arms and placed her quite easily upon his lap. "That's enough, I should think," he announced merrily as Annabelle twisted and turned in a futile effort to get away.

It was useless. Lord Westerbrook's arms felt like marble pillars, so unmovable were they. Annabelle relaxed and murmured, "As you will, my lord," for in truth it was quite a pleasant sensation to be seated so closely to the earl, although she would never have admitted that to him under any circumstances.

"It's unlike you to surrender," Cam murmured. "I shall have to watch my defences. But while we're at it, don't you think it time you begin to address me by my given name, especially since we currently seem to be on rather intimate terms?"

Annabelle's reply constituted another several moments of tussling, until Cam had once again subdued his errant charge. "Camford Singletary, you're a scoundrel," Annabelle spat out as she gasped for breath.

"Really. I thought I was a perfectly beastly man," he said just before his lips descended on hers with such force that Annabelle forgot all about fighting and concentrated instead on the devastation his mouth was wreaking on hers.

Annabelle felt lost, flooded with sensations too powerful to resist. Her arms went eagerly about his neck and she pressed herself closer to his wide chest. Her whole body was tingling, especially when his hand began to run the length and breadth of her form, causing her to utter a series of passionate little moans.

Cam shuddered and thrust the golden-brown beauty onto the seat opposite.

Annabelle appeared momentarily stunned and then began to compose herself as best she could, despite an uncontrollable shiver which had nothing to do with the cold. She knew that she would indeed have lost her virtue on this night if Cam weren't the man he was. Certainly she wouldn't have, couldn't have, stopped him.

"I'm not looking for a wife," Cam announced suddenly as Annabelle was adjusting her clothing.

Annabelle's hands stilled. "Why tell me?" she asked straight off, although she already knew the answer.

"I should think it obvious. We're attracted to each other, have been from the very first. Unfortunately, you're a young lady of gentle breeding unavailable for any kind of relationship other than marriage. I do like you, Annabelle, and we may well be seeing a great deal of each other this Season. I think it best, however, if we contrive not to be alone together. I'm simply not interested in marriage, not now, and I wouldn't have you compromised."

"What you say sounds exceedingly sensible, Cam," Annabelle conceded in the tone of voice that her aunt and uncle had come to dread. She smiled up at him sweetly, using the full force of her deeply set twin dimples. "I shall do my utmost to avoid you like the plague."

Cam's eyebrows shot up, for he'd just been insulted, albeit in such a fashion to completely disguise the swiftly delivered set down. Nevertheless, he held his tongue, which ached to retort, for he'd been nothing if not honest with the chit. He was too young for marriage. And when and if he married, it would certainly not be for love. He wouldn't go through the kind of agony his mother had suffered when his father died. Absolutely not. Much more sensible a marriage of convenience. Lucinda Moresby was the perfect choice. Her lands, in addition to his own, would certainly leave no question but that he was the most powerful man in

Sussex, and the woman herself was one for whom he would never feel anything more than a slight affection.

The carriage arrived at the Greywood's Berkeley Square townhouse moments later. Cam would've handed Annabelle down himself but she forestalled him with an uplifted palm. "Better that I go quickly," she said, accepting the tiger's hand as she jumped to the ground.

"Good night, Annabelle, and let me not catch you out again in such an outrageous scheme," Cam admonished as the golden-brown beauty stood framed in the doorway of his coach.

Annabelle smiled. "Oh, you won't catch me, my lord," she said, winking at him quite brazenly.

Cam watched her melt away into the fog and guffawed. He had to give her credit for her audacity. She really was quite intoxicating!

Betty met Annabelle at the door with a considerable sigh of relief. With her position seemingly safe, the maid hustled her charge up the steps and into Annabelle's bedroom, where the two removed Uncle William's evening attire.

Comfortably outfitted in a warm cambric nightgown, Annabelle sat before the fire in her bedroom sipping a mug of hot chocolate. Mr. Fitzroy lay at her feet, snoring contentedly. Despite the cozy domestic setting, the events of the evening ran over and over again in her mind's eye like a bad play, the worst moment coming when Cam (how delicious it was to call him that) announced that he'd no intention of marrying. Although the words had proven painful to Annabelle, she'd done her best to retain her wit, for it was far too early in the game for tears and recriminations. Still, his words had proven effective in the sense that Annabelle was now firmly dedicated to the pursuit of Camford Singletary, Earl of Westerbrook. Although she remained doubtful that she could bend him to her will, Annabelle wasn't one to back down from a challenge. The gauntlet had been thrown down, so to speak, and the contest, at the very least, would provide the kind of excitement that had heretofore been lacking in her London Season.

CHAPTER SIX

ALMACK'S WAS ABLAZE with light, but it emanated more from the fabulous jewels worn by its patrons than from the accoutrements of the establishment. Annabelle and Violet were surrounded by their usual coterie of gentlemen, which included the Marquis de Dambere, Randolph Ponfret, Freddy Merryweather, Major Jack Sprawlings—who hadn't yet given up his pursuit of the lovely Annabelle Winthrop—as well as a whole contingent of fortune-hunters drawn by Violet's enormous dowry.

Although Annabelle pretended to listen intently to the conversation which flowed about her, she was in reality not paying her suitors the slightest heed. Her thoughts were centred, as they usually were lately, on the knotty problem of how best to arrange a meeting with Lord Westerbrook. Annabelle had until recently been filled with an iron determination to fix the earl's interest. Unfortunately, she hadn't seen him in over a fortnight and was beginning to despair that she'd ever see him again. If it weren't for the fact that she occasionally overheard some small titbit of gossip concerning the earl, Annabelle would've sworn that he'd once again retired to the country. As it was, the latest on dit had it that the earl was spending the vast majority of his time in various gaming hells round Town, preferring the lifestyle of libertine to that of respectable gentleman. Violet had certainly been right when she'd said Cam had a reputation of a rake.

Because Annabelle was so deeply in thought, she didn't notice the most recent arrival at Almack's until a growing quiet throughout the room forced her to look up. There he was! The Earl of Westerbrook stood in the doorway resplendent in the required satin knee-breeches, a quizzing glass pressed rather haughtily against his eye.

In that moment, Annabelle was suddenly filled with an understanding of just what it meant to be the Earl of Westerbrook. Here was one of the most important peers of the realm. How utterly nonsensical of her to imagine that she could attract his notice. The companionable Camford Singletary that she'd known in the country was completely dwarfed by this top-of-the-trees Corinthian now standing before the assembly. Why, his very presence had completely changed the atmosphere of Almack's. A definite tension could be felt which hadn't existed before. Every mother began to think of ways to achieve an introduction. Every daughter automatically stood that much taller, straightened a wayward flounce, affixed a permanent smile—everyone except for Violet and Annabelle, perhaps. Violet because she was too embarrassed by her last encounter with the earl, and Annabelle because she was suddenly afraid to cross swords with this important, sought-after man.

The earl had no such qualms about Annabelle. Spotting her from his position in the doorway, Cam rapidly crossed the room, seemingly oblivious to those who watched his every step. The crowd round Annabelle slowly parted as it became apparent where the earl's interest lay.

Annabelle's heart began to beat rapidly beneath her pink silk bodice, so much so that she was frightened for a moment that she wouldn't be able to speak. But then she saw Cam's face, noted the disapproval he directed at those who would've fawned, and knew exactly what she had to do.

"I'm surprised you're still admitted to Almack's, my lord, in light of the gossip that you've left your entire fortune at the gaming-tables. Why, it's said that you've scarce come up for air in the past fortnight...."

Annabelle had no chance to finish her insulting tirade. Cam grabbed her by the arm and dragged her onto the dance floor with no consideration for the man to whom the waltz had been promised. "Why is it that you can't seem to act properly demure as do the other young ladies?" Cam asked, but there was no real malice in his eyes.

"If conversation concerning your most recent exploits disturbs you, my lord, we can always return to our discussion of Napoleon and the French."

"Damn Napoleon. I'm here only to lend countenance to your Season, as I promised I would. Dancing with the Earl of Westerbrook is considered very much an honour, you know. Following this waltz you'll find yourself in great demand."

Annabelle laughed gaily. "But I'm already in great demand, Cam dear," she replied sweetly as she looked upward into his twinkling, light brown eyes.

Annabelle's smile faded rapidly, however, as she found herself mesmerized by his regard. Cam too felt the powerful magnetism of their attraction and, swearing softly under his breath, drew Annabelle close so that she was forced to lower her eyes.

As Annabelle gave herself up to the joy of being held in Cam's arms, of being waltzed around the floor with an expertise she hadn't counted on him possessing, she was quite unaware of the attractive picture that she and Lord Westerbrook made. Mrs. Arthur Johnstone said as much to Aunt Charlotte, as did the Duchess of Montvale to her daughter Violet. There were those, however, who didn't view the dancing couple with the same degree of equanimity. The Marquis de Dambere regretted what he viewed as the escape of his prey, although the thought of the money he stood to make on the match soothed his wounded ego quite nicely. Freddy Merryweather and Major Jack Sprawlings stood about with hangdog faces, although neither one of them had given themselves much of a chance to begin with. It was Randolph Ponfret who was the most furious, for in his eyes Annabelle could do no better than himself. Seeing his beloved in the earl's arms awakened Ponfret to the fact that he had to intensify the level of his courtship immediately or all would be lost.

Following the waltz, Annabelle returned to her circle of friends, whereupon Cam asked Violet to dance, much to that young lady's consternation. However, he soon had her laughing and giggling, past mistakes clearly forgotten. Annabelle found herself in Freddy's arms and deemed it an excellent opportunity to begin her campaign to win the portly young sprig for Violet.

"Are there any on dits of merit that I should be made aware of, Freddy dearest?" Annabelle asked by way of an opening gambit.

She had to wait for her answer, however, for the movements of the country dance forced them to separate briefly. When they came together again, Freddy remarked somewhat petulantly, "Nothing other than the stir caused by the earl and yourself."

"Don't be ridiculous, Freddy," Annabelle chided. "Why, the earl is at this very moment dancing with the eminently suitable Lady Violet Silverton. The combined fortunes of those two individuals would surely establish them as one of the richest families in England."

Freddy brightened immediately. He was ever one for gossip. "They do say Lady Violet's dowry is monstrous."

"That it is," Annabelle replied, as innocently as she was capable. "The man who marries her will be lucky indeed, for not only does she bring an enormous fortune, she is also a most engaging companion and quite attractive with her flaming red hair."

Freddy laughed. "You sound like Lady Violet's champion."

Annabelle smiled in return. "I imagine that I do, only I've spent quite a bit of time with Violet lately and she's a wonderful friend. I would see her happy."

"Admirable, my dear," Freddy replied sarcastically, as he was wont to do at any sign of what he called "country naïveté." But Annabelle noticed later that his countenance was more than a little bit speculative as he danced with Violet.

Annabelle's next partner, much to her chagrin, was Randolph Ponfret. Over the past few weeks she'd developed somewhat of an aversion to the fellow, for he was obviously besotted with her—an emotion she didn't share. Furthermore, Annabelle was coming to realize that there was a dark side to Randolph's nature which emerged whenever he was thwarted. At those times he seemed to have difficulty accepting defeat gracefully, and although he'd never been exactly disagreeable, Annabelle sensed intuitively that he wasn't the harmless dandy his youth and appearance would suggest. That's why she didn't agree immediately when Randolph proposed escorting her to the theatre two days hence, even though he said his parents would accompany them as chaperons. Annabelle couldn't feel comfortable with the idea. She would rather attend with someone like, well, someone like Major Sprawlings. At least she knew the major was harmless, and easily controlled.

At that moment, however, Fate stepped in and determined that she would accompany Randolph to the theatre, for another arrival at Almack's, just before the doors closed, caused Annabelle's heart to constrict. Lucinda Moresby stood framed in the doorway on her father's arm, looking ravishing in a gown of white spider gauze. A quiet hush fell over the crowd in respect for Lucinda's beauty, for although there were several attractive women present, including Annabelle, none could lay claim to the blonde's sheer ability to stun.

Annabelle watched in horrified fascination as Lucinda, with her firm manlike gait, propelled herself and her father over to where Cam was chatting desultorily with Freddy Merryweather. Freddy, with his ready eye for feminine beauty, hastily made way for Lucinda and her father, and the four of them were quickly embroiled in a conversation that to all appearances looked quite animated.

Not wanting to make a total cake of herself, Annabelle tore her eyes away from the spectacle, only to meet Violet's crestfallen gaze across the room. Obviously, the redhead assumed Lucinda was making a play for Freddy as well as Cam. Annabelle rolled her eyes comically and was rewarded when Violet did the same in return.

"You know, Randolph, I think your theatre invitation sounds positively divine," Annabelle stated, impulsively squeezing the arm of the blond Lothario with whom she was dancing. Randolph wasn't the ideal choice to pique Cam's jealousy, but Annabelle was beginning to feel a sense of desperation, especially now that Lucinda was in Town!

"Splendid. I'm awfully glad you've accepted. We'll have a famous time, you'll see," Randolph replied eagerly, thrilled with the prospect of keeping company with Annabelle away from her usual throng of admirers.

The golden-brown beauty smiled winningly, but inside she felt a great deal less than pleased. She really shouldn't encourage the advances of someone in whom she hadn't the slightest bit of interest. But one sortie to the theatre could hardly be considered an act of heartlessness. Could it?

The rest of the evening passed slowly for Annabelle. She was relieved when Cam left rather early, for she hadn't wanted to see him dance with Lucinda. Ironically, though, the golden-brown beauty could muster no animation following the earl's departure. For that reason, she suggested to Aunt Charlotte that they also retire early. The older woman was of no mind to argue, for she wasn't as young as she used to be and the late nights were beginning to take their toll.

In the carriage on the way home, Annabelle got up from her usual position, plopped down next to her aunt, and leaned her head on the older woman's shoulder. The gesture surprised Aunt Charlotte, for Annabelle seemed so grown-up lately that sometimes she forgot the gel was still little more than a child.

Aunt Charlotte stroked her niece's hair and felt a film of tears cloud her eyes. How many more such intimacies would they share? In all probability, Annabelle would soon find a husband and she'd be forced to relinquish the last of her babies.

"Did you love Uncle William very much when you married him?" Annabelle asked quietly a few moments later.

"I loved him well enough, though he wasn't my first love," Aunt Charlotte answered honestly, knowing that Annabelle was suffering from some mild malaise of the soul.

"What happened to your first love, Auntie?"

"He was killed in a hunting accident, but he wouldn't have married me in any case. He was a younger son and determined to find himself an heiress."

Annabelle whipped about and stared at her aunt with widened eyes. "You must've been devastated—on both accounts."

"I was, for a while. Then I realized I hadn't really known him well enough to mourn so deeply. In other words, I was in love with the idea of being in love. A year or so later I met your uncle William. Although I'll admit to being attracted to him immediately, I've come to understand through the years that love means much more than physical attraction. It means spending time with a person, caring for that person when he's sick, agonizing over his yule-tide gifts, accepting his faults and rejoicing when he accepts yours. It means sharing the burdens of parenthood, and the mundane realities of day-to-day life."

Annabelle settled back against her aunt's shoulder. "What you're trying to tell me is that meaningful love must be built. One doesn't necessarily have to marry the man to whom one loses one's heart.''

"Well, it certainly helps if you're at least somewhat attracted to the man you would wed," Aunt Charlotte replied in pragmatic fashion, toying absently with her ever-present quizzing glass. "But if you shouldn't achieve your immediate heart's desire, you may rest assured that in time you'll undoubtedly find another.''

"But why must the process be so painful?''

"In life there are good times and bad. If we never experienced pain, how would we know the meaning of joy? And now, young lady, enough of your questions. Goodness, I feel as if you're ten years old again and forever plaguing me to tell you why the sky is blue.''

"Why are you so wise, Auntie?'' Annabelle asked, inadvertently posing yet another question.

"I'm not wise, you disobedient ninnyhammer. I'm old. When you get to be my age, provided you haven't killed yourself in one of your more outrageous schemes, you too shall have all the answers.''

"I love you, Auntie,'' Annabelle said with feeling, nestling herself into her Aunt Charlotte's arms.

"Annabelle Winthrop, if this is yet another clever ploy to coax me into buying you more gowns, you're quite out of luck,'' Aunt Charlotte replied with asperity, but there was a curious catch to her voice and she wasn't above hugging her niece to the point of breaking a few bones.

TWO NIGHTS LATER, with the assistance of Betty, Annabelle prepared for the theatre. She couldn't summon forth any joy at the prospect of the expedition, not when she was to attend under the aegis of Randolph Ponfret and his parents, yet Annabelle supposed the least she could do was look her best. Towards that end, she allowed Betty to dress her golden-brown curls high atop her head in a style which Annabelle knew to be enormously flattering. Betty then threaded a pale green ribbon through her curls, a ribbon that matched exactly the colour of her gown.

When Annabelle finally made her entrance into the drawing-room, she found that the Ponfrets had already arrived and were conversing with Aunt Charlotte, while Randolph himself busily examined a set of framed hunting sketches which hung upon the wall. Noticing Annabelle's arrival, Randolph rushed forth and complimented her profusely on her appearance. Annabelle thanked him quite prettily, although to her horror she found herself stifling a yawn. How utterly boring the evening promised to be, especially when she learned that they were to see a performance of Shakespeare's *Richard II*. Annabelle had never enjoyed that particular play. It was entirely too sad for her liking.

Yet when Annabelle arrived at the theatre, she found that the excitement which always seemed so palpable before any major performance was enough to lift her spirits quite admirably. Feeling a tingle of anticipation, she raised her opera-glass towards the stage and then surreptitiously scanned the crowd. A sea of faces drifted past, some familiar, some not, until most unexpectedly Annabelle spotted the one face that had come to dominate her thoughts more so than any other. She couldn't help but marvel again at how handsome Cam was, especially in his evening attire, but Annabelle's admiration quickly turned to anger when she spotted the heavenly creature seated next to her beloved. A statuesque redhead with milky white skin was running her hand down Cam's arm most enticingly, and worst of all, Cam looked as if he were enjoying every moment of it.

Quite without thinking, Annabelle leaned over and in whispered tones asked Randolph, "Who is that woman with the Earl of Westerbrook?"

Randolph took the glass from Annabelle's hand and then dropped it quickly as if the glass were hot. "Annabelle, I don't believe the earl's companion a fit topic of conversation for a young lady of Quality such as yourself.''

"She's a Cyprian then, isn't she?" Annabelle guessed without much effort. "Come, come, Randolph," she added, demanding the opera-glass be returned, "I may be just up from the country but I'm not a complete ninny."

"Annabelle, I simply can't bring myself to discuss such a subject with you," Randolph hissed, beginning to feel somewhat discomfited. He quickly sneaked a look over his shoulder and, seeing that his parents were engrossed in conversation, sighed audibly. Randolph had forgotten just how blunt Annabelle could be, and while he enjoyed her unaffected air, it wasn't proper that the future Mrs. Ponfret conduct herself in such a forthright manner. But then Randolph smiled. How heavenly to be the one required to instruct the Wayward Angel as to the proper degree of decorum she must learn to affect.

"Why, the creature barely has a stitch on," Annabelle commented some minutes later, more to herself than to Randolph. "And although she does possess a certain base sort of charm, she isn't really, upon closer inspection, what one would call a diamond of the first water."

"Many claim that Harriette Wilson's talents more than make up for whatever beauty she may or may not possess," Randolph was goaded into saying.

Annabelle gasped. Naturally Cam would choose as his lightskirt the most famous Cyprian of the day. Throwing the opera-glass into her lap disgustedly, Annabelle was glad to see the curtain begin to rise. She didn't at that moment feel like making small talk with Randolph Ponfret—not when she was so very angry at Cam. How dare he make such a public spectacle of himself with that—that woman! Yet Annabelle knew it was common practice for gentlemen of the ton to be seen at the theatre with women of lesser virtue. Cam was certainly not behaving in any fashion destined to place him beyond the pale. However, the fact that he was well within his rights didn't make Annabelle feel any better. She spent the entire first act of the play fighting tears and had no more knowledge of what was occurring on the stage than did her Aunt Charlotte back in Berkeley Square.

After what seemed an interminable length of time, intermission finally arrived, and feeling the need to escape the sight of the earl and his doxy, Annabelle begged Randolph prettily to stroll with her in the corridor outside their boxed seats.

"Happy to," Randolph replied with alacrity, for in truth he found the performance boring in the extreme, although he was careful to mouth all the proper tenets expected of an educated gentleman. The fact that Randolph had been asked to leave Oxford before graduation didn't factor into his image of himself as an intellectual.

Linking her arm through his, Annabelle allowed Randolph to lead her forth. She nodded her head in greeting to several friends but made no special effort to converse. Randolph found her behaviour gratifying, for it enabled him to speak at length about this subject and that as he so liked to do, without having to fend off Annabelle's usual horde of admirers. Randolph didn't notice Annabelle's air of distraction.

It was only when the golden-brown beauty spied Cam out of the corner of her eye strolling towards them with that dreadful creature on his arm that her aspect became more animated. Grasping Randolph's arm tightly, she looked up into her blond swain's somewhat vacuous blue eyes and smiled at him the smile that she'd long since learned turned most men into stammering fools.

Cam couldn't help but notice Annabelle's conduct, and to his disgust he found that the sight affected him more than he would've wished. The thought of the lovely Annabelle with that jackanapes Ponfret just didn't suit. Ponfret was a mere child in Cam's view, and a very spoiled one at that.

Convention dictated that Cam couldn't approach Annabelle or her escort, for it wasn't at all the thing to present an innocent young lady to a woman of the world such as Harriette Wilson. Cam settled for giving Annabelle a look designed to freeze even the most pedigreed aristocrat. Tomorrow he'd tell her personally just what he thought of her judgement in men. Whatever could Lady Charlotte be thinking, allowing Annabelle to be seen in the company of such a fool? Why, it could ruin the chit's reputation.

Unfortunately, Annabelle had no way of divining Cam's thoughts. She misinterpreted his haughty dismissal as a sign of disfavour and found that she was filled with anger at his cruel behaviour. How dare he dally with her in the country and then ignore her very existence in Town? Annabelle Winthrop wasn't a woman to be trifled with or ignored, and she had every intention of proving it to him.

Somehow Annabelle got through the rest of the evening. But by the time the Ponfrets dropped her off at the Berkeley Square townhouse, her head was throbbing and she felt the onset of a genuine megrim. Annabelle immediately took to bed and didn't rouse herself until well past noon the following day. She refused all callers, even when she was informed that the Earl of Westerbrook was below stairs demanding an interview. Thinking that Cam had come to accuse her of following him about Town, Annabelle began to give serious consideration to the somewhat daring scheme that had popped into her head just that morn. The plan was certainly risky and surely designed to produce a well-deserved scold from Aunt Charlotte, yet what could her beloved aunt do when presented with a *fait accompli?*

"I'll do it," Annabelle announced loudly, startling both Betty, who was at that moment sorting through her young charge's overstuffed wardrobe, and Mr. Fitzroy, who'd been resting comfortably at his mistress's side.

"Do what, miss?" Betty asked in an alarmed tone. She knew Annabelle well enough to smell something smoky.

"Oh, nothing," the golden-brown beauty replied innocently, for she knew that there was no possibility of Betty going along with this, her latest scheme. The maid definitely had her limits.

Later that night, in preparation for Lady Langdon-Smythe's musical evening, Annabelle allowed Betty to help her into a deliciously frothy ivory lace gown strategically designed to show the full measure of her well-developed figure. It was a gown which Annabelle had yet to wear, for she'd had a devil of a time convincing Aunt Charlotte to allow her to have it. In the interest of keeping the peace, she'd never worn the offending garment, but Annabelle had decided that it was time to bring out the heavy artillery.

Betty handed her young mistress an ivory fan which matched Annabelle's gown but didn't extend her usual, if somewhat dour, compliment. Instead she sniffed disapprovingly and eyed Annabelle's bodice as if she expected it to give way at the slightest disturbance. "Completely improper," Betty muttered under her breath, earning a frown and a gesture of dismissal from her mistress.

Annabelle waited until she heard Betty's slight tread fade away before she went into action. Removing her petticoat, she drenched it in the ewer which stood atop her washstand and, having stripped off her gloves, wrung the undergarment out until it no longer dripped. Then she gingerly stepped into the petticoat, trying not to mind the way it clung to her legs. Dressing as a Cyprian might surely cause no small degree of discomfort, yet Annabelle was determined to cast the voluptuous Harriette Wilson in the shade. Even if Cam wasn't present at Lady Langdon-Smythe's this evening, he'd surely hear of her appearance, and that was all that mattered.

Realizing she was keeping Aunt Charlotte waiting, Annabelle threw her new ermine-lined evening cloak about her shoulders and ran down the stairs to the drawing-room, where her aunt sat fidgeting with her quizzing glass.

Aunt Charlotte peered at her niece through her glass, her myopic blue eyes missing nothing except the fact that Annabelle was about to irreparably damage her reputation. "All ready to go, I see," Aunt Charlotte said, rising to leave. "Happy tidings, since you kept me waiting long enough."

"I'm sorry, Auntie," Annabelle said, trying not to shiver. A dampened petticoat was definitely not comfortable. To what lengths a woman went to please, or in her case, infuriate and possibly captivate, a man! "Do let us be on our way. You know how Lady Langdon-Smythe detests tardiness, especially when she's trying to placate her usual group of Italian opera singers."

"In that case perhaps we should be purposely late," Aunt Charlotte commented irritably, for she wasn't a devoted opera fan and the evening ahead wasn't one to which she was looking forward. Furthermore, Annabelle's earlier headache, which now seemed to have magically disappeared, had convinced Aunt Charlotte that she was finally in for a long-deserved evening at home. The elderly woman sighed. How she missed her simple country life. Although London had excited her at first, she was far too old to be galloping about Town like a young filly.

Despite Aunt Charlotte's grumbling, they weren't late at Lady Langdon-Smythe's gathering, although Annabelle was gratified to see that they were among the last to arrive. Sending her aunt off in the direction of Mrs. Arthur Johnstone, the golden-brown beauty relinquished her cloak to a waiting footman. She was so busy smoothing down the folds of her wet and clinging gown that she didn't notice the admiring stare of the young footman, who stood rooted in place.

The Earl of Westerbrook, however, noticed the footman's rapture, and his blood began to boil. Having spotted Aunt Charlotte, he'd come hurrying into the entrance hall to have a word with Annabelle before the dreadful evening began. Cam had it in mind to escape long before the Italians were trotted out, for he was planning to join Freddy Merryweather and a few of the other young bloods for a night of gaming at White's.

But as he strode into the foyer, his breath was quite taken away by the sight of Annabelle clothed in a gown which clung to her figure like a second skin. His pulse began to race and he experienced the all-too-familiar tightening in his groin which seemed to occur whenever she was near. By Jove, she was beautiful! Far too beautiful for Randolph Ponfret, or for the besotted footman who stood gaping at her as if he'd never seen a woman before.

That's when Cam's anger erupted. How dare Annabelle attempt to parade herself in front of High Society dressed like a common whore? What devil had possessed her this time?

Annabelle's face paled as she recognized Cam and saw him striding toward her like an angry bull. She wasn't prepared for a direct confrontation; she hadn't really expected that he'd deign to attend such an insipid gathering.

Cam grabbed Annabelle's cloak from the red-faced footman and curtly ordered him away. He then threw it about her shoulders and dragged her along with him until he reached the doorway into Lady Langdon-Smythe's music room. Signalling for Aunt Charlotte, he waited impatiently as that venerable old lady drew herself up and casually made her way across the room.

"Whatever is the matter?" Aunt Charlotte hissed angrily as she reached the doorway. "I'm not of a mind to be the cause of gossip."

Cam opened Annabelle's cloak long enough for an expression of horror to settle upon Aunt Charlotte's face. "I suggest you put it about that your niece has suddenly contracted the headache or I'm sure the gossip will be of a magnitude that you can't begin to comprehend."

Aunt Charlotte nodded her agreement and shot a look of gratitude Cam's way. The look she gave Annabelle was entirely different and set that young lady's knees to knocking.

As Aunt Charlotte went to whisper a few words in Lady Langdon-Smythe's ear, Annabelle tossed her curls and tried to wrest her arm away from Cam's grasp. "You're hurting me," she informed him icily, more embarrassed than she cared to admit at being treated so summarily like a child.

"Too bad, although this is nothing compared to what I'd like to do to you," Cam replied furiously. "Furthermore, I'm going to suggest to your aunt that you be placed under lock and key from now on, for you're obviously incapable of ordering your life in an accepted, conventional fashion."

Annabelle batted her eyelashes. "Cam, you can't possibly be upset at my mode of dress, can you? Why, the lady I saw you with last night had on less than I do now. I just naturally assumed it to be the new fashion."

"Fustian!" he replied. "You know perfectly well that the woman I was with last night was no lady. Randolph Ponfret has a large mouth and I'm sure that he informed you of all the sordid details. That brings me to another point: Randolph Ponfret. He's not the man for you, Annabelle. I've known him for years and he doesn't possess what I'd call a sterling, or for that matter an even acceptable, character."

"My personal life is none of your affair," Annabelle stated determinedly, stamping her foot for emphasis. "Much the same as your personal life is none of mine."

The two antagonists stood staring at each other in anger until Aunt Charlotte relieved Cam of what he was beginning to think of as his permanent burden.

"Thank you very much, Lord Westerbrook, for your intervention," Aunt Charlotte said, pulling Annabelle towards the door without much finesse. "And do give your mother my regards."

"You'll be able to do that yourself soon enough, my lady," Cam announced, bowing slightly as he, too, prepared to depart. "She arrives in Town next week and I expect would be delighted if you called."

Aunt Charlotte inclined her head and then, with Annabelle in tow, moved out the door to order up the Greywood carriage. Cam followed along behind, but unfortunately at that moment Lady Langdon-Smythe came charging into the foyer and, seeing that her most impressive guest was about to leave, quickly intervened.

"Surely you can't be making your departure just yet?" that good lady asked, grabbing Cam's arm and flapping her eyelashes at him most outrageously, just like a young girl fresh from the schoolroom.

Cam sighed and bowed to the inevitable. "Of course not. I was merely sharing a few words with Lady Charlotte Greywood concerning my mother's arrival in Town."

"Lady Margaret is to come to London? Oh, how divine, and about time, too, if you ask me," prattled Lady Langdon-Smythe as she inexorably drew Cam back into the music room, where he was forced to endure two hours of Italian opera before he was able to at long last make his escape.

Annabelle's punishment was much more severe. Not only had Aunt Charlotte forbidden her to accompany an expedition to Vauxhall that she'd been particularly looking forward to, but as a result of her impulsive behaviour, the golden-brown beauty caught the most severe cold that she'd had in an age. And, unfortunately, she didn't prove to be a good patient. She was cross to the extent of turning poor Betty into a watering pot on more than one occasion, and was prone to veritable fits whenever she saw herself in the mirror. For not only was Annabelle a poor patient, she was definitely not in her best looks as the cold followed its course. Her nose was swollen to an unattractive degree, her eyes were red-rimmed and teary, and her hair hung limply down her back.

Violet, upon visiting her sick friend, couldn't help but feel that there was justice in the world after all, even though she scolded herself on the way home for harbouring such uncharitable thoughts. Annabelle really was a good sort. Had she not on this very day kissed a rather annoyed Mr. Fitzroy straight upon the lips as she'd been required to do by the terms of their wager?

Cam was more amused than shocked. Accompanying his mother as she returned Aunt Charlotte's call, he used the occasion to quite boldly sneak into Annabelle's bedchamber—something unheard of in light of the necessity of preserving a young lady's reputation.

"How dare you?" Annabelle screamed as she saw who it was entering her room with impunity.

"Get back, you filthy beast," Betty threatened, brandishing one of Annabelle's best silk parasols as her mistress cringed in mortification under the bed covers.

"Ah, at long last I learn the origin of Annabelle's propensity for calling me all sorts of vile names," Cam said, his amusement growing by leaps and bounds. His somewhat snide grin vanished, however, as Betty—unmindful of his lofty position—poked at him quite ruthlessly, aiming for his ribs.

Taking a gold sovereign from within his waistcoat, Cam tossed it towards the maid, who couldn't help but chase the shiny treasure. He then placed a small packet upon Annabelle's washstand, and turned to withdraw. "I look forward to seeing you at your ball," the earl stated quickly before slipping from the room as easily as he'd entered.

"Well!" Annabelle exclaimed in outrage, flipping back the covers once she was certain he'd gone. Curiosity, however, prompted her to unwrap his gift, and she couldn't help the giggle which bubbled forth at the sight of three neatly bound books; one on Napoleon Bonaparte and the French

Revolution, another on obedience training for dogs, and the last, a primer on good manners and etiquette for young ladies of the ton.

CHAPTER SEVEN

"UNCLE WILLIAM!" Annabelle shouted joyously, hurtling herself at the great bear of a man who'd just entered the drawing-room. "I'm so glad you've arrived. It hasn't been the same without you."

"Hey, ho, my gel, it seems I've come just in the nick of time if what your aunt has been telling me is true. Did I make a mistake in allowing you to come to London?"

Annabelle hung her head and shot a quick glance at Aunt Charlotte, who'd followed her husband into the drawing-room. Fortunately, her aunt was smiling. "Well, I haven't been perfectly behaved I must admit," Annabelle began, "but I haven't done anything especially awful, either."

"Then why have I been reading about a shocking young lady they call the Wayward Angel?" Uncle William asked, running a hand over his semi-bald pate.

"Oh, that's all a hum," Annabelle answered blithely, plopping down on the pink-and-white striped satin settee. "The *Gazette* seems to give everyone some kind of silly soubriquet."

"Silly or no, now that I've come to Town you'll behave yourself, my gel, or its back to Brierly for you. Is that clear?"

Annabelle eyes widened. "Perfectly," she said after quickly gulping down the sweetmeat she'd popped into her mouth. Licking her fingers, she got up to retrieve a stack of newspapers which she'd been saving for her uncle's arrival. "Do let's go through these, Uncle William," Annabelle coaxed, smiling angelically. "It seems that few people in London are willing to take seriously the comments of women, especially young women. I've circled the articles of interest just as we used to do back home."

"Humph," Uncle William muttered, not displeased. "Don't try and turn me up sweet, my gel."

Annabelle quickly affected a crushed look, one that always seemed to fare better with her uncle than her aunt.

"Oh, all right then," Uncle William stated, motioning Annabelle to his side.

"You'll turn the chit into a bluestocking yet," Aunt Charlotte prophesied as she prepared to leave the two alone, for political discussions of any kind tended to bore her to tears. "All this education has served no useful purpose whatsoever except to encourage Annabelle's wilful behaviour," she added emphatically as she opened the doors. Aunt Charlotte sighed when she was completely ignored. Taking one last look at the two heads bent over the material Annabelle had surreptitiously collected, the older woman quietly took her leave.

Aunt Charlotte needn't have worried about Annabelle becoming immersed in scholarship, for the next few days proved extremely busy for both women as the Greywood ball—Annabelle's official come-out—was but weeks away. The invitations, which had been ordered well in advance, were now addressed and delivered. The penning of the invitations was one task which Annabelle undertook herself, since she'd a fine hand and enjoyed writing. Although Annabelle's ball wouldn't be the most lavish affair held during the course of the Season, the guest list was highly exclusive and even included, much to Annabelle's chagrin, Squire Moresby and his daughter Lucinda. To exclude them would have been considered very bad ton indeed. That didn't stop Annabelle's hand from shaking as she addressed their invitation, nor did it stop her from terribly splotching the ink when she was forced to write out Lucinda's name.

The bill of fare, which had also been planned in advance, was now the pitch of perfection—the *coup de grâce* to be ices provided by Gunters itself. Aunt Charlotte, on the recommendation of Mrs. Arthur Johnstone, undertook the hiring of a group of German musicians who were reputed to be all the crack, in addition to enlisting extra staff to ensure that the Berkeley Square townhouse was cleaned from top to bottom. Special emphasis was given to the small ballroom where the dancing would be held, and to the gilt chairs rented for the occasion, upon which would sit the chaperons and those young ladies not fortunate enough to be asked to dance.

The only bone of contention proved to be the Greywood ladies' choice of flowers. Although Uncle William loved Annabelle dearly, he almost suffered a fit of apoplexy when presented with the florist's bill and came within an inch of rescinding the order. Only Aunt Charlotte's entreaties that large bouquets of white roses were absolutely mandatory to the success of the ball managed to sway him, that and the tears his niece was able to produce.

To Annabelle's mind, however, the worst part of the whole ordeal was the endless fittings she had to endure, especially in the last few days before the ball, to ensure the perfection of her come-out gown. Not by nature a complacent person, the hours of standing and turning and being poked by all manner of needles wasn't her idea of fun. To Annabelle's credit, she strove mightily not to complain. To do so would've been churlish in the extreme, for Aunt Charlotte had insisted that for this one special gown, Annabelle be outfitted by the very best.

Madame Evangeline Roche was undoubtedly the most fashionable modiste in all of London. Her styles were studiously copied by lesser artists; her clients included only the crème de la crème of British Society. A French emigré of indeterminate age, Madame Roche was reputed to be the illegitimate daughter of a member of the French royal family. Madame certainly carried herself like royalty, for despite her diminutive stature, her regal bearing could have intimidated Prinny himself.

Upon entering Madame Roche's exclusive salon months ago, Annabelle and Aunt Charlotte had certainly been dazzled by the expensive décor—the crowning glory of which were several strategically placed Louis XV settees. As they moved farther into the exclusive shop, a servant had come scurrying out to seat them. They were then offered tea. It was only after they'd actually been served that Madame Roche herself appeared.

The tiny Frenchwoman clothed in a somber gown of impeccable design stared down her nose at them for several moments before she deigned to speak. "You wished to see Madame Roche?" she questioned in an arrogant fashion, her voice carrying only the hint of a French accent.

Aunt Charlotte's hackles began to rise. She wasn't about to be bullied by a modiste, even if she was the best designer in Town. "Yes," Aunt Charlotte replied equally haughtily. "We've come to procure a ball gown for my niece."

"Only one?" Madame Roche scoffed, as if accustomed to large orders, when in fact only the wealthiest ladies in the land could afford to order their entire wardrobes from her salon.

"Only one," Aunt Charlotte replied firmly.

Seeing that her new arrivals weren't to be intimidated, the small Frenchwoman sighed and motioned for Annabelle to rise and slowly turn. "Not as stunning as Mademoiselle Moresby," Madame Roche commented, revealing her intimate knowledge of the ton. "But in actuality much more even of feature. The figure is better, too. Poor Mademoiselle Moresby is possessed of, how shall we say, a rather large derrière. You, however, are capable of doing full justice to a Madame Roche creation. Properly clothed in white and black—"

"Black?" Aunt Charlotte interrupted with a gasp. "Surely, madame, you are mistaken. My niece is a young lady in her first season. Black isn't at all appropriate."

Madame Roche's eyebrows lifted a fraction of an inch. "I'm fully aware of Society's dictates when it comes to fashion, Lady Greywood. Mademoiselle's gown will of course be predominately white. However, I tell you right now that black is the only colour which will properly highlight her hair and skin and eyes. I will of course design the gown so that the black serves merely as an accent."

Aunt Charlotte looked ready to object. Her myopic blue eyes were widely dilated and she seemed to be having trouble breathing. That's when Annabelle jumped into the fray. "Please listen to Madame Roche, Auntie," she entreated, clenching and unclenching her hands, "for I've long known what she says to be true. Remember when we attended Aunt Sophia's funeral? Despite the sadness of the occasion, I couldn't help but note how well I looked in mourning."

Aunt Charlotte snorted. "Ruin! We shall all come to ruin over this nonsense, but I suppose it shall do. After all, I can't very well claim to be an expert in the area of fashion, having spent the past several years in the country."

As Madame Roche nodded her approval at this sage admission, Annabelle squealed and threw her arms about Aunt Charlotte. Next she turned to Madame Roche as if to hug her, too, but that good woman's stiff demeanour made it abundantly clear that any manner of physical contact was out of the question. Therefore, Annabelle merely smiled winningly and gave herself up to the task of being measured.

Preparations for Annabelle's ball weren't all so tedious, however. Happily, all four Greywood boys, although they were hardly boys now but rather fully grown men, were able to attend. William, the eldest and the heir, arrived first,

without his wife, who was in the process of presenting him
with yet another child. Henry, the second, came all the way
from Scotland, where he'd inherited a minor estate through
his mother's side of the family. Henry brought with him his
wife and their two children, twin boys, so that the townhouse was soon full of happy noise and clamour. Andrew,
the third, arrived from Bath, where he'd left his eccentric
but extremely rich and beautiful wife enjoying the benefits
of the waters. Even David, the youngest, managed to secure time off from his regiment, which was currently stationed in Manchester.

With the arrival of her boys, Aunt Charlotte was rarely
seen without a large smile lighting her face. Even Uncle
William unbent to the extent of putting aside his newspaper at luncheon in favour of family conversation.

Annabelle was ecstatic. She adored it when the whole
family was together, and as usual she took to tagging after
Andrew, who, as the handsomest and most debonair, had
always been her favourite. She even swallowed her fear of
horses and allowed him to take her driving in his curricle—
a vehicle which Annabelle regarded as highly dangerous. In
the mornings, before it was too crowded, Andrew drove her
through Hyde Park at a spanking pace, his fingers manip-
ulating the ribbons like the expert he was reputed to be by
virtue of the fact that he was a member in good standing of
the Four-in-Hand Club. In the afternoons they prome-
naded in more leisurely style along Rotten Row, enjoying the
spectacle of the ton out to see and be seen.

One morning, on an overcast day chilly and damp, Andrew none the less persuaded Annabelle to accompany him
on their usual jaunt, for he'd heard several disquieting ru-
mours about his beautiful cousin which he felt required explanation.

Pulling the horses to a stop underneath a large tree which
afforded them some small measure of privacy, Andrew
reached inside his coat and withdrew a small cheroot.

"Is it wise to keep the horses standing about in such weather?" Annabelle questioned, trying her best not to shiver. Gratefully she buried her fingers deeper inside the ermine muff which Betty had thrust upon her at the last second.

"A few moments won't hurt them," Andrew replied, lighting the cheroot and handing it to Annabelle with a smile. As a young child, the golden-brown beauty had always insisted upon doing everything exactly like Cousin Andrew. Eventually, he'd given over and had fallen into the habit of allowing her a few puffs of his cheroot from time to time. It was also Andrew who had allowed Annabelle her first taste of champagne, and it was Andrew who'd answered her embarrassing questions concerning marital relations (the ones that had so discomfited Aunt Charlotte).

Annabelle withdrew her hand from inside the warm muff long enough to grasp the cheroot, take a shallow puff and hand it back. She smiled as she did so, for it touched her that Andrew remembered their small rituals despite the fact that he was now married with a wife to please.

"Is there any truth to the rumour that you have a tendre for the Marquis de Dambere?" Andrew questioned after a short period of silent camaraderie. "I should hate to have to call him out, you know, but I tell you to your head, Annabelle, he isn't for the likes of you."

"Oh, you beast!" the golden-brown beauty raged, hitting her cousin soundly upon the arm. "Here I thought you were trying to be nice to me and as it turns out you're merely fishing for information."

Andrew grinned, and his smile, very much like Annabelle's, lit his whole face with a charm that was impossible to resist. "Annabelle, I'm only trying to help. Your life is very much your own affair. I realize that. But the marquis is a sophisticated man with sophisticated tastes and I doubt very much that you two would suit, if indeed you could bring him to the altar at all. The marquis is a man strongly opposed to remarriage. His first wife gave him his heir before she died, and he sees no need to shackle himself to one woman when several will do.''

Annabelle tossed her curls. ''As a matter of fact I haven't the slightest interest in the marquis, for I know full well his reputation.''

Andrew sighed with relief. ''Is there no one then whom you would wed?''

As Annabelle's face began to colour, Andrew slapped his thigh and yelled, ''Who? Tell me who! I can't believe it's Merryweather, or the rather timid Major Sprawlings. Let me think. Who else has been lounging about our drawing-room lately? Don't tell me you've developed feelings for the Ponfret puppy?''

A quick shake of her head caused Andrew to reflect, but then he smiled. ''It's Westerbrook, isn't it? My little cousin fancies herself a countess. But I thought the earl had an understanding with the Moresby chit.''

''Nothing official,'' Annabelle was quick to respond, confirming Andrew's suspicions. She giggled at his sly look and grabbed the cheroot for another puff. ''Only, Andrew, just imagine, I've learned the most delicious gossip about the divine Miss Moresby. I have it on very good authority that her bottom half is as big as the back end of a horse. Of course, she hides it well, don't you think?''

Andrew laughed so hard that a reply was quite out of the question. All he could do was clasp his cousin's arm and shake with mirth. Annabelle herself dissolved into a merry fit of the giggles.

Thus it was quite a scene that the Earl of Westerbrook encountered while out for his usual morning ride atop his spirited charcoal grey stallion. From a distance the earl could hardly believe his eyes, for it seemed that the impossible Miss Winthrop was actually smoking in public while laughing uproariously in a manner which in no way befitted a lady. Worst of all, she was in the company of a handsome rogue who was treating her in an overly familiar fashion. Cam spurred his horse forward, his blood at a boil, determined to confront the little termagant with this, her latest bout of misbehaviour.

Andrew was the first to notice the horseman riding towards them at thunderous speed. "Oh, Lord," he remarked, "I do believe your true love doth approach."

"What?" Annabelle shrieked, practically throwing the cheroot at Andrew, although it was apparent from Cam's expression that he'd already seen her with it.

"My dear Miss Winthrop," Cam began caustically as he pulled Merlin to a stop inches from Andrew's curricle, "dare I suggest that smoking in public isn't at all the thing for a young lady of Quality?"

Blushing profusely, for Cam looked resplendent in his bottle-green riding coat which only emphasized the sheen of his ebony hair, Annabelle affected introductions. "Lord Camford Singletary, may I present my cousin Andrew Greywood, lately of Bath, who's been so good as to come to Town for my ball?"

Nodding his head slightly, Cam felt strangely foolish, yet enormously relieved. "Greywood. Should've recognized you, of course. I believe we even sparred together once at Jackson's."

"I remember the encounter well," Andrew replied, ruefully rubbing his chin, for the earl had planted him a facer he hadn't soon forgotten. But Andrew wasn't one to hold a grudge. "I say, Westerbrook, don't blame Annabelle for the cheroot incident. I'm the one who led her down the road to perdition—several years ago, in fact. It's become somewhat of a custom between the two of us. It ain't like she smokes on a regular basis or anything. You don't, do you, Cousin?"

"Goodness no," Annabelle stated firmly, affecting rather late the air of a lady whose reputation has been grievously sullied.

A twinkle appeared in Cam's light brown eyes. "Nothing Miss Winthrop does or doesn't do would surprise me at this juncture. Well, I'd best be off. Merlin is getting restive. Greywood, nice to see you again. Miss Winthrop," Cam said, doffing his hat, and then he was gone before Annabelle even had the chance to thank him for the books he'd given her.

Watching him go, Annabelle sighed and turned to Andrew. "It's quite hopeless, I'm afraid. Camford Singletary is as determined to avoid the altar as is the Marquis de Dambere."

"Oh, I don't know, little Cousin," Andrew replied, clucking to the horses and snapping the ribbons, "His lordship the earl seemed mighty smitten to me."

THE DAY OF ANNABELLE'S ball dawned sunny and bright. The weather was perfect, neither too hot nor too cold, and the caressing breeze proved most soothing to those lucky enough to be afforded the opportunity to be outside. The Greywood townhouse sparkled. Still, Aunt Charlotte was up at the first sign of light, issuing orders to the servants much like the "admiral" Cam's mother likened her to. Annabelle herself stayed in bed a bit later than usual, although it couldn't be said that she was sleeping. Rather, she spent at least an hour gazing up at the ceiling, her thoughts ajumble, until Mr. Fitzroy drew her out of her reverie by most rudely jumping upon her chest.

"You ungrateful little cur," Annabelle teased, grabbing the dog about the legs. There next ensued at least a ten-minute romp which left them both winded but content. The noise served to alert Betty that her mistress was awake, and the maid appeared shortly thereafter, carrying a tray of hot chocolate and toast. Annabelle accepted the tray and in return handed over Mr. Fitzroy to be delivered to the second footman, whose duty it was to see that the dog received his morning walk.

"You're up a bit early, miss," Betty commented, scanning the contents of her charge's wardrobe. "Worried about the ball, I'll wager. Well, miss, it's been my experience that something always does go wrong, so it's best to be expecting it. That way you won't be disappointed when it happens."

Peering up from her chocolate, Annabelle replied, "Thank you, Betty, for the comforting advice. Please pick something simple for me to wear today. I don't anticipate visitors, and I shall be changing early in any event."

"Yes, miss," Betty replied starchly, with a small sniff to indicate that her advice, whether accepted or not, was invariably correct.

Having donned her old sprigged muslin, which had been suitably altered at the neckline to accommodate her more womanly curves, Annabelle presented herself to Aunt Charlotte, certain that the elderly woman would have a myriad tasks for her to undertake. Aunt Charlotte, however, was too nervous to allow Annabelle, or anyone else for that matter, to do the things she felt needed to be done. Although the ball was being held in her niece's honour, Aunt Charlotte knew that the occasion would be a reflection upon her efforts, and she was determined that no one would have any cause for complaint. Thus, Annabelle was shooed away without so much as a backward glance and told to rest. Aunt Charlotte refused to listen to her niece's entreaties to slow her pace. She spent the day bustling back and forth terrorizing the hapless servants, so that by nightfall the elderly woman was so exhausted that she was more than happy to take a seat next to Mrs. Arthur Johnstone, from which no amount of coaxing, even by her husband to dance, could dislodge her.

With plenty of free time on her hands, Annabelle, while unable to rest, found no time to be bored, for she kept herself busy attending to each detail of her appearance. She took a long, leisurely bath, washing her hair carefully so tha

the gold highlights were sure to shimmer and shine. The riotous mass was then ragged into scores of tight little knots
by Betty (who kept insisting that the set would never take),
in order to augment Annabelle's natural curls. The nails on
her hands and feet were then meticulously manicured and
buffed to a high sheen.

After luncheon Annabelle's gown arrived, accompanied
in person by the formidable Madame Roche, who was so
proud of this particular creation that she insisted on completing the last fitting herself. Annabelle withstood the hour-
long session without complaint and then listened avidly as
madame explained to her a few cosmetic tricks which she
could use to enhance her appearance. Although young ladies of the ton never wore "paint," it was common practice to assist nature through the use of certain subtle
products which were hardly discernable.

Late that afternoon Annabelle summoned Betty to begin
final preparations. Slowly she slipped into the requisite
number of lace-and-silk undergarments before allowing the
maid to slide Madame Roche's creation overtop her head.
Once the gown was securely in place, Annabelle turned to
the cheval mirror and was quite pleased with the results. The
gown fitted her perfectly and the black accents did indeed
make the very most of her special colouring. Small panels
of black velvet trimmed both the neckline and arms of the
gown, so that Annabelle's creamy skin was shown to advantage. A black velvet sash had been placed about her
waist to emphasize its tiny size. The majority of the dress
was composed of a white, lightly-textured brocade which
fanned over her shoulders into delicate princess sleeves and
fell into a lovely overskirt which cleverly revealed a black
velvet lining.

Betty's reaction to the dress was dramatic. "Oh, miss, you
do look lovely," she gasped. "I can only hope your appearance won't inspire rash action on the part of any of the
gentlemen."

Annabelle whirled about, hugged her startled maid, and laughed happily. "But, Betty, dear, that's exactly the kind of response I am hoping to inspire."

Betty shook her head dolefully and began to unfasten the knots in her mistress's hair. When each knot had been unbound and lay tightly curled against Annabelle's head, the maid took a heavily bristled brush and whipped the mass into a frothy halo which she piled high atop Annabelle's head. A few stray tendrils were left to curl about the ears and neck so that the end result, while carefully contrived, looked natural and totally without artifice. Annabelle was so pleased with her appearance that she forbade Betty to put any ornamentation in her hair, well aware that to do so could only detract from the perfection of the style itself.

Annabelle was just fastening her pearls about her neck when Aunt Charlotte and Uncle William entered her room. "I'm afraid the necklace will not do," Uncle William stated gruffly.

Confused, Annabelle turned to her Aunt Charlotte for explanation. "What your uncle is trying to say, in his own inestimable way, is that you'll have to take off your pearls if you're to attach our gift."

Aunt Charlotte then opened her palm and handed her niece a small but beautifully wrought onyx-and-gold enhancer which had been especially designed to hang from the centre of her pearls. Annabelle gasped and felt her eyes mist over. "You're so good to me," she whispered with bent head, trying feverishly to slide the onyx piece onto her necklace.

"Better let me take a look at that," Uncle William said, for he was never at ease with emotional scenes and felt the need to busy his hands. Annabelle quickly complied, for she too was loath to turn into a watering pot just when she'd almost completed her toilette.

Several moments later, having secured the enhancer, Uncle William fastened the pearls about her neck, and Anna belle was thrilled to see how well the onyx addition matched the design of her gown.

"You look perfectly beautiful," Aunt Charlotte insisted, kissing her niece upon the cheek. She then fled the room, for she too was suddenly filled with an uncharacteristic urge to weep.

"You do look perfectly beautiful," Uncle William added ruefully, shaking his head. "Nothing like the little hoyden who came to us so many years ago."

"I shall always be your little hoyden at heart, Uncle," Annabelle began, but the emotionally wrought atmosphere within the room was quickly dispelled as Mr. Fitzroy suddenly took it into his head to nip quite ruthlessly at Uncle William's tightly fitting satin breeches.

"Annabelle, remove this cur immediately!" Uncle William roared, so frightening the dog that Mr. Fitzroy slunk away quite of his own accord.

Annabelle put her hand to her mouth to keep from giggling. "I'm sorry, Uncle. Mr. Fitzroy has developed an unfortunate tendency to latch on to gentlemen's trousers."

"Humph," Uncle William huffed. "It was a sad day, a sad day indeed when that dog was allowed inside the house. Dogs belong in a kennel, and if you don't behave, sir," he said, pointing towards the bed under which Mr. Fitzroy had retreated, "you shall find yourself placed in one." Uncle William then turned to go, saying over his shoulder as he left, "Don't be late, gel, receiving line and all that sort of nonsense."

"Yes, Uncle," Annabelle replied sweetly, although she could hardly contain her mirth.

Following the departure of her guardians, Annabelle was next treated to a succession of short visits by all four of her cousins. While they each came to wish her well, each also brought a gift which warmed Annabelle's heart. From William she received an expensive set of long white evening gloves, which she immediately donned. Henry produced a

small vial of French perfume which must've cost him dearly.
Annabelle thanked him profusely and dabbed a bit of the
heady fragrance behind each ear. Andrew presented her with
a beautifully painted fan, which she quickly attached to her
wrist, after which he bestowed upon her a most uncousinly
kiss. From David, who was rather painfully shy, she received a carefully penned poem which he'd written himself.
Annabelle was quite amazed at his talent and told him so in
no uncertain terms, much to his embarrassment.

At long last she was ready. Annabelle made her way below stairs in stately fashion, only to complete her journey at
a run. Aunt Charlotte was urging her forward impatiently,
so agitated that the purple ostrich feather in the elderly
woman's turban began to tilt in an alarming fashion. The
door was open and the first of the guests had already begun
to enter. Annabelle joined the receiving line only slightly out
of breath and spent the next hour and some shaking hands
until her fingers began to feel decidedly sore. She did not
much mind because all of her friends were present, including Cam, who looked devilishly handsome in his black evening attire, as well as his mother, Lady Margaret, and the
Duke and Duchess of Montvale, with their daughter Violet. Aunt Charlotte had even managed to net some of the
more elevated members of the ton. Sally Jersey was present, as was Princess Esterhazy, who astonished them by ex-
tending regards from Prinny himself, who'd seen the
Wayward Angel upon occasion and found her, "A vision of
loveliness."

There were only two events which temporarily dampened
Annabelle's high spirits: the arrival of the Moresbys, followed closely by the arrival of the Marquis de Dambere.
Lucinda stared pointedly at Annabelle's gown, quite irate
that for once she seemed to have been cast in the shade.
Annabelle ignored that lady's attempt to discommode her,
but when Lucinda passed by she couldn't resist a quick
glance at the blonde's reputedly large derrière. She smiled

to herself when she recognized that Madame Roche's words were all too true.

Annabelle's smile faded rapidly, however, as the Marquis de Dambere bowed his dark head over her hand, kissing it before she could snatch her fingers away.

"You're looking charmingly feminine this evening, my dear," he said, referring indirectly to the night she and Violet had dressed in men's attire and stormed White's.

Annabelle blushed, too embarrassed to reply, and breathed a sigh of relief as the marquis passed on.

When it seemed that the arrival of guests had slowed to an erratic trickle, Uncle William led Annabelle into the ballroom, whereupon the two of them opened the festivities by sharing the first dance. Annabelle twirled about gaily, noting the beauty of the room lit by scores of candles which reflected off the jewellery of the guests. Large bouquets of white roses, tied with black ribbons to match Annabelle's gown, were festooned everywhere, lending their poignant fragrance to the air.

Following the dance with her uncle, Annabelle was besieged by young gallants, all vying for the honour of signing her card. Laughing happily, Annabelle gave the next set to Cam, as well as the supper dance when he asked for it. Randolph Ponfret received a quadrille as did Major Sprawlings; Freddy Merryweather was granted a waltz. Each of Annabelle's cousins also asked for and received a dance— Andrew insisting upon two. Thus, by the end of a very short period of time, Annabelle found that her card was completely filled.

As the music started up again, Cam made a path through Annabelle's admirers to claim his partner. Gratefully she placed her hand into his, for Randolph Ponfret was complaining quite loudly that Annabelle should have allowed him two dances instead of one.

"It certainly seems as if you're destined to be the belle of this ball," Cam stated, bowing to Annabelle as required by the dictates of the boulanger.

"Well, it's being held in my honour, so I do have somewhat of an advantage over the other ladies," Annabelle replied after she'd completed her curtsy.

"Nonsense. You're the most beautiful woman here tonight and well you know it," Cam teased. "Now if you can only refrain from smoking or some such other outrageous misdeed, I feel certain that this evening will be counted a tremendous success."

"Fiddlesticks!" Annabelle retorted, but she couldn't pretend to be angry when she was so deliriously happy.

Having failed to secure an immediate dance with his true love, Randolph Ponfret reluctantly led out Lucinda Moresby at the urging of his parents. The experience, however, wasn't the total loss he expected it to be.

"Cam seems quite smitten with the popular Miss Winthrop," Lucinda stated boldly as she matched her movements to those of her partner.

Randolph seemed momentarily startled, but then he looked across the ballroom and read Annabelle's face, upon which was written what he'd long since known but had refused to admit. "I thought the earl was promised to you," Randolph replied in confusion.

"There's never been an official engagement," Lucinda admitted, frowning. "And now I fear there never will be."

"But surely you don't think the earl will actually offer for Annabelle. He's been avoiding the altar for years."

"Perhaps he won't offer, but there can be no doubt that he's shown Miss Winthrop a particular preference since his arrival in Town," Lucinda replied, lifting her eyebrows significantly. "Therefore, it seems to me that it would behoove any gentleman with an interest in the girl to proceed quickly."

Randolph's blue eyes narrowed as he stared down at the stunning blonde in his arms. "Meaning me, I suppose."

"Let us be honest with each other, shall we, Randolph," Lucinda proposed. "I've long planned on being the next Countess of Westerbrook, but now it seems as if my position is in jeopardy. I know you've a special liking for my competitor and I'm merely suggesting that you go to her with your feelings before it's too late."

The music ceased and Randolph escorted Lucinda to the refreshment table for a glass of champagne. "It may already be too late," Randolph announced suddenly, resuming their conversation. "Annabelle stares at the earl quite adoringly." Quickly he gulped down his champagne and reached for another.

"Yes, but she's not unintelligent," Lucinda admitted grudgingly. "She knows that Cam enjoys his single state. Why shouldn't she consider seriously the suit of a handsome young man who'll someday inherit substantial property and fortune?"

Randolph preened. "You're absolutely right. Annabelle could do much worse than I. That idiot Sprawlings who hangs after her with such persistence hasn't much to offer, neither fortune nor fortitude. Merryweather doesn't seem her sort, and she's shown a marked dislike for the marquis. Why shouldn't she consider me?"

"Why not indeed," Lucinda replied, slapping Randolph on the back in her curiously masculine fashion, which drew several bemused stares.

Randolph coughed and gratefully excused himself, for his dance with Annabelle was just about to begin.

Pushing his way through the usual throng which surrounded his beloved, Randolph gently but firmly procured her arm and began to lead Annabelle away. "Do you mind if we sit this one out?" he asked, steering her towards a quiet alcove which he'd spotted earlier. "I'd much rather have the opportunity to speak to you alone."

While somewhat concerned about the nature of Randolph's proposed discussion, Annabelle couldn't help but feel relieved at any chance to rest her feet, for the evening promised to be a long one indeed.

Assisting the golden-brown beauty as she arranged the folds of her gown about her on the window-seat, Randolph carefully placed himself next to her and took one of her gloved hands into his own. Annabelle's heart began to beat erratically almost at once, because she knew instinctively what he was about and cursed herself for her short-sightedness. She should've insisted that they dance, thereby deterring Randolph before he'd the chance to embarrass them both!

"Miss Winthrop. Annabelle. Surely you know by now the depth of my feelings for you. I think I loved you from the first, certainly after you sang that outrageous song at Lady Margaret's dinner party. I realize this is rather sudden, but I'm asking you, my dear, for your permission to speak to your uncle. Annabelle, I want you to be my wife."

Gently disengaging her hand from his, the golden-brown beauty lowered her eyes as a painful blush began to creep up her face. "Randolph, I'm not unappreciative of your offer, but my answer must be no. You see, I'm simply not in love with you."

Randolph's shoulders sagged. "It's Westerbrook, isn't it?" he asked in a pained voice, which made him seem somehow more vulnerable than his usual pompous self.

Annabelle patted him gently on the arm. "Whatever my feelings for the earl, the fact of the matter remains that I'm not in love with you."

Rage quickly replaced the disappointment surging through Randolph's veins. "He'll never marry you," the blond Lothario sneered, brushing aside Annabelle's hand. "Westerbrook will never marry you, even if you wait for him forever!"

Recoiling from the look of hatred on Randolph's face, a look which distorted his appearance to the point of making him truly frightening, Annabelle jumped off the window-seat and quickly put as much distance between them as possible. Her rejected suitor propelled himself straight towards the refreshment table, where he began to drink himself into oblivion.

In Annabelle's haste to flee Randolph Ponfret's displeasure, she ran headlong into Major Jack Sprawlings, who in his scarlet regimentals looked a veritable pillar of strength despite his rather timid nature.

"I believe I've the next dance, Miss Winthrop," the major announced, taking careful note of Annabelle's heightened colour. Could she have finally developed a tendre for him as he so desperately wanted her to do?

"Of course, major," Annabelle replied with relief. Anything to take her mind off the disastrous scene with Randolph.

As they were dancing, Major Sprawlings tightened his hold on Annabelle's arm and looked into the distance. He then cleared his throat and began to stammer most alarmingly.

Oh, no! Annabelle thought in despair. *It can't be! Surely a kind God wouldn't subject me to two such painful interviews in the course of one evening?*

"Annabelle, I've long hoped that you'd come to reconsider my offer of marriage. I realize that I haven't the income of some of your other suitors, but with your dowry and my salary, I believe we could muddle along together quite nicely. We'd always be comfortable, and I'd cherish you all the days of your life. I'd treat you like a precious piece of porcelain..."

Major Sprawlings never had a chance to complete his sentence. "I don't wish to be treated like a precious piece of porcelain," Annabelle snapped. Normally she would never have been so unkind to the major, but she was feeling the onset of a giant megrim. "I wish to be treated like a flesh-and-blood woman. And as much as I've come to like and respect you, I simply do not love you."

Major Sprawlings didn't possess the temerity of Randolph Ponfret. Rather than becoming angry, he lapsed into a pained silence which was acutely embarrassing for both of them.

Relieved when the music ended a short time later, Annabelle directed one last smile at the despondent Major Sprawlings and then took her leave. Feeling a need for comfort herself, Annabelle headed towards her aunt, who, from the look of things, seemed to be in heated discussion with Mrs. Arthur Johnstone. Annabelle smiled fleetingly. *What delicious piece of gossip were they now dissecting?* she wondered.

Just at that moment, however, Annabelle caught sight of Freddy Merryweather heading straight towards her, wearing a most determined look on his pudgy face. Annabelle reacted without thinking. Lifting the hem of her gown, she quickly turned in the opposite direction, waved enthusiastically at a nonexistent friend, and fled onto the terrace. The cool night air assailed her face as soon as she stepped outside. Annabelle breathed a sigh of relief. It had grown almost unbearably hot inside the ballroom despite the fact that Aunt Charlotte had ordered each window and door opened to the fullest. It was always devilishly warm at these functions.

Strolling down the length of the terrace, Annabelle nodded at several acquaintances who'd also escaped for a breath of fresh air, before heading off into the small garden behind the Berkeley Square townhouse. She'd just leaned over to smell the fragrance of one of her aunt's flowering shrubs when Randolph Ponfret loomed up behind her, a foolish grin plastered on his drunken face.

"Kish me," he commanded, swaying alarmingly so that Annabelle was suddenly afraid he was going to fall down on top of her.

"This is the outside of enough, Randolph," the golden-brown beauty stated boldly, trying to brush past him, for in his condition there was no being certain but what he might do.

"I said kish me," Randolph repeated, but this time he grabbed her roughly by the arms and pulled her close.

Annabelle fought quite desperately but her feminine strength was no match for Randolph Ponfret—especially a drunken, angry Randolph Ponfret. Despite the fact that she squirmed and twisted, Randolph none the less forced his lips down upon her with a brutal intensity which left Annabelle icy cold with fear.

And then, just as quickly as the nightmare had begun, it was over. Cam was there, as he always seemed to be when she needed him. Jerking Randolph off Annabelle as if he weighed a mere nothing, Cam tossed the drunken young man hard onto the ground so that he landed with an expelled, "Woof," and could only stagger to rise.

"Don't attempt to get up, Ponfret," Cam warned, his light brown eyes shining dangerously in the moonlight.

"Annabelle ish mine," Randolph roared, the alcohol in his system giving him extraordinary courage. Quickly he rushed towards his adversary, ready to fight.

Annabelle emitted a small scream as she saw Randolph hurl himself at Cam, but she needn't have worried. Cam floored the blond Lothario with a single punch to the jaw. Randolph lay on the ground, eyes closed, a tiny trickle of blood dripping down his chin.

"Oh, you could've been hurt," Annabelle cried, running headlong into Cam's strong arms. He folded her into his embrace, almost crushing her with the intensity of his hug.

The sudden sound of applause awoke them to the impropriety of such intimacy, and Annabelle quickly stood away.

"Bravo, my lord," Andrew complimented, smiling broadly. "I could've warned Ponfret that it's dangerous to involve you in any form of fisticuffs but I doubt seriously that he was in any frame of mind to listen."

"But what shall we do with him?" Annabelle asked nervously.

"Don't worry, little Cousin," Andrew replied blithely. "I shall get rid of the trash, and Lord Westerbrook will escort you back to the ball." Having deftly decided the matter, Andrew withdrew a handkerchief and placed it against Randolph Ponfret's bloody jaw. He then lifted the oblivious young man onto his back and proceeded to wind his way through the garden towards the mews.

"Thank you so much for coming to my rescue," Annabelle gushed, her remaining fright making her chatter away quite distractedly. In all her years, Annabelle had never been attacked in such a fashion and it was truly a humbling experience, humbling to know that someone could touch her against her will, and humbling to know that there was not a great deal she could do about it.

"What happened?" Cam asked soothingly, sensing her fear. Taking Annabelle's elbow gently, he began to escort her back to the house.

"Randolph asked me to marry him tonight..."

"And you refused?" Cam interrupted, with an urgency which Annabelle was much too distraught to notice.

"I did, but I'm afraid he took great exception to my answer. At least Major Sprawlings had the grace to accept my decision like a gentleman."

"So you received two proposals of marriage tonight. Fortunately, you've nothing similar to fear from me," Cam said lightly, trying to improve the golden-brown beauty's disposition.

"Yes, you've made that abundantly clear," Annabelle replied quietly, in an oddly vulnerable voice clearly at odds with her usual feisty self. "Oh, and I've changed my mind about the supper dance," she added, freeing her arm from Cam's. "I'm sure Lucinda would enjoy your company far more than I." Running towards the ballroom, Annabelle didn't see Cam's frown, or the fact that he sent his fist slamming into the nearest available tree.

Somehow Annabelle managed to muddle through the rest of the evening, grateful for Andrew's support despite the humiliation she felt at being led into supper by her own cousin.

In the early hours of the morn, her head pounding in earnest, Annabelle was at last free to drag herself up to bed. Betty was snoring rather loudly in a chair next to the fireplace, but awoke with a start as her mistress entered the room.

"Did you have a good time?" Betty asked, yawning sleepily.

"No. The ball was a disappointment just as you predicted," Annabelle replied, wanting nothing more than to crawl between the sheets and forget about the disastrous events of the evening. "In fact, at present life is a disappointment."

Betty nodded her head in full agreement. "That it is, miss, that it surely is!"

CHAPTER EIGHT

ANNABELLE AWOKE LATER than usual and groaned in embarrassment upon remembering her behaviour the night before. She'd made her feelings for the Earl of Westerbrook quite obvious, and felt humiliated for having done so. While Cam certainly regarded her with some small bit of affection, he simply didn't care enough to offer marriage. Love couldn't be forced. She had to accept that fact and get on with her life. Annabelle didn't want to become a lonely old spinster dependent on her cousins for support. Besides, she'd been quite honest when she told Cam she wanted children, and one could hardly have them alone!

"It's time I begin to place more emphasis upon my future and less upon unrealistic expectations," Annabelle said to Mr. Fitzroy, who at that moment was burrowing his rather cold and wet nose into her side. Ruffling his fur, Annabelle flung back the covers and rang for Betty. She'd agreed to meet Violet today for a lengthy coze. Although Annabelle didn't particularly feel like keeping the appointment, for she was tired from the previous evening, she didn't wish to disappoint her red-haired friend, neither did she wish to be late.

Having donned a pretty blue jaconet walking dress with matching spencer, Annabelle—accompanied by a dour-faced Betty—was soon safely ensconced in the Greywood coach-and-four, rumbling through the cobblestone streets of London towards the Montvale mansion.

Violet greeted Annabelle with a certain degree of suppressed excitement. Noting her friend's high colour, Annabelle quickly sent Betty off to the kitchens for a dish of tea and followed Violet into her private sitting-room.

Once the door was closed, the redhead immediately grabbed Annabelle's hands. "He kissed me!" she whispered, her face a study in rapture.

Annabelle's eyes widened. Last night she could've sworn Freddy was on the verge of offering for her. Apparently he'd transferred his affections.

The redhead didn't miss Annabelle's look of surprise, no matter how fleeting. Motioning her friend to be seated on a lovely silk settee which exactly matched her bedroom décor, Violet hastened to explain. "Freddy was in high dudgeon when he asked me to stroll with him on the terrace last night. It seems you promised him a dance and then forgot. Freddy was livid. Naturally, I did my best to soothe his masculine pride and he did come about after a bit. By that time we were at the end of the terrace by the ivy trellis, where it's fairly dark. I must say I wasn't expecting it, but Freddy reached out and kissed me. I think it was you he imagined in his arms at first, but when the kiss was over he looked at me quite strangely. At that point I can't say he was thinking of you at all!"

Annabelle laughed. "Of course he wasn't thinking of me, you ninnyhammer. Well, I must say this is good news. I felt rather guilty about abandoning poor Freddy last night, but now that I know what happened, I don't feel guilty at all. I'm just relieved that one of us had a good time," she finished, sighing heavily.

"Why, whatever do you mean?" Violet asked, for she'd been so wrapped up in her own happiness that she'd quite missed Annabelle's rather drawn and pensive look.

Annabelle explained all that had happened at the ball, for she knew she could rely upon Violet's discretion. She left

nothing out, except the incident with Cam, which Annabelle regarded as too intimate.

"That was quite boorish of Randolph," Violet stated
emphatically, "but I can't say that I'm surprised. It's obvious he's been spoiled silly by his parents. Randolph's an
only child, you know, and he's never been denied a thing.
He's accustomed to getting whatever he wants."

"Well, in this instance I'm afraid he'll just have to accept the fact that he isn't going to get me. I could never
marry that pompous, mean-spirited, vain, callous, self-
centred popinjay."

Violet tried very hard not to giggle, but Annabelle's description of Randolph Ponfret had her clutching her sides
in mirth. After a moment or two of indignation, Annabelle
began to laugh as well, for it really wasn't in her nature to
promulgate either self-pity or depression.

"I'm glad you find my rather dismal life so vastly amusing," Annabelle proclaimed after several moments of merriment, "but today we're going to concentrate on you. It
seems our darling Freddy is all but caught. Let's examine
your wardrobe. Perhaps a strategic nip or tuck is all that's
required to bring him safely to heel."

Violet lowered her head and a charming blush spread
from her neck to her cheeks. "I've already thought of that.
What if I were to, well, what if I were to dampen my petticoats?"

"You'd be far better off lowering your neckline or tightening your waist," Annabelle replied repressively. "Remember that nasty cold I had a fortnight or so ago...?"

As VIOLET AND ANNABELLE were examining intently the
contents of the redhead's extensive wardrobe, Cam was at
that very moment just waking up. It was generally not his
habit to sleep so late, even after a long night of debauch-
ery, but last night—oh, Lord—last night he'd really dipped
deep into his cups.

Licking his lips, which were almost as dry as his throat, Cam managed to roll himself over, only to realize that he was definitely not in his own bed! He emitted a low moan and tried to sit up, only to fall back, clutching his aching head.

"That bad, huh?" questioned a sultry voice which Cam knew only too well.

"Harry, for God's sake, have done and shoot me," Cam croaked, recognizing all at once where he was, for he'd been in Harriette Wilson's bedchamber many times before.

Harriette laughed and strolled towards him. Ordinarily, she would've allowed her silk wrapper to fall open enticingly, but the Earl of Westerbrook was obviously in no condition to experience her particular brand of charms, not now, probably not ever.

"Why the pout, my dear?" Cam asked, although he was really far more interested in keeping the bed from spinning about so alarmingly than in ascertaining the mood of his current mistress.

A speculative gleam entered Harriette's eye. If she fabricated a night of passionate lovemaking, no doubt she could expect a more spectacular parting gift. Harriette had long had her eye on a sapphire-and-diamond tiara which would be the envy of all. Yet Cam had been good to her over the years and Harriette knew that she wouldn't long lack for a new protector. Why, a very rich Russian prince had been begging her for weeks to visit his newly acquired country estate. Perhaps she'd allow the Russian to purchase the tiara.

"I'm pouting, my handsome lover, because I sense that your interest in me has waned," Harriette replied honestly, studying her highly esteemed, exquisite hands.

"That's not true..." Cam began lamely, but Harriette was not disposed to prevaricate.

"When you came here last night you were more interested in obtaining a bottle than in obtaining me. Furthermore, the more foxed you got the more you kept mumbling something about an angel. You're in love with another woman, my dear, and that's something I simply won't tolerate. Why, even the married men I've dallied with cared nothing for their wives.''

Despite the protestations of his head, Cam bolted upright on Harriette's magnificently large bed and captured the Cyprian by her milky white arms. ''I'm not in love with another woman. I'm very happy with our present arrangement.''

Harriette laughed her throaty laugh and gently pulled herself away. ''Two years ago I flatter myself that you were just a little bit in love with me, despite the fact that there were others even then. I seem to remember a certain opera dancer by the name of Marie.''

Cam couldn't help the chuckle of amusement which escaped his lips.

''Yes, lover, I knew all about your other women, although I've heard that Marie has since managed to get herself married—and fairly well, too—but at least I'd the satisfaction of knowing that when we were together you were mine to command. Now I've the feeling that I could stand before you without my clothes on and you'd hardly bat an eye. Cam, our liaison is at an end, and I should appreciate it greatly if you'd let me retain my dignity by being the one to give *you* your congé. You would've wanted to do so eventually anyway, and by my guess in the not-too-distant future.''

Cam rubbed his aching head ruefully. He had to admit he felt surprisingly comfortable about ending his ''relationship'' with Harriette, and was grateful that she was so amenable. Perhaps a new romance was called for. Something less, well, less public. ''You're right, my dear,'' Cam said, picking up Harriette's hand and bestowing upon it a light kiss. ''I thought I could return to Town as if no time had passed at all. Yet I find that in the past two years I've changed to a certain degree. London simply doesn't hold for me the same allure which it did before." Cam shook his head slightly, as if he couldn't comprehend such a metamorphosis. Then he looked at Harriette thoughtfully. "You'll be all right, Harry, won't you? You may be sure that I shall be generous."

"I always manage to survive, Cam," Harriette intoned before getting up from the bed and moving across the room with the air of sensuality which had earned her the reputation as the most famous, or infamous, Cyprian of her day. "As we speak there's a certain Russian prince simply frothing at the mouth for my favours. I see no further reason to deny him. Do you?"

Cam laughed and cupped his hands behind his head as Harriette let her wrapper drop to the floor. "You were wrong about one thing, Harry," he remarked. "The sight of you without clothes certainly doesn't leave me unaffected."

Playfully, Harriette tormented Cam a bit further before she stepped behind an artfully placed screen and rang for assistance.

"I'd like to play the gallant by making a dramatic exit, but I'm afraid I can't seem to get out of bed," Cam called out as Harriette dressed with the aid of her maidservant.

"Stay where you are all day, Cam dear," Harriette replied as the maid began to button up the back of her dress. "I shan't be in, as I've it in mind to purchase a new gown. I should be in my best looks if I'm to captivate my Russian Prince. I shall instruct the servants to see to your needs and you may leave when you feel able."

Cam sighed, sank deeper into the luxurious bed, and closed his eyes. He was fast asleep when Harriette left and therefore didn't feel the curiously tender kiss she placed upon his brow just before quitting the room.

ANNABELLE AND VIOLET were at that moment sitting inside the Duke of Montvale's elegantly sprung couch-and-four heading towards the Pantheon Bazaar. Annabelle had seen a beautiful green velvet spencer there which she knew would look exceedingly well on Violet, one which was sure to catch Freddy's eye. Both girls were in a relatively merry mood despite the calming presence of their maids, since shopping invariably produced in most young ladies a singular feeling of goodwill.

That feeling of goodwill began to evaporate, however, as the carriage became ensnared in a long line of vehicles seemingly incapable of movement. Annabelle stuck her head out of the window despite the fact that such behaviour wasn't considered at all seemly. However, neither maid thought to scold, for several minutes had ticked by and the atmosphere inside the carriage was decidedly one of frustration.

"There's some manner of disturbance up ahead but I can't quite make out what is amiss," Annabelle reported finally, having craned her head this way and that.

"Perhaps I should send Tom Coachman to investigate?" Violet offered tentatively.

"That won't do," Annabelle declared, "for if the line begins to move we shan't be able to follow suit. Best I go take a look."

"I don't think..." Betty began, but she was abruptly silenced by a quelling look from her mistress.

Annabelle somehow managed to climb out of the carriage without tripping over her skirts and cautiously made her way through the growing throng until she reached the centre of the activity. What she saw there almost made her drop to her knees. A regally appointed carriage, complete with noble crest, had obviously run over the leg of a rather large dog. The dog's owner, a small boy wearing what could only be described as rags, was fiercely preventing anyone from coming close to the pain-racked animal. "Let 'im be," the lad kept repeating over and over, obviously afraid that any attempt to move the dog would spell further disaster.

Suddenly a familiar voice could be heard over the mumbling of the crowd. "I've had just about enough of this nonsense. Hand me my guns, Bob. I'll shoot the beast myself and put him out of his misery. We might've run him down, and for that I'm sorry, but I ain't got time to stand about all day while some diseased urchin and his mangy cur of a dog disrupt traffic."

Annabelle stared incomprehendingly at the Marquis de Dambere, but her stupor lasted only a second. Without considering the ramifications of her action, she ran forward and delivered to the marquis a resounding slap across his face. De Dambere's naturally dark features took on an even darker cast. "Why, you, you, you..." he sputtered helplessly, recognizing at once the identity of his assailant. Only her well-born station, and the obvious support she'd garnered from the assembled crowd, prevented him from returning the gesture, or worse.

Satisfied that she'd forestalled the marquis from shooting the dog, Annabelle then turned to the boy, who was regarding her with an emotion akin to awe. Her obvious defence of his pet prevented him from lashing out at her as she knelt next to the animal for a closer look.

"I think his leg is broken, but I know someone who can fix it if you will allow me to help you."

The boy began to cry. Somehow he gasped out, "Don't have the blunt for that sorta thing, miss."

Annabelle patted the boy kindly on the hand, and although her heart ached for him, she was grateful she had on her blue kid gloves, for the lad truly was filthy. "I'll take care of the cost," the golden-brown beauty promised.

The boy nodded gratefully and wiped his nose. Annabelle motioned for the nearest man to carefully lift the dog and take him back to the Montvale carriage.

"Just a moment, Miss Winthrop," the marquis snapped, grabbing Annabelle roughly by the arm. "If you think you can distribute such moving charity at my expense you're very much mistaken."

Annabelle tossed her curls with confidence, although her legs felt as if they might collapse. "You'd be better served, my lord," she replied chillingly, "in displaying more sympathy towards the animal you've injured and the boy whose heart you've broken, rather than worrying about your own sensibilities. But I expect you aren't that kind of man. In any case, I'm advising you to leave me well enough alone, for my family is highly protective."

"My dear Miss Winthrop, I've far better things to do with my time than to concern myself with an insipid young lady such as yourself," the marquis replied with a smirk, picking an imaginary piece of lint off his tightly fitting coat. "Others, however, aren't so generously inclined," he added, jerking his head towards a nearby carriage.

Following de Dambere's direction, Annabelle was dismayed to see Sally Jersey's cream-coloured phaeton only yards away. Although it was common knowledge that the countess cared little for the darkly handsome marquis, she wasn't known as "Silence" for nothing. This incident was just too good for her to keep to herself.

With an angry tug, Annabelle jerked her arm away from the marquis, who'd begun to laugh, and stormed haughtily towards the Montvale coach. This time her reputation was positively in shreds. One simply didn't go about slapping members of the ton, no matter how detestable said member might be. Annabelle sighed. At least she'd fallen from grace for a worthy cause. She could never have allowed that ogre to kill a dog. Only suppose it had been Mr. Fitzroy!

If the other occupants of the coach were somewhat dismayed to suddenly find themselves in the company of a large, unkempt dog and a filthy street urchin, they didn't say so. Violet smiled sympathetically, her maid emitted an of

fended snort, and Betty merely shrugged. She was well used
to the eccentricities of her young mistress.

As the carriage changed direction to make its way to a
veterinarian's office, Annabelle and Violet gently pried a
good bit of information from the downcast boy. His name
was Thomas, he told them, recently from Norwich. His father had sickened and died but a year ago, and his mother,
unable to farm their land, had packed them off to London,
where she'd a sister in service. Unfortunately, his mother
had succumbed to a fever not long after they arrived in
Town and her sister had been unable to keep the boy. To the
aunt's credit, she did try to install Thomas in a nearby or-
phanage, but he'd run away because they wouldn't let him
keep his dog.

By the end of the young lad's tale all four women were
quietly mopping at their eyes with handkerchiefs. Annabelle in particular could understand the boy's reasoning, for
she too wouldn't dream of abandoning her pet, no matter
what the cause. "Don't cry, Thomas," Annabelle extolled.
"Doubtless my Uncle William could use a capable boy in the
stables back home. You'd like that, wouldn't you? It would
mean leaving London, but Brierly is really quite beautiful."

"I'd like that 'bove anything, miss," Thomas answered,
hope beginning to shine forth from his eyes. "I'd 'ave to
take me dog, o' course, but I don't mind leavin' the likes o'
this place. London is evil, miss, pure and simple."

"Naturally you shall take your dog," Annabelle replied
quite firmly, although she had an idea that Uncle William
wasn't going to be overjoyed with this, her latest misadven-
ure. Besides the expense and uncertainty of hiring addi-
ional, and probably unneeded, staff, Uncle William wasn't
oo keen on dogs. Yet the poor boy had just lost both his
arents; he could hardly be expected to give up the only
hing he had left. And Annabelle couldn't leave him beside
he road to starve. He was abysmally thin beneath his rags.

She sighed again, a reaction which was becoming somewhat of a habit these days, then squared her shoulders. It'd
probably take a great many tears to bring Uncle William
round this time, but come round he would or her name
wasn't Annabelle Winthrop!

The visit to the veterinarian went relatively quickly and
was aided by the fact that the doctor, an older yet artless
gentleman by the name of Toggleberry, was extremely kind
to young Thomas. In no time at all it seemed as if Annabelle, Betty, the boy, and his dog had arrived in Berkeley
Square.

Annabelle bade Betty to take their guests round to the
mews, for she thought it better if she had a few moments to
prepare Uncle William and Aunt Charlotte before spring-
ing everything, and everybody, on them all at once.

As it turned out, Annabelle's aunt and uncle were already well aware of the situation. Sally Jersey had wasted no
time in spreading the shocking tale of Miss Winthrop's as-
sault upon the Marquis de Dambere, and Mrs. Arthur
Johnstone had thought it best that she inform her good
friends post-haste.

Thus Annabelle was denied the luxury of repairing to her
bedchamber to freshen up. Instead, she was summoned into
the drawing-room as soon as her dainty feet stepped over the
threshold into the townhouse.

"What's this I hear about you striking de Dambere?"
Uncle William asked in a modified roar before Annabelle
even had a chance to position herself upon the pink-and-
white striped satin settee. "I warned you that any further
trouble would mean your return to Brierly, and now it appears as if we've no other choice."

To her aunt and uncle's everlasting surprise, Annabelle
didn't try to argue the matter. Even she understood the se-
riousness of her actions. Instead, she explained to them exactly the events of the afternoon and waited meekly for their
response.

Uncle William's semi-bald pate seemed to turn a brighter shade of pink than was normal upon hearing that he'd just hired a new stable-boy, complete with dog, but he contained his anger admirably in light of the quelling glance directed at him by his rather formidable wife. "Hmm, well, yes," he muttered, fingering unconsciously the pages of today's *Gazette*. "Can't say your judgement was the best in this matter but I do understand the provocation. That reprobate de Dambere!" Uncle William shouted explosively. "It's high time someone taught that scoundrel a lesson."

"Calm yourself, dear," Aunt Charlotte cautioned, for her husband was far past the age of issuing challenges, and her four sons had once again returned to their various homes. "I've always believed that evil is rewarded in the end, as is goodness, and with that we shall have to be content. Unfortunately, I agree that we can't hope to weather this particular incident. There's little for us to do but repair to Brierly and begin preparations for next year."

"Good God, woman, do you mean we have to go through this nonsense all over again?" Uncle William asked incredulously.

Since her husband knew full well that Annabelle must be wed, Aunt Charlotte didn't deign to answer. Instead she merely lifted her quizzing glass and stared him down. Uncle William gave a loud "Humph," and disappeared behind his beloved newspaper.

Annabelle couldn't trust herself to speak, since her eyes were suspiciously moist and there was a large lump in her throat. Although London hadn't proven quite the wonderland of her imagination, she'd enjoyed the change from the quiet of the country. And, of course, there was Cam. Banished to Brierly, she knew her cause to be truly hopeless. Although Annabelle had behaved very badly towards Cam on the night of her ball, she'd found that she simply couldn't dismiss him from her thoughts. It was useless to try and fix

her interest elsewhere. At least for now. Annabelle was well
and truly smitten.

Aunt Charlotte gave her niece a sympathetic look, but
sensing that Annabelle was near tears, didn't attempt to
console her. "Why don't you go on upstairs and take a nap,
my dear," Aunt Charlotte counselled. "Mr. Fitzroy has
been rather lonely of late and would enjoy the company.
Later you might think about introducing him to his new
companion."

That suggestion brought a loud snort from Uncle William, who wasn't yet totally reconciled to the presence of
Thomas or his dog. Yet he refrained from bellowing his
outrage, for he wasn't so far into his dotage that he couldn't
understand and sympathize with the disappointment his
niece had just sustained.

Wordlessly, Annabelle stumbled from the drawing-room
to her chamber, where she proceeded to take what comfort
she could from the wriggling body of Mr. Fitzroy. Thus she
wasn't present when an elegant footman resplendent in ivory
livery delivered an envelope into Aunt Charlotte's hands.
Nor was she present when Aunt Charlotte's cry of gladness
seemed to reverberate throughout the house.

"All isn't yet lost, William, all isn't yet lost."

"Eh, what's that?" her husband asked, reluctantly tearing his concentration away from an editorial on the Corn
Laws.

"Westerbrook and his mother, Lady Margaret; they've
invited us to a house party. Is it not famous? Annabelle may
surely take part in such a small gathering."

"Go then if you wish, but I plan to return to Brierly. I've
had enough gambolling about for a while. The house party
should prove a boon to Annabelle, though. It'll ease her
transition from Town to country."

That's not all it may accomplish, Aunt Charlotte thought
to herself, but she prudently refrained from comment.

CHAPTER NINE

THE EARL OF WESTERBROOK'S London townhouse was nigh on as grand as his Sussex estate. Located on Curzon Street, the property boasted enormous sculpted grounds, which were shielded from the curious eye of the casual on-looker by a six-foot-high stone wall, whitewashed to match the house. The house itself sported the clean lines associated with Georgian architecture, but was saved from appearing truly stark by a row of Doric columns.

Since the current earl and his lady mother hadn't resided in London for over two years, the servants had been hard-pressed to put the house to order before Lord Westerbrook and Lady Margaret arrived. Room by room, dust covers had been removed, furniture polished, windows and floors washed, carpets beaten, and a myriad other tasks performed. Thus it can't be said that the servants were overly enthusiastic when it was learned that the lord and his mother planned to return to Westhaven. All their hard work seemed wasted. Though the servants said nothing, for it was their duty to serve their employers in whatever manner required, Lady Margaret sensed their frustration. Thus, that good lady lavished a host of compliments upon the servants for their sterling performance until all but the most hard-hearted were well mollified.

While Lady Margaret attended to the domestics, Cam ordered out his curricle, for he intended a personal visit upon a certain golden-brown spitfire. The earl had heard all about Annabelle's ''shocking'' behaviour in the matter of the Marquis de Dambere and felt compelled to offer what sympathy he could. In Cam's opinion, Annabelle was entirely in the right. The marquis's actions had been less than honourable. However, London Society being what it was, the gossips were already busy chastising Annabelle for her less-than-ladylike comportment. One simply didn't go about striking a member of the nobility, especially to protect a person of far lesser birth. And even though there were those who supported Annabelle's actions, the majority did not, and it was their opinion which held sway.

Knowing that the debacle was going to earn Annabelle censure from the ton, Cam's mother had suggested holding a house party at Westhaven. Cam was only too happy to go along with the idea. He'd grown quite fond of the impetuous Miss Winthrop. Furthermore, Cam wasn't at all displeased to quit London for a short spell. Surprisingly, he found himself longing for the pastoral splendour of the country.

As Cam drove himself towards the Greywood's Berkeley Square townhouse, Annabelle was at that moment closeted in her uncle's library, staring gloomily at a rather ugly hunting print which hung somewhat unevenly on the wall. Uncle William never allowed the servants to set foot in the library, for he regarded it as his own personal domain. As a result, the room could only be described as a great deal less than clean. Annabelle felt comfortable here, however, for it was one room in which a body could relax—unlike the rest of the house, which Aunt Charlotte demanded be kept immaculate.

That Annabelle was feeling rather downcast went without saying. Uncle William and Aunt Charlotte hadn't yet informed her that she'd been invited to Lady Margaret's upcoming house party. They'd left early to attend a Venetian breakfast being given in their honour by Mrs. Arthur Johnstone. All Annabelle knew was that she was being banished from London—and that meant being banished from Cam. In addition, her social ostracism was already well under way. Violet had sent round a note first thing in the morn cancelling their five o'clock jaunt through Hyde Park. The note had declared that Violet would contact Annabelle as soon as possible...meaning as soon as the redhead could evade her mother's hawk-eyed scrutiny.

Annabelle sighed abruptly and let her chin sink heavily onto her chest as she reclined against the comfortable old leather wing-chair which was Uncle William's favourite. Somehow just sitting here made her feel as if she were a little girl again. In the old days her uncle's mere presence had dispelled whatever troubles existed to plague her. With a few gruff words from him, and perhaps a kiss, Annabelle's dismals always seemed to improve. Unfortunately, she was no longer that little girl, and her troubles were far too serious to be cured by mere magic.

That's when Annabelle's eye spotted the crystal decanter on the floor next to the leather wing-chair. Smiling ruefully, she picked it up and stared through the dust to the amber-coloured liquid within. Just like Uncle William to be so messy, she thought fondly, sloshing the brandy from side to side. Her spirits plummeted again though as she recalled the last time she'd had brandy—the only time in actuality, for women weren't encouraged to cultivate a taste for the stuff. It was at Cam's country estate, Westhaven, just before Dr. Aimsbury had examined her ankle following the carriage accident. Cam himself had handed her the brandy. What was it he'd said? That he found brandy an excellent restorative? Well, if there was anything Annabelle needed right now it was to be restored excellently!

Unstopping the decanter, Annabelle sniffed the contents and wrinkled her nose distastefully. Vile stuff, brandy, but then there had to be something attractive about it, given the liquor's overwhelming popularity with the male species. Annabelle tipped the decanter to her lips and took a tiny sip. She gasped as the brandy burned a fiery trail down her throat. But oddly enough, the second sip wasn't as unpleasant as the first, the third not as bad as the second....

The Greywood butler informed Cam at the door that Miss Winthrop was not receiving. Neither Sir William nor Lady Charlotte were at home, the butler stated emphatically, and weren't expected back for several hours.

Unaccustomed to being thwarted, Cam reached inside his waistcoat and began to peel off pound notes until the servant suddenly remembered that Miss Winthrop was indeed in, and could be found in the library on the second floor.

Cam smiled tightly and took the stairs two at a time. Of all the things he expected to see, however, the sight of Annabelle tipped precariously on the edge of an old leather wing-chair attempting to sing an aria from Mozart's *Don Juan* wasn't one of them. Sadness, resignation, defeat: these were the emotions Cam had come ready to address. He was in no wise prepared for happiness, or utter joy. However, it took him but a few moments to ascertain that Annabelle was neither happy nor utterly joyous. What she was was totally, irrevocably, bosky!

Pushing his beaver hat back upon his head, Cam lounged in the doorway as Annabelle continued to sing. Trust the Wayward Angel to dispose of her problems in so unusual a fashion.

It was the earl's loud laughter which finally alerted Annabelle to his presence. "My lord," she cried, sinking into a deep curtsy from which it was impossible for her to recover.

Cam perforce was made to come to her rescue. "Annabelle," he began sternly, trying in vain to hide his amusement, "you must retire immediately. Suppose the servants were to see you in such condition? They can't be trusted you know; they talk."

"Let 'em," Annabelle yelled jubilantly, jerking her arm from Cam's grasp. "Everyone's talking already, or haven' you heard?" she asked coyly.

"Well, there's no need to further fuel the gossip," Cam replied matter-of-factly, prepared to give chase, for Annabelle had neatly dodged away and was at present taunting him from behind a massive, cluttered antique desk. "What you need is a strong pot of coffee, followed by a long nap," he added, rushing round the desk only to find that Annabelle had evaded him again by running quickly to the other side.

"Don't want no coffee," Annabelle said petulantly. "I've discovered a fondness for brandy. You were right, Cam dearest. The darling stuff is an excellent restor... restor... restorative."

"I doubt you'll feel the same way about it tomorrow morn," Cam replied wryly. Years of experience had taught him that fact only too well.

"Brandy, brandy, brandy..." Annabelle chanted as she danced merrily across the room.

Cam could take no chances. He had to get her upstairs and into the capable hands of her pinched-faced maid. Leaping atop the desk, Cam jumped quickly to the floor and in seconds had Annabelle trapped in the far corner of the room.

"Not fair," Annabelle gasped, fighting the hands which sought to ensnare her.

"For God's sake, have a care!" Cam thundered, shaking Annabelle ever so slightly, for her long, luxurious, golden-brown hair had tumbled from its pins to cascade in riotous curls over her shoulders and down her back. However would he explain her dishevelment should she be seen?

Annabelle merely giggled, but she did stop wriggling and settled down nicely against the earl's strong chest. "I love you, Cam," she slurred, nuzzling happily into the expensive blue superfine pressed up against her cheek. "You're too good for that large-bottomed blonde."

Cam gasped, but not due to Annabelle's opinion of Lucinda's anatomy. *She's drunk,* he told himself, yet drunk or no, he knew her declaration of love to be true. Worse still, Cam suddenly knew that he too loved the outrageous minx who was at that very moment clinging to him so trustingly. Using his finger to tilt back her head, Cam touched Annabelle's lips very gently with his own, and then abruptly thrust her away. "What you feel for me is nothing more than a schoolgirl fancy," he told her sternly, for the thought of love terrified him more than the thought of anything else. He'd seen firsthand how dreadfully his own mother had suffered upon his father's death. Cam had vowed then and there that he'd never consciously put himself in the position where he could experience the same kind of pain. Yet here he was, trembling on the brink of just such a situation. The solution seemed obvious. He'd attend his mother's house party, to lend his countenance to Annabelle's reputation, but after that he'd allow no further contact between them. To do so was to court the worst possible kind of disaster.

"Oh, dear, I don't think I feel so well," Annabelle announced at that juncture, disrupting Cam's introspection. The earl breathed a heavy sigh of relief, certain that Annabelle would never remember her outlandish declaration, or much of this particular meeting at all.

He'd dallied long enough. Scooping the feather-light girl up into his arms, Cam strode boldly through the doors of the library and carried her to her rooms. He did encounter the upstairs maid on the way and hastily told the servant that Annabelle was feeling unwell. He then recounted the same story to Betty. The maid agreed to put it about that Annabelle had caught a touch of the cold again.

As Cam predicted, Annabelle awakened much later that day with a terrible headache and a groggy memory of having seen the earl that morning. When her aunt and uncle returned home, much incensed about the gossip they'd been forced to endure concerning their beloved niece, the golden-brown beauty listened with as much enthusiasm as she could muster—given her condition—to the news of Lady Margaret's house party, to which they were all invited. Naturally, she assumed Cam had come by earlier to confirm their acceptance. Annabelle was thus spared the torture of knowing that she'd revealed to the earl her deepest secret.

Cam wasn't so fortunate. He spent the next several days trying valiantly to thrust from his mind the image of an intoxicatingly lovely golden-haired, golden-eyed angel who had inadvertently told him the very last thing he wanted to hear.

THE ROSE DAMASK of the Duchess of Montvale's most expensive Hepplewhite settee was most probably ruined. For on the armrest of this prize piece of furniture had fallen two days' worth of her daughter's heartfelt tears. Violet had begged and pleaded with her mother to be allowed to stand at Annabelle's side through the unimaginable social disaster which had befallen her best friend, but the duchess had thus far stood firm against the notion. She would not allow Violet to be branded an unruly hoyden as well.

Thus it was a decidedly unhappy Lady Violet who greeted Freddy Merryweather one unseasonably warm day in mid-June.

"Freddy," Violet cried gratefully, rushing towards the rather rotund young gentleman as he entered the drawing-room, "you came."

"Well, of course I came, you silly widgeon," Freddy replied good-naturedly, bowing slightly to the duchess, who sat in a wing-chair near the fireplace, surrounded by what seemed to be a horde of gossiping dowagers. "Your note did say it was urgent."

"Oh, Freddy," Violet moaned, leading him to a seat beside her on the rose damask settee. "I'm ever so worried about Annabelle," she whispered, casting an anxious eye towards the duchess. "Mother won't even let me see her, you know, but I was hoping that you might help me to do so anyway."

Freddy laughed appreciatively. "I don't know who's the more devious, you or Annabelle," he replied, adding, "Very well, I shall undertake to gain your mother's permission for a short drive."

"Wait, Freddy," Violet stammered, grasping him by the arm as the portly young sprig made to rise. "Do you think Annabelle is ruined?" she asked breathlessly, afraid of what his answer might be. For the past two days she'd been avoiding any and all of her acquaintance, unwilling to ascertain the exact extent of Annabelle's disgrace.

Freddy's perpetually jolly expression turned thoughtful. "Annabelle's certainly not ruined, my dear," he replied kindly. "I, for one, will stand by her, as will many of her other admirers. Unfortunately, as most often happens in these cases, it's the opinion of the ladies which holds the greatest weight and I'm afraid that Annabelle can't expect much help form that quarter. Although her aunt and uncle are generally well liked, they aren't a particularly powerful family, and Annabelle's own popularity hasn't been well-received by many a doting mama. It's safe to say that her Season is over. However, next year there'll be a score or more of new on dits to busy the gossips and Annabelle will be free to return to Town, a little older, perhaps a little wiser. This Season is practically over in any case. In another month or so everyone who is anyone will have left Town to escape the heat. In the meantime, we've the Westerbrook house party to look forward to."

"Why, whatever do you mean, Freddy?" Violet asked anxiously.

"I assume Lady Margaret sent you an invitation?"

Violet nodded her head. "I hadn't yet decided whether or not to attend."

"I should accept if I were you, because I've had it from the earl himself that Annabelle has been invited. I shall be there as well, although I'm not sure who else is on the guest list."

"Why, that's wonderful news," Violet cried, clapping her hands together delightedly. "Of course, if mother learns of Annabelle's invitation . . ." She bit her lips nervously.

"Lady Margaret is well aware of Annabelle's situation," Freddy replied, patting Violet's hand in a reassuring manner, "and quite fond of the gel. In fact, the house party is undoubtedly being given on her behalf. Therefore, I doubt even your mother, the duchess, would refuse you permission to attend, given the fact that Lady Margaret is well liked and respected. It simply would not be good ton."

"Freddy, you're so clever to have figured it all out," Violet gushed, for now that she'd ascertained Annabelle's future no longer seemed quite so dismal, she was prepared to turn her thoughts over to her own happiness.

Puffing out his chest, Freddy proved himself not immune to Violet's compliments despite the fact that he liked to think of himself as an inveterate cynic. "Nothing to it actually, especially when you've seen as much as I of Society."

"Such as?" Violet asked, thrusting her own chest towards the unsuspecting man about town. At Annabelle's suggestion, she'd lowered the neckline on almost all of her gowns—so much so that the duchess had taken to regarding her daughter with pursed lips whenever Violet entered a room.

Freddy caught his breath and quickly averted his eyes. It would never do to discomfit an innocent such as Lady Violet. Young girls really had no idea how their physical attributes could unsettle a man. Unfortunately for Freddy, he merely switched his glance from one attractive feature to another, for Violet's teary blue eyes glowed with a luminescence which they normally didn't contain.

Much to his amazement, Freddy found himself stammering that he'd best go ask the duchess's permission to take

Violet driving. Feeling decidedly uncomfortable, he knew only that he was suddenly filled with an overwhelming necessity to escape from those eyes, that figure, that brilliant red hair. Why, one would think it was Violet who was the object of his infatuation, not Annabelle!

SQUIRE MORESBY WAS IN A rare taking. His daughter Lucinda, usually so discerning, had stormed into the dining-room that very morn demanding they follow the Earl of Westerbrook into Sussex. Since the squire had never particularly cared to come to London in the first place, that piece of news wasn't especially unsettling. What was unsettling was the fact that he'd been forced to leave the country abruptly, at his daughter's behest, and that now, just when he was beginning to accustom himself to the noise and the dirt and the hectic pace of London, Lucinda wanted to turn round and go back to the country. Squire Moresby had quite simply had enough! That's why he finally voiced his growing belief that Cam Singletary wasn't going to come up to scratch no matter how doggedly Lucinda pursued her quarry. He advised his daughter to cast her lures out elsewhere. Surely with her stunning blond beauty and her substantial dowry, she could do quite well for herself.

The squire had been quite unprepared for the rage with which his daughter met this pronouncement.

"It's Annabelle Winthrop, isn't it?" Lucinda accused. "You think Cam has fallen for that little nothing of a creature. Well, you're mistaken. Annabelle Winthrop is in disgrace, so much so that Cam would never sully the family name with her now. Furthermore, since Cam and his mother plan to retire to the country for a brief respite, I've no intention of losing this opportunity to try and bring him up to scratch. It's what I've yearned for all these years. Just imagine it, Father—our land joined with Westerbrook land! I must go to him and strike while the iron is hot, before the scandal surrounding the Winthrop chit fades away."

The squire threw his hands up in a gesture of resignation. He'd accede to Lucinda's plans for now, just as he always did. Privately, though, he doubted that chasing Cam into the country would force the earl's hand. It had been his experience that the cornered fox always fought that much harder. Furthermore, Cam still showed no signs of seriously entertaining the thought of marriage—at least not to his daughter. The squire rubbed his chin thoughtfully. God in heaven, he hoped Lucinda wasn't becoming unhinged over this unhappy affair! If so, the squire vowed to take matters into his own hands.

RANDOLPH PONFRET NURSED a dish of tea in a secluded corner of his club. Every so often he surreptitiously removed a flask from within his waistcoat and poured into his dish a healthy splash of blue ruin. Randolph had nearly run through his quarterly allowance and was thus forced to make certain concessions to economy while striving to maintain appearances. Sipping the tea with a grimace, he stared longingly at the bottle of champagne which had just been uncorked for Viscount Cranston. Unfortunately, he wasn't an intimate of the viscount, and was thus excluded from sharing in Cranston's bounty.

Tearing his eyes away from the champagne, Randolph placed his chin into his hands and then winced. His jaw was still painfully sore where Westerbrook had landed him a facer at Annabelle's come-out ball. Westerbrook! Randolph sneered and swallowed the remainder of his tea in a single gulp. What he'd give to provide the haughty earl with his comeuppance. Westerbrook thought he was better than everybody else just because he happened to be richer than most, as well as being titled. The earl always got what he wanted, while Randolph was forced to settle for second best. It was Westerbrook who'd been accepted into White's, while Randolph had had to make do with Boodle's. It was Westerbrook who'd garnered the affections of the divine

Miss Winthrop, while Randolph was made to feel as if his attentions weren't only unwanted, but actually repugnant.

Suddenly Randolph heard the name of his nemesis mentioned aloud and he jumped as if the earl had just entered the club to inflict upon the young Lothario more physical pain. But Randolph quickly took hold of himself and located the source of the reference.

"Haven't ever been out to Westhaven before, but I've heard it's enormous. Damn nice of Westerbrook to remember his commanding officer this way. Haven't seen the young pup in an age. Been in India, you know. Glad to be back. Too bloody hot," rambled the distinguished elderly gentleman, who was known by Polite Society as Viscount Cranston. His troops had always referred to him as "Hellborn Harry." Colonel Cranston, however, had just retired from the army and was looking forward to spending the rest of his days with his feet firmly planted on English soil.

"Yes, Westhaven is rather spectacular. I was invited out there once myself several years ago when the old earl was still alive. Glad to see the family beginning to recover from his death. Lady Margaret's still quite the beauty, and from all accounts the son has handled himself exceedingly well. He ain't no fribble, that's for sure," pronounced Sir Richard Montgomery, one of the viscount's most stalwart drinking cronies.

"No indeed!" Cranston roared, earning several reproachful stares from other members of the club. "Camford Singletary was the best young man who ever served under me. Wish I'd had more like him. Would've routed Boney that much quicker."

Randolph Ponfret's expression turned ugly as he listened to the compliments the viscount bestowed upon the earl. Westerbrook certainly used his charm to great advantage. Randolph sniffed distastefully and turned his thoughts to other matters. Obviously Westerbrook was planning some sort of entertainment, and Randolph was willing to wager that Annabelle Winthrop had been invited. Randolph knew all about the scandal now surrounding the Wayward Angel's infamous encounter with the Marquis de Dambere, not that it would matter to Westerbrook or his mother. They fairly doted on the chit.

A look of pure devilment settled itself upon Randolph's attractive features. His blue eyes practically gleamed with malice. This was just the opportunity he'd been searching for. With his pockets to let he'd probably have to return home soon in any case. Why not return a few days earlier, just in time to disrupt, in any way he could, the Westerbrook house party?

CHAPTER TEN

A STEADY ENGLISH RAIN drummed down upon the roof of the Greywood coach-and-four. The dismal weather didn't, however, dampen Annabelle's spirits, for she and Aunt Charlotte were on their way to Westhaven. When the results of Annabelle's experiment with brandy had worn off, she had realized how truly wonderful Lady Margaret's invitation was. Westhaven! Life simply could not be better!

Mr. Fitzroy was stretched out beside Annabelle, his soft snores in unison with those of Aunt Charlotte on the seat opposite. Had they ever really been to London, or had it all been a dream? Annabelle smiled and stretched, and after a while she too began to doze.

A gentle shake from her aunt roused the golden-brown beauty sometime later. "Umm, what is it?" she asked, fluttering open her long, black lashes.

"We've arrived, my gel. Look lively," Aunt Charlotte pronounced, peering through the quizzing glass at the view outside.

There wasn't much to see. Even though the worst of the rain had stopped, a fine mizzle continued to fall, bringing with it a light fog. There was no mistaking the giant weeping willows, however, those magnificent trees lining the driveway which could also be found at the Greywood's Brierly estate. Nor could there by any mistaking the house. Westhaven rose out of the mist like a giant grey monument. Annabelle felt a shiver run down her spine.

In no time at all a footman clad in the familiar ivory livery was opening the coach door, his face wreathed in a welcoming smile. The staff at Westhaven had grown quite fond of the forthright Lady Charlotte and her unpredictable yet charming niece. With the arrival of these two women several months ago, Westhaven and its occupants seemed to have shed some of the gloom which had descended following the old earl's death.

Lady Margaret stood waiting for them inside the entrance hall, her foot tapping impatiently upon the marbled floor. Bajardous stood rigidly at her elbow.

"Oh, my dears," Lady Margaret rhapsodized as Annabelle and Aunt Charlotte entered the hall. "Bajardous, their cloaks."

The major-domo sniffed rather loudly. He certainly knew his duty without being told.

Annabelle giggled and accepted Lady Margaret's embrace willingly. Even though they'd seen Cam's mother in Town but a few days ago, Annabelle was extremely grateful to the countess for inviting her to Westhaven despite the scandal which currently hung over her head. After they'd exchanged the usual pleasantries, Annabelle couldn't, however, keep her eyes from wandering past Lady Margaret.

"He's in the paddock behind the stables, my dear," Cam's mother ventured, laughing gaily as Annabelle turned an alarming shade of pink.

Aunt Charlotte joined the laughter and took her turn at embracing Lady Margaret. "General," she said, giving her hostess a mock salute.

"Admiral, how good it is to have you back at Westhaven," the countess replied, earning a look of confusion from Annabelle and one of resignation from Bajardous. His family had been in the employ of the aristocracy long enough to know that eccentricity was the norm rather than the exception.

Lady Margaret steered Aunt Charlotte and Annabelle towards the staircase. "Your maids arrived several hours ago and most certainly will have set your rooms to rights. I'm sure you'll want to go upstairs and refresh yourselves before dinner. Most of the other guests, those which have arrived, that is, are similarly occupied."

Nodding gratefully, Aunt Charlotte took hold of Annabelle's arm and propelled her niece up the stairs. Annabelle went along with this gentle bullying only until she reached the familiarity of the cheerful yellow rooms she'd been assigned before. Then, ignoring her maid's admonitions, she stopped only long enough to bid a fond hello to the plump Lucy, who was helping Betty unpack, before immediately heading back down the stairs. She'd no intention of allowing Betty to help her change from her rust-coloured travelling costume until she'd located Cam. In all the bustle of leaving London, she hadn't had the opportunity to see him since that rather embarrassing encounter in her Uncle William's library—and she scarcely remembered that.

Luckily no one except a dozing footman was about as Annabelle stole down the steps, and she was thus able to reach the familiar warmth of the kitchens without any trouble at all. The cook greeted her affectionately. Annabelle returned the greeting with a grin and a rueful shake of her head. Mr. Fitzroy had lost no time at all in making himself at home and was at present seated just past Mrs. Freedly's feet, where he could catch any and all scraps of food which might happen to fall from the table. Declining the cook's kind offer of a cup of tea, Annabelle instead reached up for one of the several cloaks which always hung from the wall. She wrapped it tightly over her pelisse and headed out into the foggy mist.

Annabelle tramped through the mud past the stables, grateful indeed that she was wearing her travelling boots. Slippers would've been irrevocably ruined out in this muck. When she reached the paddock, Annabelle stopped at the wooden fence and found it necessary to strain her eyes to better look for Cam. He wasn't difficult to locate. Taller than most, Cam stood at the centre of the field, holding a rope which was haltered around a very young horse. He was gently walking the animal in a wide circle, getting the beast accustomed to taking direction.

Annabelle's heart began to beat a great deal faster at the sight of the handsome Earl of Westerbrook. Predictably, he wore no cloak or coat, so she was able to admire unhampered the wide breadth of his shoulders. Annabelle found that she was quite incapable of stopping her gaze from wandering down to his heavily muscled thighs. A rosy flush quickly suffused her delicate features and she could only be grateful that the hood of the borrowed cloak shielded much of her face from view.

As Cam continued to walk the horse, he suddenly felt a strange tingling sensation and his eyes quickly lifted to investigate the cause. He saw her almost immediately, and although she was swallowed up in an over-large cloak, he knew without a doubt that Annabelle had arrived. Only she could produce in him the sensations he was currently experiencing.

Cam called for his head groom and handed Jem the rope. Although he fully intended to train this horse personally, the mare would temporarily be in good hands with the older man.

Annabelle knew the earl had noticed her, for Cam was heading straight towards the fence where she stood, and like a fool she felt her knees begin to quiver just as they always did when she hadn't seen him in quite some time. He really was too handsome. His midnight black hair was pushed carelessly back from his ruddy face and his light brown eyes were twinkling just as merrily as Annabelle remembered they did.

Cam found himself glad that Annabelle was here, for as hard as he'd tried, he hadn't been able to force her entirely from his thoughts. Although he'd vowed to expel the errant Miss Winthrop from his life, he saw no reason not to enjoy their last few days together. Cam quickened his pace and then he was before her, the two of them grinning at each other like long-lost comrades.

"One perfectly beastly man at your service," the earl remarked with a slight bow. He couldn't see Annabelle's delightful figure or her remarkable hair, but it was enough to be looking at her angel face with its golden-brown eyes, perfect pink lips and porcelain-smooth skin.

Annabelle giggled. It was so wonderful to be back at Westhaven; it was almost like having come home. "Careful, Cam, or I shall order Mr. Fitzroy to take another nip at your breeches," she replied with spirit.

"You didn't bring that miserable creature along with you, did you?" Cam asked in mock dismay.

"I never travel without Mr. Fitzroy," Annabelle replied haughtily before she smiled. "He is at this very moment getting quite fat at the hands of the admirable Mrs. Freedly."

"The dog who dines on roast beef and capon. What do you suppose he'd do were we to toss him a bone?"

"Why, he'd turn up his nose and walk away, of course," Annabelle said, resisting the urge to throw her arms about Cam's neck. To change the course of her wayward thoughts, she quickly asked him about the young horse he'd just been putting through its paces.

"Don't you recognize her, Annabelle? You ought to. She's named for you."

"Why, whatever do you mean?" Annabelle sputtered, but then a glimmer of understanding entered her enormous, golden-brown eyes. "You don't mean . . . why, Cam, I never thought to hope . . . couldn't bring myself to ask, actually . . ."

Cam chuckled. "Yes, that's the filly you persuaded to drink from the sugar teat. Her mother eventually accepted her, thank goodness, and now she appears none the worse for wear. Good lines, don't you think?''

"Actually I don't really know much about horses," Annabelle answered honestly, "but whatever did you mean that she's named for me?"

"We call her Wayward Angel."

"Why, that's famous!" Annabelle trilled, clapping her hands together with delight. "Imagine, I've a horse named after me. But why, Cam—that's to say, I didn't really do all that much, you know."

"You helped save her life," Cam stated firmly. Then his eyes began to twinkle. "Besides, she's begun to show serious signs of fractiousness lately, making the name all the more appropriate."

"Oh, fudge," Annabelle sputtered, hitting him playfully on the arm. "Why, the horse looks the perfect lady."

"Spoken from your vast experience with the species, of course."

"Of course," Annabelle replied just before sighing heavily. "Oh, Cam, it's at times like these that I do wish I'd learned to ride."

"It's not too late, you know," he said. "In fact, I'd be glad to teach you." So much for his promise to expurgate the unforgettable Miss Winthrop from his mind. "I can start you this week while you're here, in any case," he amended hastily.

Annabelle's first impulse was to refuse. She did really have a frightful fear of horses, owing to the time she'd been thrown as a child. But several factors prevented her from obeying her impulse. First, she'd always longed for a riding habit and knew for a certainty that Lady Margaret would insist upon outfitting her in one which would show her to advantage. Second, she might not gain another opportunity to spend quite so much time with Cam, which was something she dearly wanted to do. Third, her refusal to ride oft-times excluded her from events which she'd much rather attend. Against her better judgement, Annabelle reluctantly nodded her head.

"Brilliant," Cam replied. "A fine show of spirit. We'll begin first light tomorrow morn, weather permitting, and I do mean first light, Annabelle," he added, giving her such a piercing glance that she knew it would be quite unacceptable to present herself at noon.

"Shall we say ten o'clock?" she ventured hopefully.

Cam snorted. "We shall not. I will compromise and expect you at nine. I have estate matters to tend to tomorrow as a result of my recent absence, and one of our guests, James Makepeace, is interested in purchasing several horses."

"Very well, Cam," Annabelle replied with a shudder. It really was most vexing to have to get up at the crack of dawn.

Annabelle was given little time to ponder her unfortunate fate for the drum of nearby horse hooves quickly garnered their attention. She felt her spirits plummet even further as Squire Moresby and his daughter Lucinda rode through the mist, for Lucinda, as usual, was in splendid looks, wearing a yellow riding habit complete with matching cloak. The ensemble, which would have appeared frightful on anyone else, complimented Lucinda's stunning beauty.

If Annabelle was somewhat disconcerted to be confronted by the woman she quite naturally perceived to be her rival, her feelings of animosity were nothing as compared to the furious rage Lucinda experienced upon recognizing Annabelle. It was unthinkable that the dowdy chit should show herself among refined company following her recent disgrace. Lucinda couldn't, wouldn't, acknowledge that Annabelle had been invited to Westhaven. To her way of thinking, her rival would always be the interloper.

"Squire Moresby and Lucinda, how delightful to see you again, especially in such foul weather. I hadn't realized you were down from London as well," Cam said by way of greeting.

"Yes, ahem, the noise and the congestion of Town began to take its toll so my daughter quite kindly agreed to a fortnight or so in the country," Squire Moresby explained, growing uncomfortably warm as he invented a Banbury Tale on the spur of the moment. With the unexpected presence of Miss Winthrop, it was beginning to appear increasingly clear that Lucinda was tilting at windmills.

"Father and I never allow the weather to impede our daily rides," Lucinda added with her usual air of pomposity. However, she feigned a sweet innocence as she edged her mount closer and closer to Annabelle. The silly chit's fear regarding the animals was a well-known fact.

Cam reacted instinctively, although he was hardly aware of doing so. Nonchalantly, he placed himself in front of Annabelle so that Lucinda's mount could not get too close. This gallant gesture further enraged the stunning blonde, although she was at pains not to show it.

"Actually Father and I decided to ride in your direction for a very particular reason," Lucinda stated, determined not to lose sight of her goal. The abominable Miss Winthrop hadn't won yet! "We're hosting a hunt the day after tomorrow, Cam, and wanted to be sure to invite you and your mother. Do say you'll attend."

Cam's eyes lit up at the prospect. "That sounds a fine idea, Lucinda, but my mother and I have several house guests at present and cannot simply desert them, no matter how noble the cause."

"Bring 'em along, boy," Squire Moresby roared, earning a brilliant smile from his daughter.

"There, you see, it's all settled," Lucinda pronounced, happily knowing full well that Annabelle did not ride. Just this once she would have Cam to herself without the presence of the odious Miss Winthrop. "We've invited all the usuals—the Ponfrets, the vicar, of course," Lucinda remarked, turning her large green eyes upon Annabelle. "What a shame you don't ride, Miss Winthrop. It's going to be such a lark."

Annabelle squared her shoulders. "I quite agree it's a shame that I do not ride. That's why I'm so delighted Cam has offered to teach me. Unfortunately, I don't foresee myself participating in any future hunts, no matter how proficient at riding I may become. I find the prospect of chasing after some poor little fox and watching the kill to be repellent."

"Foxes are a scourge to landowners everywhere," Cam admonished, for he quite adored all aspects of the horse and of the hunt. At the same time, though, he found himself admiring Annabelle for voicing her opinion. She'd never be a complacent woman, but then again she'd never be a boring one, either.

Lucinda pounced on what she perceived to be Cam's disapproval. "How very unEnglish of you, Miss Winthrop. So noble to set yourself up as a champion of lower-class ideology," the stunning blonde denounced in her curiously masculine fashion.

"Yes, several of my opinions seem to have prompted many in the ton to speculate whether or not I'm Newgate born, the illegitimate daughter of roving gypsies, or the spawn of the devil himself. Personally, I prefer the Newgate theory, highly dramatic, don't you think? Unfortunately, my aunt assures me that my birth was nothing if not ordinary, and since my uncle taught me to always think for myself, my views aren't likely to change any time in the near future. And now, if you'll excuse me, I find myself grown suddenly quite fatigued."

Lucinda could do nothing but sputter helplessly as Annabelle marched towards the house. However, her anger didn't prevent her from noting Cam's admiring gaze as he watched the chit go. Why, even Lucinda's father looked as if he might want to smile. Blast it all! What was it about the girl which inspired such admiration in the opposite sex? Lucinda knew herself to be at least as pretty if not prettier than Annabelle, yet she'd never earned the sort of acclaim which seemed to follow the Winthrop chit wherever she went.

Whirling her horse about furiously, Lucinda took time only to remind Cam once more about the hunt and then she was gone in the mist, expending her vexation upon her hapless horse. Squire Moresby doffed his hat and made to follow.

Annabelle was fairly shaking with rage as she stormed into the house. Lucinda Moresby was an absolute horror! Yet the warmth of the kitchens, the hospitality of the cook, and Mr. Fitzroy's large brown eyes soon restored most of her good humour. She wasn't about to let Lucinda ruin her happiness. She was at Westhaven, she was with Cam, and that was all that mattered. Grinning broadly, Annabelle bit eagerly into the warm blueberry tart given to her by Mrs. Freedly, and after petting Mr. Fitzroy upon his wiry head, she made her way back upstairs.

A large commotion in the entrance hall drew Annabelle's attention as she finished the last of her tart. At least three large trunks were being piled atop the marble floor, and were quickly followed by twice the number of bandboxes and an even larger number of portmanteaux. Finally, after it seemed that the footmen were to be kept busy unloading all afternoon, a small figure stepped through the doorway, accompanied by the watchful maid who had been trusted to act as companion.

Annabelle could not have mistaken that red hair anywhere. "Violet," she squealed, running towards her friend, "why, you must've brought the entire contents of your wardrobe."

Laughing gaily, Violet announced that since she'd been unable to decide what to bring, she'd simply brought it all. "You're not vexed with me, are you, Annabelle? Mama wouldn't allow me to come to you no matter how I begged,'' Violet said, hugging Annabelle tightly.

"Yet you contrived to come anyway, for a few moments in any case, with the help of our darling Freddy. Of course I'm not vexed. Though you're likely better off to stay away from a hoyden like me—if you value your reputation, that is."

"Don't be a goose. You're my best friend and you always will be. Now, on to more important matters. How stand things between you and the earl? Has Freddy arrived yet?"

Bajardous, who'd been waiting patiently for the two young ladies to vacate the area so that he could see to the proper disposition of the luggage, stepped forward impatiently at that juncture and was thus privy to Violet's last question. "Mr. Merryweather has indeed arrived and is resting in his rooms," the butler intoned, making it clear that he expected the other guests to follow suit.

Grabbing Violet's arm, Annabelle steered her friend towards the stairs. "Don't worry, his bark is much worse than his bite," she whispered loudly enough so that Bajardous couldn't help but overhear. The butler's outraged expression had both girls giggling furiously as they tripped gaily up the staircase, followed at a more sedate pace by Violet's maid.

When they'd finally overcome their merriment, the red head asked Annabelle who else Lady Margaret had invited to the week-long house party.

"I believe the guest list has been kept comparatively small in light of my recent misadventures," Annabelle replied with a rueful shake of her golden-brown curls. "In any case Lady Margaret is just beginning to entertain again. She's not yet a match for anything on the grand scale. Besides you and I, Aunt Charlotte and Freddy, I believe Cam's former commanding officer, a Viscount Cranston, has been invited, as well as Lady Margaret's cousin, Sir Charles Harewood. And then there's a newly-wed couple, James and Elizabeth Makepeace, who are friends of Cam's.''

"Good," Violet stated emphatically. "That means I'll have Freddy's undivided attention. If I can discourage him from mooning over you, that is."

"I doubt Freddy thinks of me much these days," Annabelle replied intuitively, for she'd seen how the portly young sprig had begun to look at her friend.

Violet coloured charmingly, which wasn't at all like her, and it caused Annabelle to giggle. "Methinks the sight of your ample endowments has wrought a change in young Mr. Merryweather's sentiments."

"Half the time I feel positively undressed," Violet confessed, squeezing Annabelle's arm, "and Mama is certainly not pleased. Nevertheless, your suggestion that I lower my neckline has seemed to produce results, so I shall just have to go about risking pneumonia until the rogue comes to heel."

"Bravo, my girl," Annabelle crowed, for a match between Violet and Freddy would prove of all things splendid.

At the top of the stairs the girls parted. Lady Margaret, just come from a comfy coze with Aunt Charlotte, had noted the arrival of her latest guest and immediately volunteered to escort Violet down the long corridor towards the suite of rooms to which the redhead and her maid had been assigned. Annabelle watched them go and then made towards her own chambers. She was beginning to feel drowsy. A long nap was definitely in order, and she wanted to have plenty of time to dress for dinner.

Betty was just hanging up the last of Annabelle's gowns as she opened the door. "There you are, miss," the maid chided. "I was beginning to think you'd got lost, or killed, or worse."

Annabelle's eyes widened. Betty's unfailing pessimism never ceased to amaze. "As far as I know there are no escaped Bedlamites running about the estate, Betty. You may rest assured that we're all safe."

The maid sniffed. "Be that as it may, it never hurts to be cautious."

"I shall make every effort to be careful. And now, if you please, I'm dreadfully tired and somewhat cold."

Betty scurried forward, for despite her eccentricities she took her duties most seriously. "I'm amazed you haven't caught your death out in that mizzle. Let me help you undress and then I think it best if you rest awhile before dinner."

Giving herself up gratefully to her maid's capable ministrations, Annabelle let Betty prattle on and on about this and that, not paying particular mind, until the maid said something so extraordinary that it caught her undivided attention. "What was that?" she enquired, slipping into the silk wrapper that Betty held aloft.

"I said that there's little about this place to please except perhaps for that handsome Mr. Bajardous."

Bajardous? Handsome? Not by the slightest stretch of the imagination could the Westhaven butler be described as physically appealing. Yet Betty, with her pinched and drawn features, didn't exactly turn heads herself. And their personalities were similar, Annabelle thought with mounting excitement. Why, love was simply blooming everywhere! Perhaps shown such stalwart examples, Cam himself might fall prey to that elusive emotion.

"I thought you found the male of the species to be an odious creature at best," Annabelle teased, waiting for her maid's reaction.

It wasn't long in coming. Betty blushed and stammered as she admitted, "Most men, miss, but not Mr. Bajardous. He's obviously cut from a better cloth."

"Well, if you find Bajardous handsome, Betty, then we' just have to see that you spend a good deal of time in hi company."

Amazingly, Betty tittered at the suggestion just like a young schoolgirl. But her dour disposition was well ingrained and seconds later she was tucking her young mistress into bed and admonishing her to go to sleep lest she fall victim to a serious case of the vapours. Now, Annabelle had never suffered from that particular malady in all her life. Nevertheless, she merely sighed and nodded, too tired to argue the point.

Dinner that evening was an exceedingly pleasant affair, served at what in London would've been an unfashionably early hour. The guests, however, were quite willing to bow to the dictates of the country.

Annabelle found Viscount Cranston to be a most distinguished-looking older gentleman, full of exciting stories concerning his life in the military. Lady Charlotte's cousin, Sir Charles Harewood, was also an older man, but he was exceedingly quiet and seemed to spend an inordinate amount of time worrying about the state of his health. James and Elizabeth Makepeace were a famous couple, clearly in love, but with enough Town bronze not to spend the entire evening billing and cooing. Instead, they kept the company amused with stories of their honeymoon on the Continent. Only Freddy, with his delectable London on dits, was able to create a bigger stir.

When finally the fruit and cheese had been served, signalling the end to an excellent meal, Lady Margaret spoke briefly before retiring with the ladies. "I'm most happy that you've all chosen to honour my son and I with your presence. Please feel free to treat Westhaven as your home for the duration of your stay. You may walk or ride or sup at your leisure. Tomorrow next our neighbours, Squire Moresby and his daughter Lucinda, are holding a hunt in which you may participate if you so desire. The following day, an alfresco lunch will be served on Westhaven's south lawn. At week's end, Cam and I shall host a small soirée to which we've invited several of the local families. And now,

having bored you gentlemen enough with the social schedule, the ladies and I shall withdraw.''

Annabelle didn't stay long in the Blue Salon. She was well
aware that she had to rise unusually early the next morn to
meet Cam for her riding lesson and she didn't want to over-
sleep. The other ladies followed Annabelle's lead, content
to call it an early night. Cam, Freddy, James, Cousin
Charles and the viscount stayed on, determined to solve all
of England's most pressing problems over several bottles of
well-aged French port.

Although Annabelle slept soundly that night, Betty was
quite unable to rouse her groggy mistress from bed the next
morn. Annabelle was simply not accustomed to rising so
early, and it was always a struggle for the maid when she was
charged with the onerous task of insuring that Annabelle
would not linger abed. It was only when a distraught Betty
began to dangle Lady Margaret's riding habit in front of
Annabelle's nose that the golden-brown beauty finally
tumbled from bed. The riding habit had been borrowed
yesterday afternoon and Betty had seen that the garment
which hadn't been worn for several years, had been steamed
and pressed. Despite its age, the habit was enchanting. It
was black, for one thing, and Annabelle knew that that
particular colour suited her well. And while it lacked the
military frogging which had become almost *de rigueur* in
recent years, the habit was cut along classical lines which
could only accentuate her figure. Furthermore, it was accompanied by a darling little hat, complete with netting and
feathers, which was designed to perch slightly askew on the
wearer's head.

Thus it was a self-satisfied Annabelle who presented herself at the stables five minutes earlier than Cam had actually specified.

"Do my eyes deceive me?" the earl mocked when he
caught sight of his somewhat leery pupil.

Annabelle tossed her curls disdainfully, unwilling to acknowledge just how devastatingly handsome she found Cam in his bottle-green riding coat. "For your information, I've been up for hours," she fibbed without the slightest degree of guilt.

Cam was doubtful in the extreme; however, he chose not to comment. "Well then, if you're ready, allow me to introduce you to your mount. We'll begin our lesson within the confines of the paddock and may then take a short ride, if we've enough time, and if you seem to be making progress."

Now that Annabelle was actually about to confront her fear, she found herself trembling, her feet completely unable to move. "Cam, I'm not certain I can do this."

The earl was instantly at her side. Annabelle had appeared so confident this morning, so cocksure and elegant in her flattering habit, that Cam had quite forgotten what a terror horses were for her. Slipping an arm round the golden-brown beauty's incredibly tiny waist, the earl fought to keep himself from stealing a kiss. "Naturally I'll not force you to do anything you feel you cannot, but I do think you very much can, angel. Won't you try?"

Annabelle looked up at him, her magnificent eyes large with hesitation. After several seconds, she nodded once, making the feathers on her jaunty hat dance quite charmingly. Cam resisted the urge to smile as he led her forth into the stables.

They stopped before the stall of an exceedingly gentle little mare by the name of Daisy. Under Cam's direction, Annabelle reached out to stroke the horse's nose and found herself surprised at the velvetlike texture of Daisy's coat. "I'll fetch a saddle and we'll put it on together. It's important that you know as much as you can about an endeavour if you're to be successful at it."

Annabelle nodded her understanding, feeling a bit more confident now that she'd actually met the horse Cam was determined she mount. In fact, Annabelle was feeling so charitable with the creature that she reached into the pocket of her habit and withdrew the tasty titbit she'd stolen from Mrs. Freedly's kitchens in order to curry the animal's favour.

Daisy sniffed curiously at the offering in Annabelle's hand but made no move to eat it. "What's the matter, girl? Stuffed yourself at breakfast?" Annabelle queried innocently.

"What in God's name are you trying to feed that horse?" Cam thundered, startling Annabelle, who'd been so engrossed in watching Daisy that she hadn't heard him return.

"Well, I couldn't find where Mrs. Freedly keeps the apples so I thought an orange would do just as well," Annabelle replied, a defiant gleam in her eye.

"Annabelle, horses don't eat oranges," Cam stated matter-of-factly, until the humour of the situation overcame him and he began to guffaw quite loudly.

"I don't find it at all amusing, Camford Singletary," Annabelle retorted as the earl continued to laugh. She stamped her foot angrily and turned her back.

"At least you could've peeled it for her," Cam replied, laughing even harder.

Since Annabelle wasn't the sort who minded a good joke, even if it was more or less at her expense, she was ultimately unable to keep a straight face and for several moments the two of them stood inside the stables, laughing heartily as the groomsmen listened in amazement.

When finally they managed to control their mirth, Cam instructed Annabelle on how to attach the side-saddle and other accoutrements before he led Daisy from her stall and out into the paddock. Lifting Annabelle by the waist, the earl set her atop the horse before the golden-brown beauty had the opportunity to think better of it. Handing Jem the reins, Cam mounted his own stallion, Merlin. Taking hold of both horses, the earl led Annabelle about the paddock several times until she felt more comfortable. Only then did he allow her to attempt to control the mare on her own.

Annabelle found the lesson much more enjoyable than she'd imagined. There was something about sitting atop a horse which gave one a feeling of power, a feeling of freedom which was quite unlike anything else she'd ever experienced.

"Oh, Cam, do let's go for a short ride," Annabelle pleaded when she'd mastered the rudiments. Daisy was such a sweet goer that she'd long since abandoned her fear of being thrown.

"In case you haven't noticed, young lady, we've been at this for the better part of the morning. I think that will do for now. I won't have time to instruct you tomorrow because of the hunt, but I promise a long lesson on the following day, complete with a short ride."

Annabelle was of a mind to pout, but she recognized the truth in Cam's words. It was getting on. Luncheon would undoubtedly be served soon and she needed time to change into proper dress. Furthermore, despite her newfound enthusiasm, she was beginning to notice a decided soreness in her nether portions, also a new experience, albeit one she definitely did not think she was going to enjoy.

Cam tried to ignore the rosy flush of Annabelle's cheeks as he lifted her off Daisy, and her excited smile. He couldn't remember having so enjoyed a morning, despite the fact that Annabelle was a novice horsewoman. He'd definitely miss the chit when she left, but leave she must. It'd be all too easy to become permanently attached to the angelic Miss Winthrop, and all too easy to despair should something tragic befall her.

"Learning to ride, Miss Winthrop?" questioned James Makepeace as he strolled towards the paddock. He'd spent the past several moments from afar observing Annabelle and Cam.

"I'm attempting it in any case," the golden-brown beauty said to the slim young man with the light brown hair. "I realize that I'm beginning my tutelage rather late, but I think now I understand a bit better why the English are so completely horse mad."

James laughed and complimented Annabelle upon her seat. "I do believe that with a few more lessons you might become quite the horsewoman yourself and join our equestrian ranks."

"You're exceedingly kind, if slightly prone to exaggeration, for I do know that it will require more than a few lessons to firmly establish me as an equestrian," Annabelle replied with a wry grin. "And now, if you gentlemen will excuse me, I'll bid you farewell, for I understand, Mr. Makepeace, that you're anxious to tour Lord Westerbrook's stables."

James admitted that he was indeed anxious to have a look about. Leaving the gentlemen to their business, Annabelle hurried back towards the house, where she spent more time than was usual in completing her toilette. Unfortunately, she found it necessary to enlist Betty's aid in the application of a soothing ointment to areas of a "sensitive" nature, and was thus not ready for luncheon until the gong sounded for the second time.

The rest of the day passed relatively uneventfully. Annabelle spent the afternoon in the Blue Salon with the other ladies, plying a needle and thread, although sewing was not in truth her favourite activity. Still, it was pleasant to listen to all the chitter-chatter, and after tea had been served Annabelle even found time for a private coze with Violet. It seemed that Freddy was studiously avoiding the redhead, a fact which was causing Violet no end of worry. "Just when I thought he was coming round a bit," she whispered with a sigh. "It's hopeless, I tell you. I'm bound to spend the rest of my life as an eccentric spinster alone but for my money."

"Stuff and nonsense," Annabelle replied, borrowing one of Uncle William's favourite phrases. "You do plan to go on that horrid hunt tomorrow, do you not?"

"Yes, Annabelle, I do," Violet admitted rather guiltily. She knew full well her friend's sentiments concerning cruelty to animals, but she'd been raised with the hunt and found it exhilarating.

"Well then, here's what you must do," Annabelle stated firmly, instructing Violet on the intricacies of a plan which she might have put to use herself had she been more comfortable atop a horse.

"Oh, are you sure?" Violet questioned uncertainly. The plan seemed rather drastic to the redhead, yet Annabelle had been of enormous help thus far in assisting her in garnering Freddy Merryweather's reluctant attention.

"I cannot see that it could do any harm," Annabelle replied with assurance. "At the very least you'll have a better measure of Freddy's true sentiments."

Violet nodded her head in agreement, but further conversation was then forestalled as Lady Margaret summoned both girls over to sample Mrs. Freedly's special Madeira cake. Not long after, the gentlemen rejoined the ladies, having spent several hours at the billiards table.

It was a lively assembly which gathered for dinner that evening, particularly since Lady Margaret had decreed no one need dress. In fact, the cook had prepared a sort of indoor picnic. After helping themselves to a variety of delectable dishes which had been placed upon the cherry wood dining-table, the guests then returned to the Blue Salon to sup. All agreed that the informal meal had proven splendid fun.

Following dinner, the guests removed to the beautifully decorated music room. First Violet played the piano, followed by Annabelle, who managed this time to bring no discredit upon Aunt Charlotte. Next, Lady Margaret and her cousin Sir Charles sang a charming duet. James and

Elizabeth Makepeace between them recited a poem which so clearly reflected their newly established marital bliss that the ladies in the company were soon plying their handkerchiefs. When the Makepeaces were through, Annabelle was recalled to the piano, where she accompanied her aunt, who delivered a relatively credible ballad. Since Viscount Cranston was adamant that he had no talent of which to speak, he instead enthralled the assembly with a tale of one of the more horrific battles in which he'd been wounded. As dramatic as was his tale, it was Cam and Freddy who stole the moment. Obviously forewarned, the two had practised, and now proceeded to perform a Scottish sword dance which required considerable skill as well as considerable wind. In fact, the sight of portly Freddy Merryweather prancing about on his toes was so hilarious that the men received a standing ovation upon the completion of their dance.

Annabelle went to bed happy that night—an emotion that was, unfortunately, not to last. The simple evening had been a resounding success. She enjoyed frolicking in such fashion much more than she enjoyed sophisticated (and starchy) London entertainments. Nestled in her bed with the candle out, Annabelle expected to review the evening, to perhaps enjoy another chuckle upon remembering Freddy's incredible dexterity. Yet for all her happiness, she found her thoughts turning instead to the upcoming hunt. She simply could not wrest her mind from the poor hapless fox who was to provide the morrow's sport. So rather than ending the evening with a smile, Annabelle found that she cried herself to sleep, weeping much harder than she had at any time in recent months.

Cam noticed Annabelle's wan face at breakfast the next morn and couldn't imagine what had occurred to overset her so. That she'd been crying was obvious, for her eyes were red-rimmed. Furthermore, Annabelle usually never came downstairs for breakfast. Her habit was to sleep well into the morn. Because they were the only two who'd yet to make an appearance, Cam reached over and covered Annabelle's hand with his own. "What's amiss?" he asked gently. "May I be of service?"

"It's silliness, pure and simple," Annabelle replied, "and I shall shortly be fully recovered." She favoured him with a weak smile.

Cam attempted a few more bites of his beef, for he believed in eating a large meal before strenuous activity, but found that he simply could not be satisfied with Annabelle's evasiveness. He was so accustomed to her cheerful disposition that this episode of the blue devils was most perplexing. "Now see here, Annabelle," Cam began more forcefully than he intended, "you must tell me what the matter is, lest I fret about you all day."

A small kernel of joy leapt in Annabelle's heart at Cam's words. It was a thoroughly pleasant sensation to know that he cared enough to be concerned. "It's picturing the kill—" she began, but her words were interrupted by the exuberant arrival of Freddy, closely followed by James and Elizabeth Makepeace.

"All set to run the wily fox to ground?" Freddy asked of the assembled group.

Hearing those words, Annabelle hurriedly snatched the napkin from her lap, flung it on the table and fled the room. Freddy stood looking after her, an expression of pure amazement on his pudgy face. "Whatever did I say?" he questioned of no one in particular, for although he was beginning to suspect that he didn't in fact love the Wayward Angel as he'd once thought he did, Freddy was still very fond of Annabelle and loath to cause her pain.

Cam stood up and clapped Freddy soundly on the back. "You couldn't have known, old man. It seems that Miss Winthrop finds the hunt rather barbaric. Her sympathies, my dear fellow, are firmly with the fox."

A look of relief entered Freddy's eyes. "Ah, a tender heart," he said, seating himself at table. "Admirable sentiments to be sure, but hardly practical," he commented, spooning a healthy portion of buttered eggs onto his plate.

Violet entered the breakfast room at that moment, looking absolutely charming in a green riding habit which served only to emphasize the brilliant red of her hair. Freddy gazed at her with admiration, having no notion that Violet, while a veritable pocket Venus, could hardly breathe. Since one couldn't very well ride in a low-cut habit, unless one wished to risk truly humiliating consequences, Violet had opted instead to wear a corset, which flattered her waistline but made breathing a difficulty.

As Freddy continued to covertly watch the redhead while she was seated, he found himself thinking it fortunate that Lady Violet was made of sterner stuff than Annabelle. Freddy didn't think he could take to wife a woman who did not approve of the hunt. Immediately, the direction of his thoughts caused Freddy's heart to hammer most alarmingly. Why ever would he associate thoughts of Violet with marriage? The enormity of the situation prompted Freddy to double his determination to avoid the redhead for the remainder of the week.

Following breakfast, those who'd chosen to join the hunt, which turned out to be everyone except Annabelle and Lady Charlotte, were mounted by Cam's excellent groomsmen according to need and skill. The ride to Moresby Field was relatively short and the group found themselves in high spirits as they came upon the merry scene. It seemed as if every hunter for miles around had elected to participate, so that the start point was full of horses, riders and excited dogs.

Lucinda reined in next to Cam and the earl found that he wasn't totally immune to her stunning blond beauty, which was always shown to advantage atop a horse. It almost seemed that when Lucinda rode, a side of her which under other circumstances was not apparent was revealed, lending the blonde an air of excitement and abandon which made her rather more attractive. Lucinda's green eyes glittered, her ash blond hair shone, her cheeks were rosy red.

"All ready, Cam?" she enquired, noting with pleasure the absence of the Winthrop chit. It promised to be a marvellous day!

"Without a doubt," he replied with a smile, keeping careful hold of his mount. With all the activity, Merlin was restless, anxious to be off.

Several moments later the horn finally sounded and the hunt was on. Lucinda and Cam raced to the fore as they always did. Lady Margaret and her guests were content to settle somewhere in the middle of the pack, Sir Charles Harewood hanging even farther back. He wasn't about to risk a broken neck, which he felt sure was a common occurrence in the midst of such confusion.

Although Violet had doubted that Freddy would ride beside her, she was elated to see that he'd nevertheless jostled into a position which was quite close to that of her own. It was absolutely essential to the success of her plan—or rather Annabelle's plan—that he be within viewing range.

Violet waited until the throng had cleared out somewhat, for she'd no intention of receiving an injury, or possibly injuring someone else. Then there was the necessity of locating just the right spot. At long last she spied it. Not a quarter of a mile ahead was a relatively small ditch which the participants were electing to either jump or circumvent. Spurring her horse forward, for it was important that she be ahead of Freddy and his mount, Violet took the jump. In mid-air, she pretended to lose her balance. The startled horse looked back at her strangely, for he'd cleared the hurdle easily and knew it full well. Violet almost laughed, but instead, as carefully as she could, she slid off the horse's back and onto the ground.

Freddy was at Violet's side within seconds, cradling her head in his arms, a look of terrible fright upon his portly face. The redhead peeped up at him from beneath her lashes and felt a powerful twinge of guilt. But she steeled herself by recalling the necessity of the deception. Moaning most pitifully, Violet kept her eyes securely shut.

"My dear!" Freddy cried, rocking her to and fro. "Violet, can you hear me? Blast and damnation! Someone get a doctor."

Deeming this to be a prudent moment to make a partial recovery, Violet slowly opened her eyes and asked in a weak voice, "Freddy, is it you? What happened? I feel quite queer."

"You fell off your horse, darling," Freddy replied anxiously, oblivious to the concerned group of onlookers who by this time had gathered round them. "Can you move? I think it best I get you back to Westhaven as soon as possible."

"I might be able to move if you help me," Violet answered, opening her eyes more fully. She made a feeble effort to sit, and then fell back.

Ignoring the advice being offered by those in the crowd, Freddy gently gathered Violet up in his arms and carried her to his mount. Sitting her atop his horse, he handed the reins of her own mount to a groom, and then climbed on behind the redhead. Violet leaned back against his broad chest and sighed. Even if Annabelle's plan proved all for naught, this alone was worth the effort.

As he wheeled his horse about, Freddy's concern turned more to anger. "Whatever happened, Violet? You shouldn' participate in the hunt if you aren't capable of keeping up."

Biting back a swift retort, Violet maintained her weak voice. "I simply do not know what happened, Freddy. I'm usually an excellent rider, to which any number of people can attest."

"But you scared me," Freddy complained.

Violet's heart began to beat a bit faster. "It was only minor accident, Freddy. I shall be fine."

"Nevertheless you could've been seriously injured. I absolutely forbid you to ever ride again."

Violet issued a derisive sound. "Really, Freddy, you are in no position to dispatch such a command."

Suddenly the horse stopped. Turning her head to see what the matter was, Violet gasped at the expression on Freddy's face and felt her heart begin to pound even faster. "Freddy," she whispered, then lowered her eyes in confusion and fell silent.

"I find that I've c-come to care for you very much, Violet," Freddy admitted, stammering only the once. "And that gives me every right to look out for your interests."

"Yes, Freddy, I believe it does," Violet agreed just before they kissed.

Well up ahead, Cam, Lucinda and several of the more fervent riders had absolutely no idea that one of their number had taken a fall. Most of them wouldn't have stopped in any case.

The chase was almost over. The dogs were braying loudly now and seemed to have cornered the unfortunate fox. Cam felt a surge of exhilaration, for the ride had been swift and full of worthy obstacles. Lucinda had kept pace with him throughout and they sat their mounts side by side as the momentum slowed and then stopped.

"The dogs will be on to it any second now," Lucinda prophesied, her green eyes flashing brilliantly.

Cam felt a momentary pang of unease. Would it really be so horrid if the dogs were now called off and the unfortunate fox allowed to slip free? He shook his head ruefully. Nonsense. A kill was a fit ending for a scourge.

"This is my favourite part of the hunt," Lucinda announced loudly as she watched the dogs with keen interest. "The culmination of all our efforts."

"Really?" Cam questioned, noticing for the first time, thanks to Annabelle's fuddled remark, just how large Lucinda's backside was as she sat on her horse. Cam resisted the urge to laugh, for the blonde certainly would find no humour were he to tell her the reason for his mirth. In truth, Lucinda found little humour in anything. Could he really consign himself to eternity with such a woman? For suddenly it seemed that there was a great deal more to Lucinda than Cam had ever noticed before, and none of it good.

All at once the stunning blonde shrieked, as did several of the other nearby riders, thereby startling Cam out of his reverie. "The dogs have let the fox escape," she cried, turning to Cam with a look of disgust etched upon her vivid features.

Cam resisted the urge to smile. All he could think of was how delighted Annabelle would be to receive the news.

CHAPTER ELEVEN

A LARGE TABLE swathed in yards of Irish linen and French lace had been placed upon Westhaven's south lawn. Atop the table, silver and crystal glinted in the sunlight. Mrs. Freedly had once again outdone herself. What was supposed to be a simple collation for a small number of people looked more like a Carlton House feast. Mrs. Freedly wouldn't have it said that she couldn't compete with the best. Why, her cooking was far better than that of the Moresbys' uppish French chef!

Around the table, like so many decorative butterflies, milled Westhaven's residents and guests. Annabelle, looking particularly fetching in a gown of white muslin, stood beside James and Elizabeth Makepeace. She was content to nibble on one of cook's delicious lobster patties as James rhapsodized over the horses he'd purchased from Cam. Aunt Charlotte sat only a few feet away, listening in sympathy as Sir Charles Harewood listed, and then proceeded to describe, his many physical ailments. Privately, Aunt Charlotte thought Sir Charles looked in excellent health, positively in the pink, but she wasn't going to spoil for him what had obviously become the focal point of his life. Viscount Cranston and Cam stood directly opposite the table, discussing the whereabouts of the men with whom they'd served.

Only Violet and Freddy remained somewhat apart from the crowd, and for that they had good reason. It was obvious to all and sundry that the vivacious redhead and the portly man about town had formed a tendre. Following yesterday's hunt, and Violet's minor accident, the two had been apart only as long as propriety dictated. Furthermore, the fulminating glances they shared, as well as their tremulous sighs, left little doubt as to the nature of their aborning relationship.

Watching covertly, Annabelle couldn't help but smile as Freddy gently removed a bit of crumb from the corner of Violet's mouth. How his friends would crow if they could see him now. Ever the sophisticate, Freddy Merryweather was currently acting like the greenest of boys where Violet was concerned. Annabelle sighed. She was truly happy for her friend, but she couldn't help feeling a certain amount of envy. Annabelle glared at Cam. He wouldn't be as easily cozened.

From within the house, Lady Margaret took a moment to watch her guests through the windows of the Blue Salon. She was anxious to join them, for it was truly a lovely day, and from the look of it, Mrs. Freedly had been up at the crack of dawn slaving over her ovens. Alas, Bajardous had demanded an interview just before the countess was able to make good her escape, and she'd been unable to put him off. It was with a great deal of curiosity that she awaited her treasured, if somewhat imperious, major-domo. Bajardous knew better than to interfere with her duties as hostess. Lady Margaret waited anxiously. Whatever could the matter be, and what in heaven was taking him so long?

Fortunately, the countess was saved further anxiety several seconds later as Bajardous opened the double doors to the Blue Salon and stepped quickly inside. "My lady," he intoned with a dignified bow.

Lady Margaret nodded impatiently and waved him closer. Bajardous obediently complied, but not before he'd ascertained as he shut the doors behind him that there was no one loitering about in the corridor.

Why ever all the mystery? Lady Margaret wondered.

As soon as the doors to the Blue Salon were safely closed Bajardous's whole demeanour took on a drastic change

Rushing over to where his mistress stood, he grabbed the hem of her gown and knelt at her feet.

"You must stop her, my lady," Bajardous pleaded with what sounded suspiciously like a loud sniffle.

"Get up at once," the countess ordered. "You forget yourself. Now come and be seated and tell me what this is all about."

"Beg pardon, my lady," Bajardous apologized morosely, rising to his feet. He was obviously so upset that he actually took Lady Margaret at her word and for the first time in his tenure sat with his mistress upon the blue satin settee. "It's Miss Winthrop, my lady. She's got some maggoty notion into her head that I need a wife. Furthermore, she's of a mind to supply the candidate. Wherever I go, whatever I do, that maid of hers, Betty, simpers about. I've never done much complaining, my lady. I like my position here very much. But this I can't tolerate, won't tolerate. You must implore Miss Winthrop to cease!"

Lady Margaret schooled her features into a solemnity befitting the occasion, although she wanted very much to laugh herself into apoplexy. "I'm sure Miss Winthrop means no harm, Bajardous," she comforted, patting the major-domo on his hand. "But unless I miss my mark, we're going to be seeing a great deal more of that particular young lady in future. A great deal more. You may as well accustom yourself to her rather exuberant nature. However, it is possible that in this instance, Miss Winthrop has gone slightly, well, shall we say, beyond the pale. I'll speak to her, Bajardous, you may be certain of it."

"Thank you, my lady," the major-domo said with conviction. Now that he'd actually taken the proper steps to solve his horrific dilemma, Bajardous felt that much better. Gathering himself up with as much dignity as he could salvage, he executed a perfectly rigid bow and then excused himself.

Lady Margaret counted the seconds until he was gone. Only when the doors had closed firmly behind him did she give vent to her hilarity. In fact, Lady Margaret was so amused that she scarce heard the doors reopening. It was only when a slight cough sounded behind her that she realized she was no longer alone. Clasping an anxious hand to her mouth—for Lady Margaret very much feared that Bajardous had returned, letter of resignation in hand—that good lady was vastly relieved to see Viscount Cranston standing near the doors.

"You must think me the veriest madwoman," the countess remarked, putting a hand to the back of her hair. The viscount was an extremely attractive man, for all that he was older, and she found herself much more concerned with her appearance whenever he was near.

"Nonsense, Lady Margaret," the viscount replied in a somewhat gruff manner that was belied by his smile. "The others sent me to locate you before the food disappears. However, now I find myself much more curious about what has you so very much amused."

"That I am, I can assure you," Lady Margaret stated emphatically, beginning to feel somewhat more comfortable. Viscount Cranston, with his distinguished white hair, wasn't only handsome, he was charming as well. "And if you promise to stand mum, I shall tell you all."

"Fear not," the viscount promised as Lady Margaret rose. Lending her his arm, he listened with growing interest as Cam's mother spun him the tale.

Outside, the guests had almost finished their luncheon as Lady Margaret, escorted by the viscount, finally made an appearance. She apologized profusely for her tardiness, citing a minor domestic crisis. Viscount Cranston moved to prepare her a plate.

Standing beside his second cousin, Cam listened somewhat impatiently as Sir Charles went through a lengthy description of his last bout with the influenza. The earl found himself musing over an acceptable reason to excuse himself, yet he knew his mother would never forgive such gross impropriety. And, despite Sir Charles's eccentricity, he was a kindly man, undeserving of such cavalier treatment.

Still rather occupied with his own thoughts, Cam at first missed the fact that his cousin had changed the subject. "Don't you agree?" Sir Charles prompted as Cam finished off the last piece of Mrs. Freedly's Madeira cake.

"What's that, Charles?" Cam asked with an embarrassed grin. "Afraid I was doing a bit of wool-gathering."

"I said, young fellow, that your mother is looking simply splendid these days. Quite recovered, I would venture, and not above a minor flirtation, if my failing eyes don't deceive me."

"Hold your silly tongue," Cam hissed quite rudely, despite his earlier resolution to treat his cousin well.

Upon receiving the rebuff, Sir Charles—perhaps realizing his gaffe—silently melted away.

Cam didn't notice. His attention was suddenly fully riveted on his mother, his beautiful, young-looking mother, who at this very moment was laughing quite gaily with her escort, Viscount Cranston. Cam had never thought that his mother might establish a new relationship. He found the very notion repugnant. His mother belonged to his father; it could be no other way. Furthermore, had they not shared a great love? Whatever could his mother be thinking? Cam started towards the couple and then stopped. What could he do, or say? He had no right to interfere.

Annabelle and Violet were laughing merrily at Freddy's less-than-flattering imitation of the Marquis de Dambere when Cam stormed the group. "I need to talk to you," the earl stated imperiously, grabbing Annabelle by the arm.

Too stunned to object, the golden-brown beauty found herself hurtling along behind the earl as he dragged her towards the gardens. She stumbled forth as best she could until they reached the reflecting pool, the one which sported the statue of Neptune, and then she found she could go no farther. A small stone had lodged most determinedly in one of her satin slippers.

"Stop," she ordered finally, when her efforts to jerk her hand free had failed. "Stop, Cam, you're hurting me."

Camford Singletary, Earl of Westerbrook, did indeed stop, but the look he gave Annabelle was in no way apologetic or comforting. Instead, he sent her a glance of such pure malevolence that Annabelle found herself cringing. She'd never seen her beloved like this before and it scared her no small bit.

"I'll wager it was all your idea," Cam accused, practically shouting down at Annabelle from the advantage of his considerable height. "Nothing so outrageous used to happen round here until you turned up."

"Whatever are you speaking of, Cam?" Annabelle questioned in confusion. To the best of her knowledge she'd been surprisingly well-behaved this past week. Why, her record had nary a blot on it.

"I'm speaking of my mother and Viscount Cranston. Was it your idea to play matchmaker in that direction?"

"I've done nothing of the sort, Camford Singletary," Annabelle snapped, for she'd quite a temper herself when roused.

"You need not deny it. The whole household knows you've done your best to throw that pinch-faced maid of yours at my major-domo. You seem to have some misplaced notion that an unmarried person cannot be happy."

Annabelle's face reddened slightly, for she'd no idea that her machinations on Betty's behalf had been so transparent. Nevertheless, she could not take credit for attempting to match up Lady Margaret and Viscount Cranston—not that it was such a bad idea. "How dare you accuse me? I've done nothing to suffer such a scold. Furthermore, I don't believe that everyone need marry, especially if they find themselves likely to marry someone like you!"

"You don't mean that, as well you know," Cam said condescendingly, grabbing Annabelle roughly by the arms.

She fought against his embrace, yet, just as before, Annabelle's strength was little match for that of Cam's.

His lips crushed down on hers, searching, seeking, as if her kiss would reveal the answers he sought. Annabelle felt her resistance weaken almost at once. Cam ignited in her a fire that she'd never experienced before, scarcely knew how to define. Slowly her arms fell away from his chest to clasp the hard muscles of his upper arms. She gasped as his tongue invaded her mouth, swirling, teasing, inviting her response. She didn't deny him, although her actions were much more tentative than his. Desire was all so new to her.

Cam's control slipped, egged on no doubt by his murderous fury. His hands began to roam over Annabelle's body, delighting in the slimness of her waist, the rounded curves of her hips. She was so sweet, so innocent, so young. His hands couldn't help but dip into the tempting valley between her breasts. He felt her stiffen almost at once, yet that didn't stop him from cupping her flesh, from taunting her hardening nipple with his thumb.

A dizzying sensation swept over Annabelle as Cam intensified the intimacy of their embrace. She knew there was much to learn and that she wanted only Cam to teach her. Yet Annabelle realized she was courting disaster. Cam had already advised her he'd no intention of offering marriage. Abruptly, she pushed away from him, sobbing out her frustration as she did so. Cam roared and pulled her back, yet this time she didn't accept his embrace. Annabelle remained stiff, unyielding, and after several seconds, when reason began to resurface, Cam dropped his arms and stepped away. Running his hands through his tousled black hair, he turned his back on the golden-brown beauty, trying to marshal his thoughts.

"Look here, Annabelle," Cam began eventually, but when he turned about to apologize, he found that she'd gone.

ANNABELLE HAD NEVER BEEN so miserable in all her life. Not only was Cam uninterested in marriage, suddenly her knight in shining armour had fallen quite firmly off his horse. How could he have been so horrid to her? How could he have been?

Annabelle spent the remainder of that day locked inside her rooms. It seemed as if nothing could improve her humour: not the cheerful yellow décor within her bedchamber; not even Mr. Fitzroy's more outrageous antics; certainly not Betty's commiseration.

On the following day, when Annabelle again failed to show herself, Aunt Charlotte decided it was time to intervene. That venerable lady presented herself in her niece's rooms directly before luncheon, intending to demand Annabelle rejoin the house party. Aunt Charlotte wasn't prepared for the visage her niece presented, including swollen eyes and dripping nose—despite the fact that Annabelle seemed to do little more than cry these days.

"Would you care to tell me about it, my dear?" Aunt Charlotte questioned, far more gently than she'd originally planned.

"Oh, Auntie," Annabelle replied, throwing herself into the older woman's arms. "I love him, you know, and he cares naught for me."

There was no need to ask of whom Annabelle spoke; Aunt Charlotte knew full well the way the wind blew. "There, there, my dear," she crooned, much as she had when the gel was young and sick with fever. "It'll all come right in the end, you'll see."

"No, it won't, Auntie. He doesn't want me, and I must accept that. I must try to forget him. I think we should leave. There seems little point in staying on."

"Annabelle Winthrop, would you have it said that you lack courage?"

Annabelle looked at her aunt uncertainly.

"Best to brazen it out, my gel. Keep your chin high. Show him the stuff of which you're made. That way, no matter what the outcome, he'll know you're a woman of strength and character. Furthermore, Lady Margaret has gone to considerable trouble to arrange this house party. I think you owe her better than a clandestine departure."

"You're right, Auntie, as you invariably are. I'll stay. I'm not going to let Camford Singletary best me. I shall make an appearance at dinner tonight."

"That's my good gel. And just so you know, everyone thinks you've been suffering a terrible case of the headache."

Annabelle nodded as she pulled the bell cord to summon Betty. She wanted to look her best tonight and that was going to take the better part of the day to achieve!

Leaving Annabelle in her maid's capable hands, Aunt Charlotte slowly retraced her steps along the expensively carpeted corridor. Had she made a mistake in encouraging a match between Annabelle and the earl? It seemed Lord Westerbrook had done little else than cause her young niece misery. Tapping her quizzing glass against her hand, Aunt Charlotte suddenly found herself longing for the simplicity of her own home.

By the time Violet popped her head into Annabelle's chambers an hour or so later, the golden-brown beauty and her maid had made considerable progress towards turning Annabelle from a watering pot into one of London's reigning belles.

"May I come in?" the redhead enquired, proceeding to do so only when Annabelle had nodded in the affirmative. "How are you feeling? Not too terrible, I hope? I know the headache can be an awful thing. My mother suffers from them as well. Anyway, I've missed you dreadfully. There's so much to discuss."

Annabelle smiled and directed Betty to take her gown downstairs to be pressed. After the maid had gone, Annabelle rose from the dressing-table and led Violet towards one of the yellow-and-white striped, satin wing-chairs which flanked the fireplace. "I'm amazed you managed to pull yourself away from Freddy long enough to seek me out," she teased as they were seated.

Violet blushed becomingly and admitted that Freddy had gone for a ride with James Makepeace. "I just can't believe it's all come about so well," the redhead gushed. "And I owe everything to you, Annabelle. Do you know that Freddy plans to approach my father when we return to London? I can't imagine there will be any objection. After all, Freddy will be a viscount one day, and it isn't as if his pockets are to let, although his fortune can't be said to be as great as mine."

"No one's fortune is as great as yours," Annabelle retorted, rising swiftly to place a kiss upon her friend's cheek. "I'm so glad for you, Violet. I know you and Freddy will be famously happy."

"Well, now that my future has been secured, it's time we put our heads together to consider yours. Tell me, what delicious plan have you concocted to bring the fabulous Cam Singletary up to scratch?"

Annabelle managed to smile weakly, although she felt her heart might break. "That's all over with, Violet," she proclaimed with far more control than she actually felt. "I've come to the conclusion that it's ridiculous to set my cap for Cam. He's one of the most eligible bachelors in England and I feel sure that when and if he decides to marry, it'll be to someone far more suitable than I; someone less likely to tumble into constant trouble. Someone like, well, someone like Lucinda Moresby."

"Oh, pooh," Violet scoffed. "He cares no more for Lucinda than he does for me. Whatever happened to unseat you so? If anyone can bring the Earl of Westerbrook to the sticking-point it's you, Annabelle, and everyone knows it."

"Everyone except the earl," Annabelle replied.

Although Violet remained for the better part of an hour, she was unable to restore her friend's usual confidence, nor her good cheer. Annabelle tried to feign happiness but Violet knew her well enough to realize that she was definitely blue-devilled. That's why, when she left, Violet resolved to discuss the matter with Freddy. Surely he could think of something to bring Cam to his senses.

Dinner that night was a tedious affair for Annabelle, although the food as usual was excellent and the company delightful. Fortunately, Cam had excused himself from table, ostensibly to see to urgent estate business. Annabelle knew better. He was no more anxious to endure her company than she was to endure his.

Pretending that she was still suffering somewhat from the headache, Annabelle retired early that night, forgoing the game of charades that Lady Margaret had planned as the evening's entertainment. Only one more night remaining. After tomorrow, and Lady Margaret's soirée, she and Aunt Charlotte would leave Westhaven for good. How she longed for the comfort of Brierly and all that was familiar. For while Annabelle had never dared to dream that she'd take the ton by storm, she'd also never thought that she'd return home such a dismal, dreary failure.

It was foggy the next morn, but by noon the mist had burned off, leaving a sunny yet wondrously cool day. All in all, everyone agreed, the weather so far this summer had been the best in recent memory.

Lady Margaret was kept busy all day attending to the last-minute details of the evening's soirée. Considering the relatively small number of guests who'd been invited, she decided to use the music room for the event. Such a small number of people would've been lost in Westhaven's enormous ballroom. Better the intimacy of a smaller chamber. And the music room, with its gold rococo ornamentation and antique tapestry, was the ideal setting.

Employing several footmen, Lady Margaret spent the early morn rearranging the furniture and instruments within the music room so that none of the more valuable items could be damaged by the crush. She then had the cherry wood chairs from the dining-room brought forth so that the guests would have something on which to sit.

Once the room had been arranged to her satisfaction, Lady Margaret organized a cleaning detail over which she personally presided. When the chamber was virtually sparkling, she spent half an hour in the gardens directing which flowers were to be cut and how they should be arranged.

That left Lady Margaret with just enough time to dress. She surprised her maid by rejecting the blue organza she'd chosen earlier, opting instead for a low-cut red gown that she hadn't worn since before her husband's death. Lady Margaret didn't allow herself to consider too closely why she'd decided to don the more flattering red. She had more important details on her mind: she had to be downstairs in time to greet the musicians, a local group who ought none the less to be able to perform at least the rudiments of the current favourites; she had to make certain Mrs. Freedly had the refreshments well in hand; she had to double-check the wines and liqueurs Bajardous had brought forth from the cellars....

The musicians had just begun to warm up when Annabelle descended the staircase that night. Unfortunately, she couldn't have chosen a worse moment to make her appearance, for Cam stood at the bottom of the stairs looking as handsome as ever in his black evening attire. Remembering her aunt's advice, Annabelle lifted her chin, as well as the hem of her gown, and slowly proceeded downwards. It was perhaps inevitable that their eyes should lock. She resisted the urge to turn and flee.

The aquamarine dress which Annabelle had elected to wear made her look more beautiful than ever before, Cam mused, wondering what foolish pride kept him from running to her side and begging forgiveness. An aquamarine ribbon had been threaded through her shimmering golden-brown curls as well as round her slim white neck. Her skin looked as smooth as English cream. The low, low *décolletage* of her bodice reminded the earl of how he'd touched her there just a short while ago and how he longed to touch her there again. The short, puffed sleeves of her gown emphasized her slender white arms. Cam felt himself begin to shiver. Ridiculous! Ridiculous to let himself be so affected by a mere schoolroom chit.

"Miss Winthrop," Cam intoned, executing a slight bow as the beauty passed by.

"My lord," she replied coldly, giving lie to the fact that she'd ever laughed with this man, or held him in any kind of esteem.

With a heavy heart, Annabelle joined the others who'd gathered for a small drink before the guests were due to arrive—not that they were long in coming. The local gentry hadn't been invited to Westhaven in nigh on two years. Within minutes, it seemed, they were filing past Cam and his mother and on into the music room.

Annabelle didn't recognize many faces, for most true fashionables were still in London. She did, of course, remember the vicar, as well as the elder Ponfrets. Her heart did a quick somersault when she saw their son, Randolph, stroll casually through the doors, but she assumed that Lady Margaret hadn't been informed of his less-than-gentlemanly behaviour. Annabelle couldn't help but glance at Cam as Randolph headed immediately towards a pretty little maid carrying a tray heavily laden with champagne. The earl scowled in Randolph's direction, but there was little he could do at present without creating an embarrassing scene.

Violet lost no time in abandoning Freddy as she, too, noted the latest arrival. "What on earth is he doing here?" the redhead asked in horror as she reached Annabelle's side.

"Taking advantage of Lady Margaret's hospitality, I should think," Annabelle replied, pursing her lips with disdain. "I wonder that he dares taunt Cam so after what happened last time."

"Thwarted love often makes people act irrationally," Violet stated as if she were an expert on the subject. "He's up to no good, whatever the case."

"Do me a favour, Violet. Could you and Freddy stay close tonight? I'm in no mood to deal with a disgruntled suitor just now."

Violet nodded and summoned Freddy with a wave.

"Here comes another of our favourites," the redhead announced seconds later, having caught sight of Lucinda Moresby and her father. Violet immediately threaded her arm through Freddy's.

The dress Lucinda had elected to wear could only be described as shocking. Already many of the guests within the music room were beginning to comment. Obviously, they tittered, the squire was no authority on propriety or he'd never have allowed his daughter to leave the house dressed in such fashion. Lucinda wore a green gown which exactly matched the brilliant colour of her eyes. Yet the neckline was cut so low that only an act of God would keep her breasts confined within the bodice of the gown for the duration of the evening. Furthermore, it was obvious that Lucinda had dampened her petticoats, for the gown clung to her so revealingly that even the more adventurous matrons of the ton would've hesitated to wear it.

"My word," Freddy sputtered as Lucinda lurched into the room, for despite her stunning beauty, she'd still not managed to tame her masculine stride. Freddy's reaction wasn't atypical. Every man in the room was staring at the blonde. Why, even the vicar had a strange smile pasted on his usually sanctimonious face.

The reaction to her gown was all Lucinda could've hoped for. As the stunning blonde made her way farther into the room, she was instantly surrounded by the eligible bachelors, as well as several other men who weren't so eligible. The satisfaction was made more significant when she espied her rival standing quite alone in a corner, save for the presence of the odious Violet Silverton and the portly Freddy Merryweather.

The opening set was about to begin. As tradition decreed, Cam took his mother's arm, Violet set forth with her beloved Freddy, and Annabelle, quite dismally, found herself in the arms of the vicar. She glanced at her Aunt Charlotte enviously, for although Sir Charles Harewood wasn't the ideal partner, he was a far sight better than the vicar, who'd already begun to pontificate on the evils of the waltz. Annabelle sighed and resigned herself to a deadly dull evening. She couldn't have been more wrong!

The trouble began when Lady Margaret accepted the second dance with Viscount Cranston. For all intents and purposes, Cam surrendered his mother gracefully, yet Annabelle knew at a glance that he was furious. He stood with his back to the wall, barely suppressing a glower each time the couple danced by. Annabelle found herself suddenly quite nervous, so much so that she couldn't concentrate on the movements of her feet as she struggled to follow the lead of the extremely young man who'd asked her to dance. She was enormously relieved when the set ended, but found to her dismay that Randolph Ponfret had singled her out, seemingly oblivious to the protective presence of Violet and Freddy.

"Just wanted to apologize for my behaviour when last we met," Randolph stammered, quite red in the face. "Hugely disappointed, you know, when you rejected my suit."

"Really, Randolph, I don't think this the time or the place," Annabelle began with a quick glance at her companions.

"I know. But I didn't think I'd have a chance to talk to you otherwise. Please, Annabelle, won't you accept my apology?"

He certainly looked sincere. Annabelle graciously nodded her head, despite a disapproving frown from Freddy.

"Will you dance with me then?" Randolph asked, holding out his hand.

Annabelle knew she shouldn't. Randolph, despite his seeming air of innocence, wasn't a man to be trusted. And Cam was in a black enough mood already without her further inflaming his ire. Yet Annabelle could think of no way to refuse Randolph without creating a scene, especially since he was gazing at her so beseechingly.

"Very well," she agreed with a heavy sigh.

Cam couldn't believe his eyes. Had his mother and Annabelle both gone mad? Each had elected to dance with men of whom the earl couldn't approve. He began to think seriously of retiring for the evening when he noted Ponfret twirling Annabelle closer and closer to the French doors which led to the terrace outside. Cam's eyes narrowed suspiciously, though no one else seemed concerned. Freddy and Violet were practically locked in each other's arms by the refreshment table. James and Elizabeth Makepeace were similarly occupied. Lady Charlotte, bless her kindly soul, was entertaining Sir Charles, and his mother was talking quite animatedly with the viscount. Cam ground his teeth and turned his attention back to Annabelle and Randolph—only they were nowhere to be seen!

Cam threaded his way through the music room, careful to draw no undue attention. Annabelle's reputation had suffered quite enough damage for one Season. Had the earl known Randolph's intent, he would've moved that much quicker.

Outside on the stone terrace, Annabelle struggled to extricate herself from Randolph's grasp. She would've screamed save for the scandal such a display would invariably have caused.

"Do stop wriggling," Randolph commanded forcefully albeit in a hissed whisper. He always tried to maintain some sense of decorum when his parents were present. "If you cease to struggle, then I shall release you forthwith. I wish only to ask of you one small favour."

Curiosity, and the realization that she could do little else, made Annabelle comply.

"There, that's better," Randolph stated, well-pleased as he let go the golden-brown beauty's arm. "I brought you out here to request from you a last kiss."

Annabelle tossed her curls angrily and all but slapped Randolph's pompous face. "I think the kiss you took, nay stole, when last we met must suffice," she retorted furiously.

"Please, Annabelle, I realize I behaved badly at your ball. But as I've already explained, I was desperately disappointed that you turned down my offer of marriage, and quite bosky into the bargain. I only request this favour now because I find I can't put you from my mind. What I'm asking for, my dear, is a goodbye kiss so that I may acknowledge to myself the futility of future pursuit."

"I hardly think your reasoning sound, Randolph. If I kiss you now, you may find your situation worse, n-not better," Annabelle stuttered, feeling acutely embarrassed.

"Trust me to know myself," Randolph pleaded, taking one of Annabelle's hands into his own. "Please, my dear, bestow upon me this one last favour and I shall never bother you again."

Annabelle sighed, her embarrassment turning to exasperation. Randolph was staring at her, the same beseeching look in his blue eyes that he'd used earlier. Would she never be rid of this plaguey nuisance? "Very well," she replied against her better judgement. "Only be quick about it. I don't want anyone to see."

Randolph smiled beatifically. Since Annabelle's back was to the French doors she couldn't know that the one person he did indeed want to witness this tender little scene was already heading directly towards them.

Cupping the golden-brown beauty's chin in his hand, Randolph leaned forward and placed a chaste kiss upon Annabelle's upturned lips. She pulled back immediately, but was already too late.

"So sorry to interrupt your romantic tryst," Cam stated coldly as he lounged nonchalantly in the doorway, "but I just couldn't let the opportunity pass to tell you what a splendid pair the two of you make."

Annabelle gasped and rushed to the earl's side. "Please," she began, "it's not what you think."

"I think," Cam replied just before he stalked off, "that the Wayward Angel enjoys being kissed rather too much."

Annabelle turned to Randolph. "Well, you certainly got your revenge," she choked out, struggling to keep the tears at bay.

"I must admit that I had a difficult time not seeking you out sooner," Randolph replied, straightening an imaginary crease in one of his ridiculously high shirt points. "But when this plan suggested itself, I found it too good to bypass. Let it be a lesson to you, my gel. No one gets the better of Randolph Ponfret."

Resisting the urge to insist that she'd never in fact done anything to earn his enmity, for Annabelle realized how useless it was to try to argue with someone of his character, the golden-brown beauty stumbled away. She fled down the steps of the terrace and into the gardens below. She simply wasn't up to facing anyone just yet.

For one moment, Randolph considered following her, but two things stopped him: common sense (even he realized he could only push the earl so far) and Freddy Merryweather.

LUCINDA SAW CAM LEAVE the music room and, disengaging herself from her rather-too-persistent admirers, made to follow. She'd wanted to lure Cam outside herself, but he hadn't paid her the slightest heed, despite the daring nature of her gown. Lucinda shrugged. What did she care how her plan came about, as long as it came about?

Cam headed towards the stables. That's where he always went to think when he was upset or confused. He'd spent a great deal of time there when his father died, and now he felt again the need for the comforting smell of animal, hay, leather and ointment.

As he neared the stables, Cam could hear the low rumble of the groomsmen talking as they prepared to bed down for the night. The earl turned away from the talk and headed instead towards Merlin's stall. The charcoal grey stallion snorted a greeting as Cam stroked the horse's nose.

"Fine-looking animal, I always thought," said a female voice from behind.

Cam whipped about only to be confronted by the sight of Lucinda Moresby, dressed for all the world as if she'd just stepped out of a brothel. He hadn't noticed her attire before, but he noticed it now, as she so obviously meant for him to do. Unfortunately for Lucinda, Cam had had enough of women for one night. Besides, most of the time these days he found himself completely uninterested in the blond stunner's charms.

Somewhat disconcerted by his lack of response, for Lucinda had always known he appreciated her physical attributes if nothing else, the blonde nevertheless pressed forward with her plan. "I really didn't return to the country for my father's sake, Cam." She began moving closer to the earl.

"Is that so?" he questioned absent-mindedly.

Lucinda cleared her throat. "No. Fact of the matter is I returned to the country for you, Cam dearest. It's time we make public our plans for a more permanent liaison. I've waited patiently all these years." Lucinda's face flamed alarmingly but she persevered. "I won't wait any longer."

Lucinda had certainly managed, if nothing else, to snare Cam's full attention. Unfortunately, he found himself embarrassed more than anything—embarrassed for both of them. Gently he took her hand and told her what he'd been meaning to tell her for quite some time. "I know I've led you to expect that one day we might marry, but I find I can't wed simply to increase my acreage," Cam explained, surprising even himself as he added, "especially when my heart's elsewhere attached." The admission seemed to lift a heavy weight form the earl's shoulders, and suddenly he knew exactly what he had to do!

Grimacing, Lucinda chose to ignore what she viewed as Cam's obvious bewitchment. "Alas, I've long planned on becoming the next Countess of Westerbrook," she said, gaining in anger the confidence she'd always heretofore lacked with the earl.

"Please don't make this any more unpleasant than it already is."

"You've provoked the need for unpleasantness, not I," Lucinda replied, and with a blood-curdling scream, she proceeded to rip her bodice so that her milky white breasts were suddenly exposed to Cam's startled gaze.

Jem and the other groomsmen came running.

Trying to cover herself as best she could, Lucinda ran towards Jem and threw herself into the amazed head groomsman's arms. "Send for my father," she begged. "I've been attacked."

Lucinda's ploy wasn't as stupid as it seemed. Although she knew Jem would never act without Cam's approval, all of the groomsmen were witness to the scene. Surely one of them was open to bribery. Furthermore, her scream had almost certainly been heard up at the house.

"By all means send for the squire," Cam agreed with casual wave of his hand. No one, however, missed the dangerous gleam in Lord Westerbrook's eye. The earl wasn't about to be bamboozled into anything he hadn't agreed to especially marriage.

Fortuitously, Cam was never forced to confront the squire, for at that moment Freddy Merryweather presented himself in the stables with an unwilling Randolph Ponfret in tow. (At times, Freddy's bulk did have its advantages. Although his original plan had been to give Randolph well-deserved thrashing, Lucinda's scream had drawn his attention and her patently obvious ploy had given Freddy better idea.

"I'd like to suggest an alternative," the portly man about town stated, earning the earl's grateful attention.

And that's how Lucinda Moresby came to be Mrs. Randolph Ponfret. For when her father reached the stables, found that his daughter had been compromised by

Ponfret pup. Although both Lucinda and Randolph kept insisting they were the victims of a conspiracy, the squire had had enough of his wilful daughter's outrageous behaviour. Besides, there were scores of witnesses to attest to Lucinda's humiliation—the guests of Lady Margaret's soirée, as well as the earl's groomsmen, each of whom swore to a man that it was Randolph Ponfret who'd ripped the bodice off the squire's daughter.

Annabelle heard Lucinda scream as did everyone else. And being a person of more than passing curiosity, she made her way to the stables with the other interested ladies. Needless to say, Annabelle found herself as amazed at the events which came next as did the others, amazed and pleased. For although she knew she couldn't have Cam, perversely, she didn't want Lucinda to have him, either. In fact, Annabelle's unhappiness vanished altogether until the last of the locals had departed and the evening came to an abrupt end.

As the hour was still relatively young, Lady Margaret's house guests were reluctant to take themselves to bed, especially following all of the excitement. What a delicious on dit Lucinda's misadventures would make when they returned to London and their respective drawing-rooms.

Annabelle found herself ensconced in the Blue Salon with the others, carefully dissecting the delicious scandal. However, she was becoming more and more uncomfortable, for she felt Cam's eyes upon her, which in fact they were. Threading her way casually to the doors, Annabelle prepared to make her escape. She never got the chance. The earl, following close behind, was most insistent that they talk. Annabelle hesitated, for she didn't want to experience another bout of Cam's anger, yet she did want to explain what had occurred earlier between her and Randolph Ponfret. Reluctantly, she agreed to a private tête-à-tête.

Cam led Annabelle to the study, his own private sanctum, telling the others he'd agreed to lend her a book. He needn't have bothered. Lady Margaret's guests were far too busy discussing Lucinda Moresby's humiliation to pay attention to something so trivial as the loss of two of their number.

Once inside the study, Annabelle seated herself upon the rust-coloured leather couch as Cam proceeded to pace aimlessly back and forth. She let her attention wander to the Thomas Gainsborough landscape, but found she couldn't concentrate on the artist's masterful perfection of strokes. Her hands were shaking and, to her horror, Annabelle found that she'd begun to perspire. Cam didn't notice. In fact, he seemed far away, locked in a world all his own.

"Annabelle, I've determined that it's disastrous in marriage to actually love your partner," Cam stated unexpectedly a bit later.

Annabelle jumped. Of all the things she'd expected him to say, that wasn't one of them. However, they didn't call her the Wayward Angel for naught. "Rubbish! Love is mandatory for a good marriage. Who wants to endure a lifetime of complacency?"

"Ah, therein lies the rub. Love seldom lasts a lifetime."

"That's true. I lost my parents when I was quite young and it was a devastating experience. And still, I wouldn't change the person I am for a different set of parents. Nor would I call back all the wonderful years I've spent with the Greywoods. But more to the point, I doubt your mother would give up the years she spent with your father, give up the union that produced both you and your sister. Love can be painful, Cam. But my Aunt Charlotte says one need not live without it. Love comes in different forms and it comes at different times in our lives."

"Are you sure you're just eighteen years old? You sound so wise," Cam remarked softly, staring out of the window at the blackness beyond. His hands were clasped tightly behind his back.

Annabelle blushed. Indeed she wasn't worldly-wise enough to be doling out such philosophical advice. That was Aunt Charlotte's realm. "Cam, did you have something specific you wished to discuss? It's getting rather late and I really shouldn't be here with you like this...."

Cam spun round, walked towards her, and as he neared said, "I wished only to tell you that when I saw you kissing Randolph Ponfret earlier I truly felt as if I could kill the young popinjay."

Annabelle's heart quickened. "He made me kiss him. He manipulated me in order to anger you. Do you really think I care anything for that fribble?"

"I hope not," Cam said, sitting down next to her. "I hope instead that you care for me. I love you, Annabelle. I've been fighting it forever, but dammit, there it is. I suppose I have to accept the fact that love entails a certain amount of chance."

"Oh, Cam," Annabelle sighed, nuzzling her cheek into the earl's broad shoulder. When she lifted her head, he kissed her gently, a kiss full of promise for the future. Annabelle smiled and touched his forehead with hers. Then she took his hand. "Cam, will you marry me?" Annabelle asked, unable to wait for the inevitable.

Cam laughed. Life with the Wayward Angel would certainly never be complacent. "Yes, my dear," he said, "I think I'd better."

EPILOGUE

THE NEWS OF THE EARL of Westerbrook's engagement to Miss Annabelle Winthrop was met by a wide variety of reactions, not the least of which were many a disappointed sigh by the young ladies and gentlemen of the ton.

Annabelle's Uncle William, the first to learn the news, since Cam rode immediately to Brierly for his blessing, was quite pleased, for despite the loss of his beloved niece, he was overjoyed that he needn't be plagued by the stuff and nonsense of another Season. Furthermore, he was delighted when Cam met well the one condition of the engagement: that the earl land the Marquis de Dambere a solid facer. The marquis, while sporting for quite some time a rather blackened eye, wasn't too dejected, for he won a rather vulgar sum of money on the match via his wise bet at White's. Major Jack Sprawlings was a bit more downcast, but only until he managed to shock Society by snagging the following year's reigning belle.

Aunt Charlotte and Lady Margaret were both as pleased as punch and for quite a while thereafter went about referring to each other as "General" and "Admiral," although that did stop somewhat when Lady Margaret became Viscountess Cranston.

Violet and Freddy were exceedingly smug about the engagement, for was it not they who'd brought the pair together in the end? Without Violet's intuition, Freddy would never have known to confront the pompous Randolph. As for the new Mr. and Mrs. Ponfret, they were naturally quite vexed at first until, bowing to the inevitable, they turned their energy instead towards attempting to make their combined property the finest in all of Sussex.

It took Bajardous, with the aid of several bottles of the earl's finest French brandy, a while to come about, but come about he did, to the extent of marrying the new countess's maid, Betty. When that good woman ultimately took on the role of housekeeper, Lucy finally received her promotion to lady's maid, serving none other than Annabelle herself. As of this writing, Lucy was still trying to convince the second footman that they were now prosperous enough to officially declare their engagement.

As for the other Westerbrook servants, villagers and tenants, they were happy that the earl was finally to marry and assure the succession. None had relished the prospect of the properties and land falling to a wastrel landlord. And their happiness was justified as, in time, Annabelle presented Cam with a son—but not before she'd first borne him three daughters, each more beautiful and wayward than the next!

HARLEQUIN®
REGENCY ROMANCE™

IF YOU THOUGHT ROMANCE NOVELS WERE ALL THE SAME ... LOOK AGAIN!

Our new look begins this September

Framed by its classic new look, Harlequin Regency Romance captures all the romance, charm and splendor of the Regency period.
Romantic and flirtatious, lively and fun, these love stories will transport you into the entertaining world of Regency Romance.

Watch for a sneak preview of our new covers next month!

HARLEQUIN REGENCY ROMANCE—
Elegant entanglements!

OFFICIAL RULES • MILLION DOLLAR MATCH 3 SWEEPSTAKES
NO PURCHASE OR OBLIGATION NECESSARY TO ENTER

To enter, follow the directions published. If the "Match 3" Game Card is missing, hand print your name and address on a 3″×5″ card and mail to either: Harlequin "Match 3," 3010 Walden Ave., P.O. Box 1867, Buffalo, NY 14269-1867 or Harlequin "Match 3," P.O. Box 609, Fort Erie, Ontario L2A 5X3, and we will assign your Sweepstakes numbers. (Limit: one entry per envelope.) For eligibility, entries must be received no later than March 31, 1994 and be sent via first-class mail. No liability is assumed for printing errors, lost, late or misdirected entries.

Upon receipt of entry, Sweepstakes numbers will be assigned. To determine winners, Sweepstakes numbers will be compared against a list of randomly preselected prizewinning numbers. In the event all prizes are not claimed via the return of prizewinning numbers, random drawings will be held from among all other entries received to award unclaimed prizes.

Prizewinners will be determined no later than May 30, 1994. Selection of winning numbers and random drawings are under the supervision of D.L. Blair, Inc., an independent judging organization, whose decisions are final. One prize to a family or organization. No substitution will be made for any prize, except as offered. Taxes and duties on all prizes are the sole responsibility of winners. Winners will be notified by mail. Chances of winning are determined by the number of entries distributed and received.

Sweepstakes open to persons 18 years of age or older, except employees and immediate family members of Torstar Corporation, D.L. Blair, Inc., their affiliates, subsidiaries and all other agencies, entities and persons connected with the use, marketing or conduct of this Sweepstakes. All applicable laws and regulations apply. Sweepstakes offer void wherever prohibited by law. Any litigation within the province of Quebec respecting the conduct and awarding of a prize in this Sweepstakes must be submitted to the Régies des Loteries et Courses du Quebec. In order to win a prize, residents of Canada will be required to correctly answer a time-limited arithmetical skill-testing question. Values of all prizes are in U.S. currency.

Winners of major prizes will be obligated to sign and return an affidavit of eligibility and release of liability within 30 days of notification. In the event of non-compliance within this time period, prize may be awarded to an alternate winner. Any prize or prize notification returned as undeliverable will result in the awarding of that prize to an alternate winner. By acceptance of their prize, winners consent to use of their names, photographs or other likenesses for purposes of advertising, trade and promotion on behalf of Torstar Corporation without further compensation, unless prohibited by law.

This Sweepstakes is presented by Torstar Corporation, its subsidiaries and affiliates in conjunction with book, merchandise and/or product offerings. Prizes are as follows: Grand Prize—$1,000,000 (payable at $33,333.33 a year for 30 years). First through Sixth Prizes may be presented in different creative executions, each with the following appproximate values: First Prize—$35,000; Second Prize—$10,000; 2 Third Prizes—$5,000 each; 5 Fourth Prizes—$1,000 each; 10 Fifth Prizes—$250 each; 1,000 Sixth Prizes—$100 each. Prizewinners will have the opportunity of selecting any prize offered for that level. A travel-prize option, if offered and selected by winner, must be completed within 12 months of selection and is subject to hotel and flight accommodations availability. Torstar Corporation may present this Sweepstakes utilizing names other than Million Dollar Sweepstakes. For a current list of all prize options offered within prize levels and all names the Sweepstakes may utilize, send a self-addressed, stamped envelope (WA residents need not affix return postage) to: Million Dollar Sweepstakes Prize Options/Names, P.O. Box 4710, Blair, NE 68009.

For a list of prizewinners (available after July 31, 1994) send a separate, stamped, self-addressed envelope to: Million Dollar Sweepstakes Winners, P.O. Box 4728, Blair, NE 68009. MSW7-92

BIG SUMMER READ

Summer Reading At Its Best

In July, Harlequin and Silhouette bring readers the Big Summer Read Program. Heat up your summer with these four exciting new novels by top Harlequin and Silhouette authors.

SOMEWHERE IN TIME by Barbara Bretton
YESTERDAY COMES TOMORROW by Rebecca Flanders
A DAY IN APRIL by Mary Lynn Baxter
LOVE CHILD by Patricia Coughlin

From time travel to fame and fortune, this program offers something for everyone.

Available at your favorite retail outlet.

BSR